Sandy's War

A story of intrigue
and deception

Hawk Kiefer

Copyright 2024 by Hawk Kiefer

All rights reserved. This book or any portion thereof may not be reproduced or used in any manner whatsoever without the express written permission of the publisher except for the use of brief quotation in a book review.

Inquiries and Book Orders should be addressed to:

Leavitt Peak Press
Email: info@leavittpeakpress.com
Phone: 1-888-549-0988

ISBN: 978-1-965679-59-3 (sc)
ISBN: 978-1-965679-60-9 (ebk)

Also by Hawk Kiefer: *Soldiers Never Sleep*

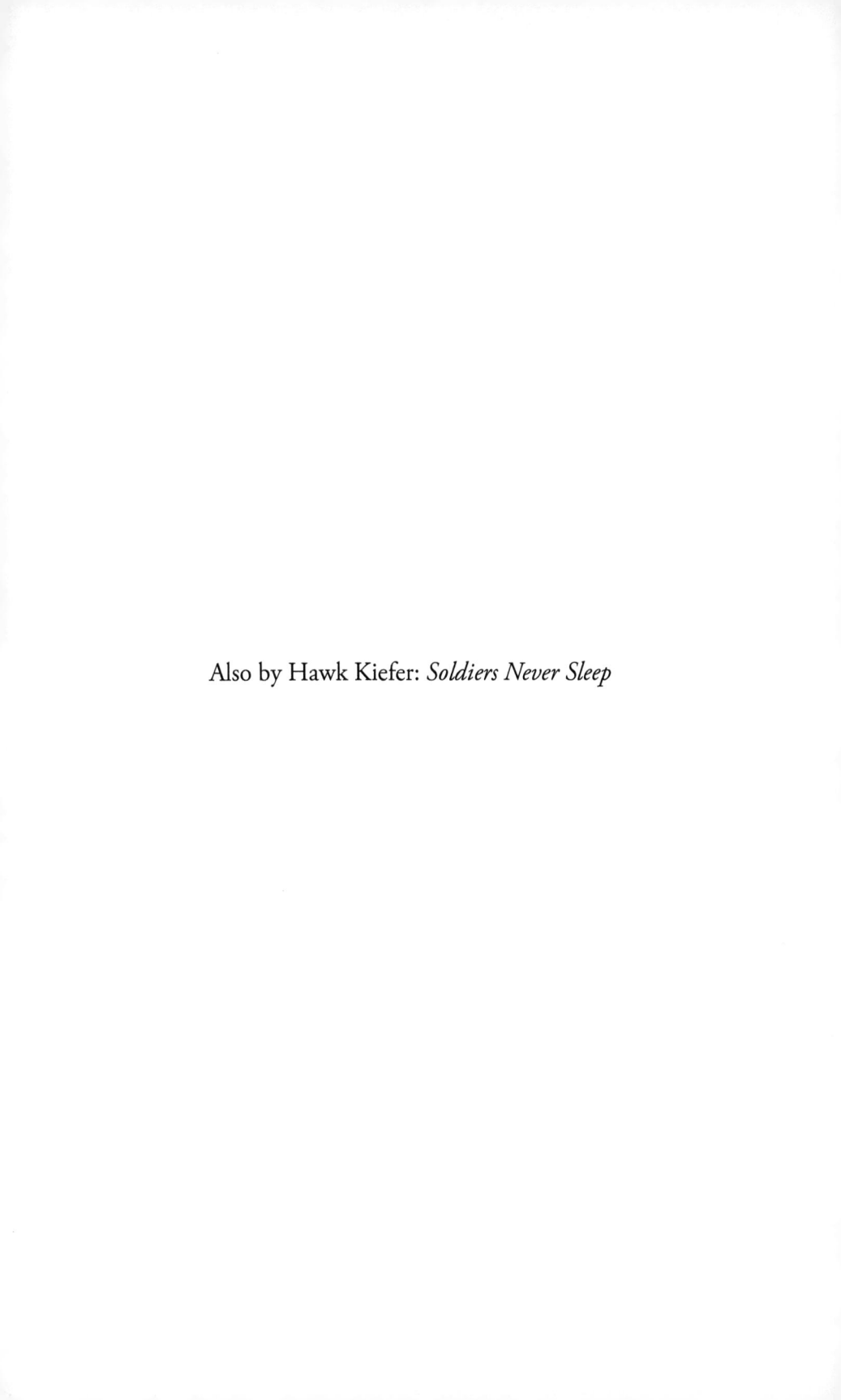

ACKNOWLEDGMENT

To my editor, who deplores my ignorance and yet teaches me; to my friends, who listen to my stories and still encourage me; to my children, who endure my idiosyncrasies and do not criticize me; to my readers, who reward my efforts and critique my work; and to my wife, who has lived with me for over forty years and still loves me, I am in awe.

THE WALKER FAMILY

Joshua Walker eloped from southwest Virginia with teenaged *Sara Austin* around 1835. They had one child, *Joseph Andrew Walker*, who was born in Ohio around 1842.

Joseph Walker married *Ida Sanford* at Cincinnati in 1865. They had one child, *Joseph A. Walker Jr.*, who was born in 1867.

Joseph Walker married *Kate Beirne* at Cincinnati in 1890. They had three children: Jeanette, born in 1892 at Fort Robinson, Nebraska; *Rose*, born in 1894 at Fort Laramie, Wyoming; and *Andrew*, born in 1903 at Cincinnati.

Andrew Walker married *Penny Nugent* at West Point in 1925. They had two children, both born at Fort Sill, Oklahoma: *Sanford* in 1926 and *Kathleen* in 1927. A year after *Penny's* death in 1973, *Andy* married *Helen Vincent* at Alexandria, Virginia.

Sandy Walker married *Nancy Down* at West Point in 19487. They had two children: *Walter*, born in 1949 at Fort Sill, Oklahoma, and *Sara*, born in 1950 at Destin, Florida.

Walter Walker married *Cathy Plummer* in 1967. They had two children, both born at Hilton Head, *Paul* in 1968 and *Beth* in 1969.

Paul Walker married *Jo Weibel* at Hilton Head in 1987. They had one child, *Steven*, born in 1988 at Fort Benning, Georgia.

PROLOGUE

Andy Walker was born in 1903 after his father returned from three years of fighting Aquinaldo's guerrillas in the Philippine Insurrection. Andy became part of a military tradition, for the Walker men had all been warriors. Back in 1861, when President Lincoln first called for volunteers, Andy's grandfather, Joseph, had enlisted as a Private in the Ohio Guthrie Grays. He emerged from the war with the Medal of Honor, a badly damaged right leg and a Regular Army commission as a Captain. Having seen the elephant, Joseph could not bring himself to return to Cincinnati and become a banker. In 1865l, therefore, with his bride, Ida, he led an infantry company on the Old Oregon Trail west from Fort Leavenworth, Kansas, to fight the Sioux and Cheyenne in a war against Chief Red Cloud. After twenty-five years of irregular conflict against the Plains Indians, and three years of regimental command in the Far East, he was promoted to Brigadier General. Tragedy marked the end of his life, for while he was far from her in the Philippines commanding Buffalo Soldiers in combat, his beloved Ida became ill with the Spanish flu back home in Cincinnati. To Joseph's great sorrow, she died before he could complete his hasty journey home to her bedside. Saddened, he retired from the Army to spend his remaining years speaking and writing in a vain attempt to secure better treatment for refugees and other innocent noncombatants who become trapped on the heartless fields combat. The futility of his effort was demonstrated when, three years after he had retired, he received dismal news from the Far East. The Philippine Constabulary under the command of General Leonard Wood has slaughtered over nine hundred Moro men, women and children in an extinct volcanic crater near Mt. Dajo on the island of Jolo. In deep sorrow over his wife's recent death, the news shattered him, and he fell into a deep depression. It was a bottomless pit from which he could not emerge. Alone with the memories of the twisted and frozen bodies at Wounded Knee, he suffered the agonies of the damned. When he could stand it no longer, he committed suicide.

Andy's father, whose nickname was Junior, graduated from West Point in 1890, just in time to ride with Joseph from Fort Robinson in Nebraska north to the Standing Rock Sioux Indian Reservation. Their mission was to persuade Sitting Bull, the influential old Sioux Medicine Man, not to join in rebellion with others of the Plains Indians. A new Ghost Dance craze was then sweeping the Dakotas, and within it were the seeds of open warfare. Because of his age and stature, Sitting Bull alone had the power to stop the Sioux from joining the suicidal movement. Joseph's long relationship with the elderly Indian made him the logical one to urge caution. The mission was unsuccessful, for the animosities were far too deep, but the results were dramatic. Sitting Bull cursed Joseph and then gave the Ghost Dance his blessing. Three months later, the old Indian was murdered as the strange religious craze swept through the Dakotas. That killing touched off the massacre of three hundred of Big Foot's people by the Seventh Cavalry near Wounded Knee Creek, where Junior first encountered a young lieutenant named Black Jack Pershing, who was soon to become famous. After meeting on that tragic battlefield, the two went on to serve together on Mindanao in the Philippines, where Pershing once more distinguished himself, this time as a Moro Province commander. President Teddy Roosevelt responded by promoting Black Jack from Captain to Brigadier General in one quick move over the heads of many more senior officers, and Pershing's star had ascended.

When the United States entered World War II, Pershing had just finished a two-year campaign on the Mexican border against Pancho Villa. With young George Patton at his side, he led his Buffalo Soldiers in a masterful effort. Although their campaign failed to catch Pancho, the underfunded and ill-equipped operation was so well managed that President Wilson rewarded Pershing by selecting him to command the American Expeditionary Force about to go to

France. Pershing in turn called Junior to his staff and directed him to mobilize a million men for the war effort.

The nation responded to the call, and a year later, the First Infantry Division, nicknamed the Big Red One, landed in France. It may have lacked equipment and training, but the Big Red One was over there. It was a proud outfit with its own motto: if you're going to be one, be a big red one.

Unfortunately, Junior's veteran Buffalo Soldiers were not to be a part of that effort, for they had been relegated to guard duty on the Mexican border. Stripped of their leaders and spread out in Texas and New Mexico, they were harshly treated by the citizenry and subjected to extreme discrimination. In Houston, the sheriff was especially harsh in his treatment of the Black soldiers.

In the heat of August after two months of harassment, therefore, they mutinied. During the resulting riot and rampage, eleven white citizens died. Military investigators recommended clemency because of the harsh treatment the Buffalo Soldiers had received, but Washington overruled. The longest mass trial in military history then took place in Texas. After a month of deliberation, eighteen Black soldiers were found guilty and summarily executed. Because the country was at war, the hangings were carried out without judicial review. Thirty-six more soldiers were given life at hard labor. No action was taken against the two white officers of the battalion. The NAACP cried out for vengeance.

Junior Walker was devastated. Under great pressure to form new fighting units, his office had searched the nation for leaders to command in France. Among those chosen and sent overseas were the best leaders of the Buffalo Soldiers. Without competent commanders to restrain them, the Houston battalion rioted, and Junior felt personally responsible. He thus appealed to General Pershing, requesting that he intervene on behalf of the soldiers with whom they both had served against the Indians, Spanish, Filipinos, and Mexicans. The General replied that soldiers had no business meddling in politics. Because he believed the trials were pure politics, and nothing more, he would not act. When Junior pointed out that the lives of the Buffalo Soldiers were at risk and that in the best of units, loyalty must go down as well as up, the General did not answer. That silence saddened Junior beyond measure, and he gave up his commission rather than render tacit approval to what he saw as unfair trials, harsh sentences, and hasty executions.

Back home in Cincinnati, young Andy Walker was caught up in the patriotic fervor that had swept the country. Our doughboys were going over to France to fight the hated Boche, and at fifteen years of age, Andy tried to sneak an enlistment into that conflict. Quickly discovered and rejected, he then tried for and won an appointment to West Point, as a member of the class of 1925. On his first day at Beast Barracks, he began an enduring conflict with Bob Harrison, an upperclassman from Georgia who resented the role Andy's grandfather had played in what Harrison called the "War of Northern Aggression." Starting at their first meeting, Harrison hazed Andy in an overt attempt to make him leave the Academy, Under Superintendent MacArthur's watchful eye, they fought on the football field and in the boxing ring, as Harrison tried unsuccessfully to make Andy give up and resign.

All was not conflict at the Academy, however, for at a mandatory Sunday Tea Dance in Cullum Hall, Andy met Penny, the beautiful daughter of a prominent Westchester attorney. For two years, they saw each other whenever she could ride the New York Central up to West Point from Marymount College in Tarrytown.

A year before graduation he took her to Flirtation Walk, and under Kissing Rock, he proposed. She accepted, and they planned to be married in the Cadet Chapel just after he received his Regular Army Commission as a Second Lieutenant at graduation. Fate intervened to postpone that happy day, however, for Junior had wasted away since resigning his own Commission. By the time of Andy's graduation, Junior had become seriously ill. His hair was white, his speech halting, and his complexion sallow. As Andy strode across the stage to accept his diploma and begin life as an Army engineer, Junior rose, staggered toward the rostrum, and fell to the floor, the victim of a massive stroke.

Andy and Penny quietly married, canceling their planned reception and postponing their honeymoon. Andy applied for and

Sandy's War

received emergency leave to care for his father. The rumor was that General Pershing personally approved Andy's petition. Back in Cincinnati, Andy spent three months at Junior's bedside, as his dying father struggled to tell him about the tragic events of

1890: the failed mission to Sitting Bull's remote cabin and Wounded Knee. Most of all, Junior seemed to want Andy to know about some sort of curse Sitting Bull had placed on the Walker family. Junior died on September 5th, the anniversary of the day he had met Sitting Bull and the same date government agents at Fort Robinson had murdered the great Sioux war chief Crazy Horse many years before.

After Junior's death, Andy and Penny went on their delayed honeymoon. For a month in Andy's Model T they toured the Indian battlefields that Junior had described. The Rosebud was smaller than they had envisioned, and the Little Big Horn was sobering as they imagined the great mass of Sioux and Cheyenne warriors surrounding Custer's 250 doomed men. They found the site of the fort Joseph had commanded along the Bozeman Trail, but the ruins were on lands now owned by an Indian, and he would not let them enter. When they confronted him, he repeated the exact curse Sitting Bull had placed on Joseph thirty-five years before.

Fifteen difficult years followed. The Depression, forced leave without pay, and the responsibility for their children, Sandy and Kathleen, wore them down. Penny's romantic illusions of glamorous military life generated by her experiences at West Point were dashed in hot, dry, dusty places like Forts Sill and Polk. As an engineer officer, Andy had to build latrines and barracks instead of bridges and buildings. Their marriage strained. Some relief came when Andy was sent to the Engineer District at Pensacola. That was when Penny's mother left her some money, and they bought a small cottage on the beach at nearby Destin.

Then, Federal money became more available, and the Army sent them from New York on the USS Washington down the East Coast, through the Panama Canal, up to San Francisco, and out to Hawaii.

In the summer of 1941, military life in Hawaii was more to Penny's liking. She had help with the housework, time on her hands, and a dance every Saturday night at the officers club. On the other hand, Andy was assigned to a combat engineer battalion that seemed to have no interest in preparing to fight. His attempts to whip his unit into shape were frustrated by his commander and complicated by the arrival of Lieutenant Colonel Harrison, his old nemesis from West Point. Such complications became more vexing when Harrison began to take an interestin Penny. At one Saturday night dance, she and Andy quarreled over Harrison. The following morning, the Japanese attacked.

Penny's sleepy Hawaiian scene turned to chaos. Andy dashed off to defensive positions on the north shore of the island. And that night, when the Army jammed their apprehensive dependents onto ancient yellow school buses for transport from Schofield Barracks to Honolulu, nervous soldiers frequently stopped them at hastily established roadblocks. Occasionally, they heard rifle fire. Once, in panic to avoid bullets, they scrambled onto the floors of the buses. The Army kept them in the city for two weeks before permitting them to return to their homes. There, everything had changed. No dances. No household help. No officers club. After a week, Andy came home briefly to tell her that she was to be sent back to Florida, while he was headed for the South Pacific. This was not what she had bargained for back at West Point, and she let him feel her anger. Three weeks later, when the Army herded her and the children like cattle onto the USS *Lurline* for evacuation to San Diego, she boarded ship without saying goodbye.

Promoted to command of his battalion, Andy took his unit to the Fiji Islands. For months they worked to expand the main island airfield so that it could accept heavy military traffic. Every day, they received reports that the relentless Japanese were advancing ever nearer. Night and day, Andy drove his men hard, in spite of incessant rains and the violent opposition of native islanders who did not want him to disturb their lands. Finally, the task was finished, just in time to support the battle of the Coral Sea and the Marine landings on Guadalcanal. The engineers were then able to rest and relax while they prepared for a move to New Guinea. At several picnics and volleyball games, Andy spoke with Helen Vincent, a Red Cross Volunteer who worked at a nearby aid station. Once, when rain interrupted an outing, they ran together for his Jeep. He had intended to drive her to the Red Cross bivouac area, but on impulse he stopped at his place so they could dry out. They had a drink of sour mash bourbon and danced to the strains of "Sleepy Lagoon" on the radio. The moment was too intense to resist, and they became lovers.

Andy and Helen were together only a month before she was sent to Australia and he took his unit to Port Moresby on the Island of New Guinea. He lost track of her as he fought to build the Buna Road through the jungles, mountains, and Japanese on the eastern part of the island. Once that was successfully accomplished, he built airfields for the Sixth Army as it island-hopped its way west to the Philippine Islands. There, he assembled men and materiel in preparation for the invasion of Japan. Those preparations forecast that a half million Americans would become casualties, and he readied his unit for the grim task. Suddenly, atomic bombs destroyed Hiroshima and Nagasaki, and the war was over.

Promoted to Colonel, Andy joined General MacArthur's staff for the occupation. One of his tasks was to assess the damage done by the atomic blasts. The destruction was overwhelming, and Andy began to question the political decision to use such weapons on civilians in undefended cities. When informed of Andy's doubts, General MacArthur sent him home.

Andy's reunion with Penny was strained, and they clashed almost immediately over his assignment again to Pensacola. Penny was tired of Florida and yearned for her New York home. In a huff, she left Andy for a visit with her father there, and she never returned to Florida. Although she and Andy never formally separated, and they occasionally corresponded, the marriage was effectively over. Six years later, Andy made his only visit to New York, where he was to testify about Atomic weapons before a committee of the United Nations General Assembly. While there, he encountered Harrison, now a Brigadier General with the United States mission to the United

Nations. When he discovered that Harrison was dating Penny, Andy was crushed. He returned to Florida and resigned his Commission.

For twenty years, Andy remained alone in the little Destin cottage, brooding about his failed marriage and obsessed over the atomic tests being conducted in the Marshall Islands. He drank too much and became isolated from family and friends. During that time, his grandson, Walter, was drafted, went to Vietnam, and was at My Lai on March 16, 1968, the day of the massacre. Interrogated, but exonerated, Walter left the Army and went to law school in Columbia, South Carolina. For Walters graduation, Penny and Harrison flew down from New York to congratulate him. On their way out of the airport, a car hit them, and all three were killed. A Vietnamese immigrant drove the offending vehicle. The date was September 5, 1973.

Andy spent the following year on the wagon. He undertook an exercise and diet program, and he lost twenty-five pounds. His cholesterol, blood pressure, and body fat dropped to acceptable levels. His doctor could not believe the improvement. At the end of the year, Andy hired a private detective to find Helen. She had never married and was living in Alexandria, Virginia, near a girl's school where she had taught English Composition. Andy then flew up to National Airport, rented a car, and called her. She hesitated, but finally agreed to meet. After a quiet dinner at the Army Navy Country Club, he proposed marriage, she accepted, and they moved to Mobridge, South Dakota near the Standing Rock Indian Reservation and the Sioux Indians his grandfather had fought for so many years.

CHAPTER ONE

Sandy Walker was on a losing streak. Two months before he was to leave for Vietnam, Nancy had served divorce papers on him. Then shortly after he arrived at Saigon in November, the South Vietnamese paratrooper battalions he had been assigned to advise had tricked him in order to conceal the coup they were about to attempt against President Diem. Finally, his commanders had sharply criticized the report he had submitted about the causes of that failed revolt. And just now, in spite of clear evidence of how the French failed using that policy, newly inaugurated President Kennedy had sharply increased the number of American combat advisors like Sandy in Vietnam, increasing their ranks from five hundred to fifteen thousand. The new American Administration back home was evidently determined to continue and escalate a policy Sandy considered flawed. Frustrated, he had decided to take extreme measures.

He contacted Mac, his West Point classmate. Old Ripsaw, as they still called him, was working with security elements at the American Embassy in Saigon, and Mac agreed to meet Sandy at the Tan Son Nhut airbase's officers club just outside of town. After warm initial exchanges, some reminiscences about West Point and the Army, and a second beer, Sandy explained why he had sought out Old Ripsaw.

"The parachute battalions I'm advising were involved in that coup attempt last November," he said, "and the American mission in Saigon ordered me to investigate. They directed me to find out why my paratroopers wanted to kick Diem out."

"Did you?"

"Sure, at least I think so. But it's a real mess, and that's why I wanted to talk to you."

"What kind of a mess? Were you involved? Were you working with them? That would be really bad, old buddy, maybe even court-martial stuff. Did you have any idea they were about to attack Diem?"

"Not a clue," Sandy said. "Three weeks before the attack, they sent me out west to Cu Chi. Their explanation was that they wanted me to help train and set up an artillery battalion there. In retrospect, I think it was just an excuse to get me out of the way so I wouldn't discover what they were doing."

"Okay, so you're clean, and you did a postmortem. What'd you find out?"

"The paratroopers are elite soldiers," Sandy said. "They're very patriotic, willing and anxious to carry the fight to the guerrillas. But they've lost faith in President Diem and the henchmen he has around him."

"Why do you think they've lost faith?"

"They don't like what Diem's doing. He uses his soldiers more against his political enemies than the insurgents. He acts like a French colonialist, and because the South Vietnamese people have hated the French for such a long time, they're starting to hate him. Under Diem, the ARVN isn't the Army of Vietnam, it's a gang of government bully boys. And when ARVN does get off its ass and go into a field operation, it acts like the peasants are the enemy, instead of citizens it's supposed to defend. They terrorize villagers, torture people, burn down houses, and torch crops. Almost everything they've been doing turns innocent or neutral villagers into communist sympathizers. The paratroopers decided to attempt that coup because they thought their country was losing a fight it could win. They still think that, and they want new leadership. I'm not so sure they're wrong."

The discussion went on for three more beers and two more hours. Sandy made repeated arguments that President Diem was leading his country in the wrong direction, ARVN forces were disorganized and ineffective, and Diem's own people were turning against both him and the Americans. To Sandy, the evidence was overwhelming. Finally, the beer, time, or the arguments won Mac over to Sandy's side.

"Okay, old buddy," Mac said, "I know someone in the embassy that might be sympathetic and able to help. And you're in luck, because next Sunday, a group of American officers and embassy staffers are going on an outing down to My Tho. That's the capitol of Dinh Tuong province, just South of Saigon. I'll meet you there and introduce you."

Checking the map and Mac's directions, Sandy found that My Tho was indeed just some fifty kilometers south of Saigon on Route 4. So, he arranged to leave the city the following Sunday as soon as the first part of the highway to the south had been cleared of mines and ambushes. He set up a Jeep, to be driven by a paratrooper lieutenant he had befriended. In the back were two of the lieutenant's best sergeants. They had families at My Tho, and they were happy to accompany him as bodyguards. They told him that My Tho was a beautiful city of some forty thousand people on the north branch of the Mekong River. The place had been a favorite of the French, and now the Americans prized it as an easy, relatively safe field trip away from the capitol, where they especially enjoyed a certain Chinese restaurant on the north bank of the river.

For this trip, Sandy and the Vietnamese lieutenant wore combat fatigues and paratrooper berets. They were armed with 9mm French automatic pistols. Two American M-1 rifles were in slings on the sides of the Jeep. The sergeants in back were serious about their roles as bodyguards. They wore American steel helmets and carried French 9mm MAT-49 submachine guns. They had plenty of grenades in an ammunition box at their feet. The road might have been cleared by the ARVN that morning and pronounced safe, but the paratroopers knew they had to be ready to fight. That need was clearly demonstrated by the bullet-pocked concrete blockhouses that guarded the narrow, steel-trestle, single-lane bridges the French had built along the way. Nervous, dispirited, and glum ARVN soldiers guarding those bunkers were clearly frightened and apprehensive as they waved the paratroop Jeep through. A little over halfway to their destination, they checked in at Tan An, the capital of Long An province. There, the ARVN district command duty officer claimed that the rest of the road was also clear, so they started out again. By then, the paved highway had turned into a dusty, rutted tract filled with bicycles, taxis, trucks, and peasants carrying packages of all sizes and shapes. In spite of the crowded, deteriorating road, however, by ten o'clock, they arrived safely at My Tho. Their objective was the palatial home of the ARVN commander in that area. Because he was one of President Diem's buddies, he had had enough clout to commandeer the residence of the former French governor of the province, and he was hosting a party on what was now his own private mansion and tennis court.

When the paratroopers dropped Sandy off at the compound in question, he was impressed. Up to now, he had seen nothing outside of Saigon to compare with this. Most of the villagers he had seen were living in poor conditions and grass huts without running water. The My Tho ARVN commander here obviously wasn't sharing their pain. His grounds occupied an entire city block, with an eight-foot, pink-stucco wall surrounding the buildings, gardens, and tennis court. Noting armed soldiers at each outside corner and two each on the front and rear gates, Sandy guessed that guerrillas were active in the area, and he reckoned that an ARVN infantry squad was on duty around the compound at all times. Just inside, their squad leader would be in radio contact with a nearby platoon reaction force. Sure enough, an ARVN noncommissioned officer met him at the front gate. He asked for Sandy's pistol, but Sandy refused to surrender it, and his paratroopers stood by to back him up. Instead of surrendering his weapon, Sandy forcefully told the ARVN sergeant that he wanted to see the American Embassy security officer inside. For a moment, the man hesitated. After sizing up the paratroopers, however, he went back to his radio. Shortly thereafter, Old Ripsaw appeared and vouched for Sandy. As Mac walked Sandy past the soldiers on duty, however, he warned Sandy that the guards would be watching closely. Their mission was to protect their commander, and if Sandy were to take his pistol from its holster for any reason, they would react.

As the two of them worked their way through the sparse crowd and tropical landscaping toward the tennis court to pay respects to their host, Sandy noted about an equal mix between Vietnamese and Americans, half in casual clothes and half in sports attire. The Vietnamese women were particularly attractive in their national dress, the au dai. It combined loose, white, long trousers with a white, high collared, knee-length tunic split up the sides to the waist. Their slender bodies were completely covered, but the figure-hugging design of the tunic created a particularly sensuous effect. One woman, a bit taller than the others, particularly attracted him because of her erect carriage and shapely figure. He wondered if she was a native of My Tho. Among the men, Sandy was the only one in uniform and armed. At over six feet and two hundred pounds, he was hard to ignore as he moved through the smaller Vietnamese.

Mac introduced Sandy to their host and several guests. Then he suggested they take some light food and iced tea from the buffet table and find a quiet seat in the shade. Soon they were seated and enjoying their snack, as Sandy reflected on the contrast between the easy life of an embassy officer and combat duty with the paratrooper battalion. The differences between the haves and the have-nots also permeated Vietnamese society. That meant a long fight lay ahead in Vietnam. At first, no one joined them. Then the Vietnamese woman Sandy had particularly noted earlier approached their table. Up close, she was stunning, with the straight, black hair and clear, radiant, bronzed complexion of the best of her race. But her cheekbones were not quite as prominent and her features were not as coarse as others Sandy had seen in Saigon. She was also several inches taller than the average Vietnamese woman, and her au dai revealed more than ample curves.

"Hello, Avril," Mac said. "May I introduce a West Point classmate of mine, and good friend, Major Sandy Walker? Sandy, this is Avril de Castries."

For some reason, the direct gaze of Avril's large, brown eyes seemed to fluster Sandy, and he stumbled as he rose from his chair and took off his beret. As she took the chair that Mac offered, Sandy stammered that he was pleased to meet her. She nodded quietly, saying nothing.

"Sandy," Mac then said, "Avril is the Executive Secretary to the Cultural Attaché at the embassy. She has been there longer than any other member of the staff, and she knows just about everybody. She may be able to find an embassy officer who might be willing to hear you out."

The fact that Avril looked ten years younger than Mac gave Sandy reason to question Mac's information about her tenure at the embassy and her ability to solve Sandy's problem. But he had no reason not to trust Mac's judgment, so he decided to go along for the time being.

"Why don't you tell Avril what you told me?" Mac said." I guarantee you can trust her."

"Miss de Castries," Sandy said, "I am the military advisor to several Vietnamese airborne battalions stationed near Saigon. Those battalions joined in that failed coup attempt against President Diem last November. My superiors asked me to determine why the troopers had attempted a revolt. My findings and report are what I would like to discuss."

"Please call me Avril, Major Walker" she said. "I would be happy to hear what you have to say."

Again, Sandy was flustered, this time at her accent. She spoke English as if she were French, rather than Vietnamese. For some reason, he thought of Edith Piaf and "Le Vie en Rose."

"Avril," he said, savoring the name, "I believe that those paratroopers are good patriots who just want what is best for their country. They staged that coup in order to change a leadership that they believe is acting poorly and going down a losing path."

"And what path is that?" she asked.

"They think that what's now going on is an attempt by President Diem to establish a dictatorship based on his personal power and modeled after the defeated French colonial regime. In that effort, Diem uses ARVN and my paratroopers more against the religious sects like the Hoa Hao Buddhists and the Cao Dai, as well as crime rings like the Bihn Xuyen, than he does against the guerrillas. And whenever he does move against insurgents in the provinces, he directs more violence and reprisals against the peasants than the communists. He even dresses and acts like a colonialist, wearing that white suit like a Frenchman, rather than put on Vietnamese clothes, and chain-smoking. His policies and actions have driven masses of the Vietnamese people into joining or sympathizing with the insurgents. That's why the villagers down in Ben Tre Province revolted a while back. They were reacting to oppression and being forced from their villages into the new strategic hamlets. Those are some of the reasons the paratroopers think the country's leadership is driving the people into supporting North Vietnam. They want change."

"You certainly present a negative picture of what the paratroopers think," she said. "And you, tell me what do you personally believe."

"I believe the whole situation here is too complicated for someone like me who has been here only six months. It's for people like you who have been here a lifetime to judge."

They talked for an hour, during which Sandy became deeply impressed with her intelligence and grasp of the situation. Why would a mere secretary know so much and be so concerned? He was disappointed when she rose to depart, but his disappointment disappeared when she said she would call him in a week to set up a meeting with someone of authority who would listen. As she left them, he marveled at her grace and beauty. He could hardly wait to see her again. It was going to be a long week.

"That is some gal," he told Mac.

"Looks and brains," Mac said. "I thought you'd like her."

"Thanks for introducing her," Sandy said. "You sleeping with her?"

"No. I once made a pass, but she quickly shut me down.

Oh, I'm sure she's had male friends in the past, but not for some time. To my knowledge, right now, she's alone."

"Why is that?"

"I can't rightly tell you," Mac said. "I guess it's because she's all business, sort of unapproachable."

The paradox deepened. She was a beautiful woman, and yet, in a city full of lonely men, she was unattached. It was hard to believe. His business done, however, Sandy took the first chance he had to thank Mac and his host, leave the compound, and walk over to the Chinese restaurant on the river where he was to meet the Jeep. A few hours later, as the paratroopers drove him back to Saigon, he was silent, lost in thoughts of the mystery woman he had just met. The next week would be a long one.

CHAPTER TWO

The explosions never stopped. Safe in their protective caves and redoubts, the enemy gunners were directing artillery fire at pointblank ranges with devastating effect, and their infantry was dug in less than six hundred yards away. And now, he had no howitzers capable of answering their destructive and demoralizing fires. For over two months, the surrounding enemy soldiers had slowly dug their trenches and tunnels closer each day, inching their heavy guns ever nearer. He had suffered heavy casualties, almost three thousand dead and three times that number of wounded. Now, no supplies could reach him and his exhausted men. No planes could land, and no more paratrooper reinforcements dropped out of the dark clouds above the ruined airfield. And there was no way out. The airstrip was so full of holes and mud that even the bravest of pilots could not land. And he could not escape. The enemy soldiers were too numerous, and all protective cover had been stripped away by their constant shelling. Without water, ammunition, or food, he and his men would soon die, even if the enemy did not mount a final charge. Suddenly, as another massive barrage began, and masses of black-pajama-clad North Vietnamese soldiers in their cone hats swarmed at him. Dazed, he raised his hands in surrender, waiting, even hoping, for some enraged enemy soldier to shoot him, and then through eyes blued by blood, he saw the command bunker overrun. And in a few moments, General Christian de Castries emerged with a white flag held above his bloodied and bandaged face. ...

Startled, Sandy awoke, his body covered with perspiration. Eyes now wide open, he sat upright on his cot. What had he dreamed? Then he remembered: He had seen General de Castries surrender at Dien Bien Phu. And that was her name: Avil de Castries. How could that be? The mystery deepened. What was the relationship? Who was she? He lay back and by recalling her striking face, he tried to erase the nightmare scenes of dead and dismembered French soldiers lying face down in the muddy hills of North Vietnam, but the contrasting images kept mixing together so that he could not separate them. And he didn't want to sleep and dream the horror again.

He had been distracted for a week by the impact of the dream and the memory of her dark eyes. Then to his relief, she called. They were to meet at the Hotel Continental in the center of Saigon at cocktail hour on the following Saturday afternoon. The location was a convenient one, because the Vietnamese army had provided living space for Sandy and the other American advisors in the Brinks Hotel near the French Quarter. They were adjacent to and just east of the headquarters of the United States Military Mission to Vietnam. Their rooms were sparse but far more comfortable than the rice paddies of the Delta. An attempt was made to provide some security so that the American officers could rest and recuperate when they were not out in the field with ARVN forces. From his rooms, Sandy could easily walk to the Continental. Much of the way lay through an old French colonial residential section, where the houses were concealed behind high walls and surrounded by tropical gardens. Through occasional black iron gates, he could see beige stucco buildings with red tiled roofs. The neat, rectangular structures all seemed to be made from the same form out of weathered alabaster walls. The roads and sidewalks were wide, and the whole area had an air of prosperous stability that was marred only by the fact that everywhere he found clear evidence of a continuing deterioration that revealed a lack of care and maintenance. The French had been gone for almost seven years now, and apparently, they had taken their money with them.

The rambling Continental Hotel was astride a corner and occupied almost an entire Saigon City block. A former billet of British and French officers, it was in a section of the city where fine shops sold everything from furs to the best of Oriental lacquerware. On the corner and running the length of the hotel's front was a porch, half under cover of rolled bamboo awnings. The porch was two-tiered, separated by wrought-iron railings and palm planters. The upper tier was under the marquee that bore the hotel's name in great white letters. The porch was brightly lit and cooled by ceiling fans. Thus, sheltered from the heat and rain, the white-jacketed, affluent clientele relaxed as they observed a never-ending stream of Renault taxis, Lambretta motorbikes, street hustlers, rickshaws, pimps, and prostitutes crowding the ample sidewalks and avenues. Above the sheltered porch rose two beige-colored stories punctuated by great, arched windows, the hallmarks of former French colonial elegance.

Sandy emerged from the crowd and moved easily through the great white columns and wide doors of the main entrance. He was dressed casually, in khaki trousers, sport shirt, and a light jacket for protection from the rain. He carried no weapon as he moved under the high ceilings, past the marble walls, and over the tiled floors toward what she had described as the main bar. Like Humphrey Bogart in that hotel in Casablanca, he paused at the entrance to permit his eyes to become accustomed to the dim light. Sure enough, what looked like white-suited Frenchmen were mixing with exotic Vietnamese women and fat Oriental gangsters. Glasses clinked and cigarettes in long, black holders poured smoke into the thick air of the congested bar. Music came from somewhere nearby. It was "As Time Goes By," and he would been surprised to see Hoagy Carmichael at the piano. Peering through the crowded room for the piano player, he saw instead that Avril was at a corner table with a middle-aged, nondescript American. Across the crowded room, she was stunning, a goddess, and the sight of her took his breath away. He went to her.

"This is Jon Bourne," she said. "Jon is the Economic Attaché at the embassy. He can help."

Sandy barely heard the name as he shook the man's hand. His attention was fixed on the fascinating woman whose image had so disturbed his sleep since they had last met. Was it just a week ago? Silver earrings and a delicate silver chain holding what must have been a birthstone set off her white, high-collared tunic. She wore a silver bracelet with a matching ring that was not a wedding band. Against her clear, cream colored skin, the effect was lovely. Who was this Avril de Castries? What was the source of the spell she had cast over him? She was sipping a white wine, and Bourne had what appeared to be scotch and soda. Sandy ordered a beer.

"Avril tells me you've definite views about what we're doing in Vietnam," Bourne said. "I'd like to hear them."

Brought back to reality, Sandy reluctantly shifted his attention to the embassy bureaucrat. With an effort, Sandy tried to size the man up. It was no use. The guy was a nothing. Why had Avril brought someone who couldn't help him? Oh well, Sandy would make an effort.

"That's right," Sandy said. "Headquarters wanted to know why my paratroopers attempted that coup against Diem last November, and when I took a closer look, I came to definite conclusions."

"Would you share them?" Bourne asked.

"The cause of the coup was failure of leadership at the highest levels," Sandy said. "All across the board."

"Assuming what you say is true, did you report this to your higher headquarters?" Bourne asked.

"Sure, but I got no response. Nobody cares."

"They may still be analyzing what you said. These things are complicated. They take time."

"Spoken like a true diplomat," Sandy said. "And you may be right, but I can tell that they've read and rejected it. I'm getting the cold shoulder already."

"Ignore that for the time being," Bourne said. "Let's assume you're correct in your analysis of the current situation. What would you have us do in Vietnam, or for that matter in Southeast Asia? If you were the new American President, what changes would you make?"

"That's an unfair question. The President has a multitude of avenues he can use, many I'm sure I've never even heard of. I'm just a military guy. We fight wars, but the President can use diplomacy, economic pressure, personal alliances, the CIA, and I'm sure there are other approaches I'm not aware of. I wouldn't know how to use those at all."

"Let's change the question then, how would you alter the American military approach here in South Vietnam?"

"You mean if I had full authority?"

"Yeah. Let's appoint you emperor for a day."

"First of all, if I were emperor, we probably wouldn't be here at all. One of the few axioms I remember from military history back at the Point is one that said, 'never get involved in a land war in Asia. The place is too big, and they have too many people." I would apply that one to Indochina and rule out the use of our troops here."

"But what about Ho Chi Minh and his aggression against the South? And the millions of people who fled from North Vietnam just six years ago to escape Communism? Now there may be as many as fifteen million people here in the south. Would you ignore them and condemn everyone to slavery under Communism?"

"I've thought a lot about that question, and I think you're looking at the trees, when you should be studying the forest. At the heart of this situation there's a larger question, one that my father pointed out to me just before I came over here. That one says that the enemy of my enemy is my friend. I would suggest that based on what happened in Korea, the Chinese are our real adversaries in Asia. If you realize that the Vietnamese and the Chinese have been fighting one another for more than a thou sand years, you would have to conclude that the Viets should be our friends, not our enemies."

"But they aren't."

"They were at the end of World War II. Our OSS worked well with them against the Japanese occupation. We gave them guns and bullets. We told them about freedom, and we were the best of friends back then. After the war, they loved us. Ho Chi Minh repeatedly sent messages to President Truman and our State Department asking for help in gaining the freedom our advisors had described. General Marshall was the Secretary of State, and the recommendation of the State Department to the President was that he ignore Ho in order to please the French. That's what he did, but my point is that we might be able to build on that history and be allies again."

"How?"

"Talk to them. I mean really sit down and talk to them. Work out our differences at the conference table, not in the jungle, rice paddies, and villages."

"But you said you were a military man. What you're talking about is geopolitics. You're not addressing military strategy or tactics on the ground. What about those?"

"If Diem is going to fight the guerrillas, his army has to contest the night and the jungles, on a man-to-man basis with his enemies. If he continues the way he's going now, he loses. This search and destroy business will do nothing more than alienate the villagers. The French lost a hundred thousand men in Indochina trying to sweep and destroy. When the searchers march through, the insurgents melt away, only to come back when the outsiders have gone. No, the ARVN has to stay on the ground and win the loyalty of the villagers. American soldiers can't do that. Only the ARVN can, and its leaders won't let them."

"Why do you think that is?"

"President Diem needs his army. It is his source of power. If he sends them out to fight for the villages, his soldiers will take casualties, maybe enough to make them want to change national leadership. So, he keeps them close to home and rewards commanders who don't lose men. If that keeps up, his enemies will eventually take over the whole countryside. And when that happens, he's finished. That's a loser."

"And what's your conclusion?"

"Either Diem takes off that colonial white suit and starts leading his country and winning the support of his people, or you find someone who can. What's going on now is wrong. He has to inspire the ARVN to fight, or you get rid of him. Remember how Ramon Magsaysay eliminated the Huks in the Philippines. He was a popular leader, one who was always out among his people, and he won. You need a man like that here, or you better sit down at the table and bargain with Ho Chi Minh."

"Can you be more specific?"

"Sure. All the airborne soldiers in my group, and that's five battalions of them, from their commander on down, all they want to do is fight for their country. They are being prevented from doing that."

"How so?"

"Most of their operations are with the ARVN 7th Infantry Division in the northern part of the Delta, and the Division Commander, Colonel Huynh Van Cao, is typical of the problem. He is only thirty years old, and he doesn't have the experience or knowledge to command a Division in combat. Time and again, my paratroopers join his Division and are within inches of trapping major elements of the insurgents, only to have Colonel Cao waste the opportunity. I was recently on one such mission myself. We had surrounded a Main Force guerrilla battalion on three sides, and all Cao had to do was commit his reserve force to close the gap. He didn't do it. And by failing to do so, he allowed a major guerrilla unit in Dinh Tung Province to slip through the net and fight again some other day."

"Why would he do that?" Bourne asked.

"I can think of three possible reasons: he may be inept, he may be afraid of taking casualties, or he may be a Communist sympathizer. In any case, his conduct is no way to defeat the insurgents in battle."

"And you think he is typical?"

"So, the airborne officers tell me, but they also tell me the problem goes even higher, to the civilian leadership of the country. As a result, the troopers revolted against President Diem because he represents that failed leadership."

"What did they see as failures?"

"President Diem uses the military more against political opposition than the guerrillas. My troopers have been in more fights with the Saigon criminal gangs, the Buddhist monks, and the other religious sects than they have against the soldiers and guerrillas of the north. And Diem acts like he wants to be a French Colonialist. He even wears that dirty white suit while constantly smoking a small, white, French cigarette, just like one of them. And just as the people hated the French, so they're starting to hate him. Over ninety percent of the people are Buddhists, but Diem is a Catholic. Instead of accepting them and trying to win them over, he's separating himself from them. He stays in his palace near the American embassy, rather than going out to listen to his people. That's why the guerrillas control three quarters of the Delta. That's why the airborne soldiers staged that coup to bring about change at the top."

"But the Saigon regime has to start somewhere," Bourne said. "They have to build on something. The Saigon gangs are lawless and corrupt."

"Sure, but Diem is on the wrong tack," Sandy said. "Even the programs he's started have alienated the people. Take that plan to start moving the villagers into strategic hamlets. That would take them away from their homes and make them refugees, and all they want to do is tend their fields the way they always have. Taking them away from the homes of their ancestors won't make them his friends. And that's typical. The government approaches every decision from the point of view of its own interests, not those of the people."

"And the paratroopers think the government is losing the support of the people," Bourne asked.

"Sure. The insurgents are out in the villages every night working with the peasants, while the ARVN hunkers down in their bunkers, afraid to fight in the dark. The guerrillas act as if they are part of the people, fighting for the farmers, while the government ignores the wellbeing of the peasants. It torches their fields to deny rice to the enemy. It kills their chickens and buffaloes. If it suspects a guerrilla unit is holed up in a village, it sends bombers and artillery to bombard the entire place, ignoring the fact that innocent villagers are living there too. The problem seems to be that Diem treats his people like peasants rather than voters. He uses force, rather than persuasion."

"And what should he do?"

"Two things: he needs to win over his people, and he should start talking to the North Vietnamese."

"How would you win over the people?"

"Back home at Fort Bragg, the Special Warfare Center has done tons of research on how to win the hearts and minds of the people. But over here, Diem isn't doing any of what we know has to be done. He has to make the people want to follow him rather than the insurgents. The villagers need to be secure in their own villages and not to fear the guerrillas. The ARVN has to stop those absurd search and destroy sweeps and establish a permanent presence in each village and hamlet, one location at a time. It's like when you throw a rock in a pond. The ripples work out in ever-widening circles. You'd start in Saigon and other government-controlled areas, and work out from those places.

Of course, that'd mean a larger ARVN with much better quick-reaction forces, like my paratroopers, ready to respond to attacks night and day. American advisors can be with every unit, showing them how this would work. The worst thing we could do is to turn the fighting over to American units, yet I hear talk about bringing American combat units over here. They would be like the French all over again. It was wrong back then, and it's wrong now. The South Vietnamese must win this one through their own efforts. All we can do is show them how."

"And you would talk to the North Vietnamese?"

"Sure. And the stronger President Diem's government gets, and the more the people support him, the more the North will listen. Before I came over here, my father lectured me about China. He said that China is our real enemy in the Far East, not Ho Chi Minh. China and Vietnam have been fighting for a long time. Ho was so afraid of China after World War Two that he agreed to let the French come back in rather than have the Chinese replace them. He reminded his people that the last time the Chinese came, 'they stayed a thousand years.' If it is really true that the enemy of my enemy is my friend, we should be making friends with Ho rather than fighting him. And remember, as I told Avril down in My Tho, we did just that at the end of World War Two. Our OSS fought at his side against the Japanese. Back then, we told him we were fighting for the freedom of his people, and he loved us. We need to build that relationship again, rather than let it slip away."

"If we and Diem talk to Ho Chi Minh," Jon said, "what is our objective? We talked to them at Geneva six years ago. The outcome was to be free elections that were to decide the future of Vietnam. It didn't work back them. Why would it work now?"

"It didn't work for two reasons: South Vietnam wasn't strong enough to compete against the North, and your State Department sabotaged the elections. If Diem wins the hearts and minds of his people, that would remove the first obstacle. And if our State Department stops looking at the trees and starts looking at the forest, we can pull out of here. Communism isn't unified at all, and we shouldn't see Ho as a tool of the Soviet Union and China. He could be a buffer against Chinese expansion into all of Southeast Asia."

The discussion continued for over an hour, as the two of them exchanged views. Avril seldom entered into the dialogue. As before, she held back as if she were studying Sandy and his views. Occasionally, she would nod or shake her head, but she did so quietly, so as not to interrupt them. Finally, the exchanges ended, and Jon rose to go.

"I give you my word that I'll pass your views on to the appropriate people," he said. "But I must warn you that the other side holds strong ideas about these matters. They'll need good reasons to make changes now, more than what I've seen here. But let's agree to meet again next week."

They shook hands, and he left them. As Sandy watched the man leave, he was discouraged. Try as he would, he could find no reason to think he had had made any progress in convincing the other to agree with him. Indeed, Bourne had remained skeptical, and Sandy felt frustrated. Avril interrupted his thoughts.

"You were quite persuasive," she said.

He turned his attention to her. She had been so quiet that he had thought she was almost disinterested in the problems they had been discussing. And her stunning beauty was in such sharp contrast to the problems of ugly guerrilla warfare that it again took his breath away. He didn't want the meeting to end.

"How 'bout another glass of wine?" he asked.

CHAPTER THREE

"I thought I'd try one of your beers," she said. Then she suddenly brightened. "And the chef here is very good. Why don't we look at a menu?"

Suddenly, he was starving, and he signaled for a waiter. As they discussed the various menu entrees, he studied her. Her dark eyes and black hair beautifully set off the high cheekbones and creamy complexion that had so attracted him back in My Tho. Yet she seemed to wear no makeup and he caught only a faint hint of perfume. Everything about her was delicate, even exotic, and her every aspect hinted of the mysterious Far East. Yet her English was impeccable, and her disconcertingly direct gaze was certainly not oriental. Curiosity consumed him.

"Who are you?" he asked.

"What a question," she said. "You know who I am."

"On the contrary," he said, "you are a puzzling enigma, and I haven't a clue. Are you Vietnamese, or French? And how come my buddy Ripsaw picked you as my embassy contact? You're in the office of the cultural attaché. Why not pick an American who is involved in security matters? And why did you select Bourne as the one to meet me? He isn't your cultural attaché. He says he's an economic representative, but he sure doesn't talk like one. You speak excellent English and from what I just heard between you and that waiter, even better French. Even your name, de Castries, is a mystery. That was the name of the final French commander at Dien Bien Phu. What goes?"

"My father was a French banker, actually a cousin of General de Castries. When the French arrived in Indochina a hundred years ago, they began a program of economic development. Primarily, they created a vast irrigation system of dikes and dams that turned the southern part of the country into the rice basket of Southeast Asia. French banks financed that and the prosperity that followed, and my father benefited because he was a third generation part of the financing effort."

"Did the bankers finance the opium trade too?"

"Unfortunately, they did that also," she said. "Opium was a big part of the system back then."

"From what I hear, it still is."

"True, but my family never had anything to do with that, even though my mother was from a prominent Vietnamese family. They were businesspeople who dealt in commerce other than opium. That's how speak: French and Vienamese."

"And the English?"

"When my father left Vietnam after the war, my family stayed here. My mother used the money he gave her to send me to the best schools in the country, at Da Lat and the University of Saigon. I studied English because I thought that in the years to come, it would become the world's universal second language."

"Your father stayed here during World War II? Was he Vichy French? Did he collaborate with the Japanese?"

"No, he protected the country from the Japanese," she said. "When France fell, Vichy France negotiated a treaty with the invaders that restricted the number of Japanese soldiers who would be garrisoned here. In return, the French were permitted to maintain law and order. As a result, my father was a part of the system that protected all of us until the last months of the war. That was when the Japanese moved in, assumed power and began a systematic purge of the French. Father had to fee then to avoid persecution.

"He didn't take you with him?"

No, the Japanese staged a sudden coup, and immediately they began killing great numbers French. When they came they to our house, he barely escaped into hiding, and he had to leave the country very quickly. I'm not sure my mother would have gone with him anyway. Here, she was a member of a respected family. In France, she would have been a foreigner."

"And your family now doing business with the Americans?"

"No, my family was devastated by what happened after the war. When Japan was defeated, the Communist Viet Minh moved in and took revenge on those they thought were a part of the Vichy French government here. They killed many. Then the French came back and retaliated against those who seemed to be sympathetic with the Viet Minh. They were the ones that killed my mother, and after that, they confiscated the family business. I was fortunate to be away at school, or I would have died too. After the chaos, I emerged with only our home to show for my father's many efforts. I'm alone now, just trying to survive."

"But you have a job with the American Embassy."

"As I told you, I had studied English. Fortunately, when the Americans came, they needed multilingual nationals with an education. President Truman upgraded the American Consulate to Embassy status in 1950, and that's when they hired many of us. I've been with the embassy for ten years. That's why I know so many people there."

"How old are you?" he asked.

"A gentleman wouldn't ask such a question," she said. "I would rather ask about you. Why are you in my country?"

"I'm a soldier," he said. "I come from a long line of soldiers. I'm here because my President thinks I should be. My assignment is to help organize, train and employ the ARVN parachute forces."

"Your father was also a soldier?" she asked.

"Yes. He was and engineer. He graduated from the United States Military Academy in the mid-twenties. My sister and I were raised during the Depression, in the great Army dust bowls of America. Then things got better, and just before World War II, we were sent to Hawaii, and we were there when the Japanese attacked those islands. Mom, sis, and I were sent home, and dad moved to the Southwest Pacific for four long years. I went to West Point, married Nancy after graduation, had two kids, and almost got killed in Korea."

"You are married?" she asked.

"Was married, but not any more," he said. "Nancy couldn't stand the separations and uncertainty of military life, and she divorced me when I became a parachutist and was sent over here. She said the kids needed a live father who would be around to raise them, not a dead hero. That's one of the many ways Army life can be rough on families."

"How do you feel about the divorce?

"Failure hurts, especially the kids."

"Where are your children now?"

"With their mother at a place called Destin, a small town in the panhandle of Florida, on the northern coast of the Gulf of Mexico. Nancy was raised there, and her parents now help with the kids."

"How old are they?" she asked.

"Walter is eleven, and Sara is nine. They go to school in nearby Pensacola."

"You must miss them," she said. "Do you see them often?"

"I take annual vacations with them, and I write them when I can. They write now and then. It's not a good arrangement, but it's the best I can do."

"I think I would agree with Nancy," she said. "If you were my husband, I wouldn't want you jumping out of planes. And I can see why she would rather have you with her than off in Korea or Vietnam. I know I would."

"It's a tough world," he said. "My grandmother once told me about a poet that wrote that life is a continual farewell. I didn't know then what he meant. But now, as I listen to you talk about your life in Vietnam and compare mine, I think I have a better idea of what he had in mind: people come and go all the time, and one generation replaces another. A lot of life is saying goodbye."

"My view would be that life's also continually new," she said. "And as for your previous question, I'll answer now: I'm thirty. How old are you?"

"Thirty-four," he said. "You know what todays is?"

"The first day of the rest our lives?"

"Good answer," he said. "It's also Valentines Day. Back home, people think a lot about love on Valentines Day."

"Here too," she said.

At that moment, someone at the jukebox selected a current hit, the "The Hawaiian Wedding Song." For reasons he could not explain, it was one of his favorites.

"Dance?" he asked.

For a moment, she hesitated. Then she nodded. On the small dance floor, he took her in his arms. She seemed unexpectedly light as she moved easily in rhythm to the sound of Hawaiian steel guitars and the slow beat of the music. At first she held herself a chaste six inches away from him, but then she moved closed, and he felt her body against him. Encouraged, he put both arms around her waist, she responded by outing her arms around his neck. He buried his face in her hair, and he was again aware of the exotic scent he had first noticed in the garden back at My Tho. This time, however, it was not as faint. Indeed, the closeness of their embrace caused him to be almost overwhelmed. He gave himself to the moment, closed his eyes, and drew her closer. It was heaven, too soon over. When the music ended, he took her hand as they walked back to the table. There, he held her chair for her, but she stopped.

"I must go," she said. "Thank you."

For a moment, she seemed about to say more. Then she brushed her hand against his cheek, gazed at him questioningly, turned, and quickly disappeared in the gathering crowd of the bar. Stunned, he stared after her. He started to follow her, but it was too late. She was gone.

CHAPTER FOUR

The nine aircraft flew in a "V" of "V's" with the first three planes forming a triangle and the other six making two triangles behind the first and abreast of each other. Each triangle held the combat elements of an infantry company, so that the formations carried the fighting soldiers of an entire paratrooper battalion. Sandy has positioned himself in the lead aircraft with the group commander, Major Tho. Leading the first battalion, they would initiate the attack, Sandy from the left door and Tho from the right. Their objective was a large complex of rice paddies to the west of the village of Phu Phuan Dong. Coincidentally, their direction of flight, east to west, took them almost directly over My Tho, where Sandy had met Avril, just a few weeks ago.

They had risen at four o'clock, assembled at the airfield, and taken a less than an hour ago. The operations plan had them hitting the ground at the beginning of morning nautical twilight, about a half an hour before sunrise. In an attempt to achieve surprise, they had discussed but eliminated an aerial bombardment of the area, and no Pathfinders had jumped into the area early. In this way, they hope to catch General Do, the enemy commander in that area of the Delta, asleep. The arrival of Sandy's Paratroopers would be the signal of the ARVN 7th Infantry Division to attack the enemy on the road network from the east and south, hoping to drive the guerillas into the guns of Sandy's battalions on the west. If the insurgents attempted to flee into the extensive mangrove swamps on the north, Colonel Cao had a Ranger Battalion in reserve to commit and catch them in the open. The primary objective of the operation was to wipe out the main guerrilla command and control elements for the entire area of the northern Delta.

Sandy had already taken his place in the side jump door of the old American C-119 aircraft. With his hands gripping the edge of the door, he positioned his feet so that he was ready to launch himself out. Ready to go, he glanced down at the ground less than a thousand feet below. Through the twilight haze, he could make out the lights of My Tho, and he was barely close enough to make out individual houses in the dim light. He searched for and found what he thought was the large compound where he had met Avril. For a moment, his mind wandered back to that first encounter. Then the plane lurched and brought him back to reality. He glanced back into the aircraft to size up the soldiers who were waiting to follow him out the door and into the dangers of combat. The Vietnamese paratroopers were crammed tightly into the plane and their equipment. Small in stature and suffering the nervous anxiety of the moment, they looked almost childlike wearing large American helmets, strapped into main and reserve parachutes, and holding duffel bags of equipment between their legs. From his lead position in the open door of the aircraft, Sandy wanted to offer encouragement. He repeatedly yelled "Airborne" back at them until they began to relax and started to yell back the conditioned response, "all the way." Satisfied, he then turned his attention to the red light on the tail boom outside. He was none too soon, for almost immediately, it turned green, and he threw himself into the twilight. The old American airplane flew slowly, and thus the opening shock of his parachute was not great. Soon he was floating quietly with four hundred troopers toward the rice paddies below. Because they had jumped from about eight hundred feet, they were on the ground quickly, and they immediately rushed to establish the blocking positions they had planned. The rice paddy had been easy to spot from above, even in the dim light, its brighter waters contrasting sharply with the dark dikes and woods nearby. And they had suffered no casualties in the jump. The planes were, headed back to Tan Son Nhut airfield to pick up another battalion of jumpers. Three lifts would place three battalions of Sandy's airborne group in place to block General Do's escape to the west.

Their positions ready, the paratroopers sent patrols toward the areas that intelligence had told them the guerillas were occupying.

Hawk Kiefer

Soon those scouts reported contact, and the battle was joined. Major Tho was pleased. The Americans were right. Extensive training was paying off, his men were ready, and the operation had been well planned. He knew the enemy would not stand and fight against the armored personnel carriers and half-tracks of the 7th Division coming at them from the other side. Soon General Do's men would be attacking his own men.

And attack they did. In less than a half and hour, hundreds of black-pajama-clad soildiers carrying AK-47 rifles swarmed across the dikes toward then. When the enemy was without cover in the open rice field, Major Tho fired a signal flare, and the paratroopers opened up with machineguns, mortars, and rifles. With good, interlocking fields of fire and well protected in covered positions, the troopers did their work well, taking a severe toll on the disorganized insurgents. As quickly as it had begun, the enemy attack ceased, and an apprehensive quiet took over the field. Sandy and Tho ranged up and down the paratroopers in their lines, looking for casualties and urging the soldiers to reload and prepare for the next assault. When they returned to the command post, the commanders compared notes.

"We lost two scouts and five wounded in Alpha and Bravo companies," Sandy said, "How about Charlie company?" "Three scouts dead and four wounded," Tho said. "We're in good shape. Will they attack again?"

"We have to find out," Sandy said. "You should send out patrols from each company. Try to establish contact and find out what they're doing."

"I'd prefer to hold our positions," Tho said. "We've lost five scouts on patrols already. No use in losing more."

"We have to find out if they are moving north, so we can tell Colonel Cao to commit the Rangers."

"My mission is to hold this line. I don't want to lose more men doing something I'm not tasked to do."

"Damn it, that's our mission," Sandy said. "Give me three men with a radio. I'll take them over there and report what the guerillas are up to."

Reluctantly, Major Tho finally agreed, and Sandy asked for the men who had been with him en route to MyTho. Quickly, they set out across the rice paddy toward the enemy positions. Bent over and running low, they dodged back and forth as they went. They were able to reach the next dike without taking fire, but when they started across the next field, they immediately met resistance. Rifle fire and grenades cracked and thumped around them. As was his habit, the enemy concentrated fire on the radio operator, and he soon took a hit. In another explosion, Sandy sustained some sort of a cut on his forehead, and he had to wipe blood from his eyes. He could tell from the light volume of fire and the absence of machineguns or mortars, however, that he and the two others faced only a small rear guard. Sandy told the lieutenant and the remaining sergeant to cover him while he made his way to the right in an attempt to flank the enemy position. He wiggled through the mud and down a small stream until he established himself on the dike south of the point from which enemy fire was coming. In that way, he and the two ARVN unhurt in the paddy had the enemy soldiers in an effective crossfire. With grenades and small arms, they cleared the dike. Once safely under cover, Sandy could see into the fields to his east. The guerillas were indeed moving toward the swamps on the north.

"Tell Major Tho the plan is working," he ordered the sergeant who taken over the radio. "If Colonel Cao commits the Rangers right away, he'll catch large numbers of the VC out in the open. It's a chance to inflict heavy losses, and it might not come again. He should do it now."

The sergeant made the call, but nothing happened. Colonel Cao continued to hold his Rangers in reserve, and he failed to press his own frontal assault against the guerillas. He later said he feared the situation was a trap set by General Do. That may have been the case, but as it was the main enemy force with General Do was able to fade into the mangroves to the north. In Sandy's mind, the operation was a failure. Such was not the view from Saigon. Because Colonel Cao's 7th Infantry Division had suffered no casualties, President Diem gave Cao a victory parade in Saigon and promoted him to the rank of brigadier general. The little Vietnamese president was now convinced that he knew far better than any of his American advisors how best to deal with the insurgents.

The Vietnamese battalion aid station cleaned the cut over Sandy's right eye, and he returned to duty disgusted again at the failure of the ARVN to carry out and operation that had been well-planned and on the brink of success. This was no way to win a war.

CHAPTER FIVE

Colonel Bob Newton was the Chief of Staff of the United States Military Assistance Advisory Group, Indochina. MAAG, as it was called, was formed in September of 1950, just after the outbreak of hostilities in Korea. Washington's decision to establish the MAAG in Vietnam was based on the belief that Communism was intent on mounting a coordinated worldwide offensive against the free world. Korea and Indochina were assumed to be just two theaters in which that conflict would be fought, and President Truman actually expected the Russians to attack in Europe in conjunction with the North Korean surprise attack in 1950. So, the mission to assist the South Vietnamese was set up at the time in anticipation of war in that area. Today, eleven years later, Newton was a year away from becoming Chief of Staff of the U.S. Military Assistance Command Vietnam (MACV). This was to be greatly expanded role for the United States, for newly elected President Kennedy had personally just approved the expansion. While MACV was working out its new organization back home, however, Newton's job was to control the activity of some five hundred advisors like Sandy who were already in Vietnam. Their numbers would grow to over eleven thousand by the following Christmas. When that happened, Newton wouldn't even have to move his office. MACV's new headquarters would still be in Newton's Saigon, in the same building, a former French cavalry compound along the wide, well-traveled avenue from Saigon to the Chinese section of the city in Cholon. Newton was co-located with, and the advisor to, the ARVN Corps that was responsible for defense of the Saigon Military District and its surrounding area, as well as the northern part of the Delta. As such, he was Sandy's direct superior.

Newton and his staff were housed in a three-story stucco building with the ubiquitous red-tiled roof found throughout the city. A large, slow-moving fan directly above him provided some cooling to his high-ceilinged office, and in order to provide a modicum of air circulation, he kept the swinging doors to the adjoining veranda and his windows wide open. In spite of those efforts, the office was uncomfortably warm when Sandy reported as ordered. Newton's bad mood added to the heat, and he didn't waste time with pleasantries when Sandy saluted him. Sandy's bruised forehead and black eye set Newton off.

"Major Walker," he said, "you aren't here to lead combat missions. Look at you: black and blue. You're a disgrace. You're supposed to be an advisor to that airborne group, not its combat commander. Do I make myself clear?"

"Absolutely, sir?" Sandy said.

The contrast between the two was also clear. Newton was stocky, maybe five foot eight inches tall, and he was twenty pounds overweight. Like his face, his body was square. What there was of his thinning blond hair was cropped short and flat, adding to his rectangular effect. Because of his appearance, he had earned the nickname "Brick." Rumor also had it that Brick was addicted to a certain massage parlor on To Do Street where apparently he had two favorite girls. The story was that he visited them two or three times a week. After bathing him, they put him on his back and began working on him from opposite ends with tongues like butterflies Their goal was to meet in the middle. In contrast to Brick, Sandy was over six feet tall, muscular, and trim, and he had never been to To Do Street. His black hair was neat but not shaved into a military cut, and he carried his two hundred pounds effortlessly. He held Brick's massage parlor in contempt. A powerful-looking man, he easily dominated any room he entered, including Newton's office, and that infuriated old Brick.

"Then what in the hell were you doing on that combat jump at Phu Phuan Dong last Tuesday?"

"The airborne battalions had just recently been organized," Sandy said. "They had never conducted such an operation before.

My job was to advise them on how to do it. And that requirement included preparations for that combat jump, instructions on how to assemble quickly on the drop zone, and guidelines on how to organize an immediate defense on the ground. Because they were so new at it, I thought they needed me with them, and that included the jump."

"If they needed you with them, you haven't been training them well enough, have you? And training is supposed to be your job, not splashing around in some rice paddy. And what's worse, I'm told you personally led a combat patrol. That was just plain dumb. What kind of wild hair got into you?"

"I thought I could help," sandy said.

"Well, apparently thinking may not be your strong suit," Newton said. "You know the rules. American advisors aren't supposed to be in combat."

"Then why are we armed?" Sandy asked.

"Don't be a smart ass, Walker," Newton said. "Your sidearm is to protect you, not for use in offensive operations. If we start taking American casualties, the politicians back home will have a major problem with the press. And that'll mean you and I are dead meat. I'm talking about Leavenworth here, and I mean the prison, not the Staff College. Do you have any question about that?"

"Just one, sir," Sandy said. "Everybody has problems. The ones back home are different than the ones here. They have theirs, we have ours. Do we concentrate on winning the war here? Or do we have to worry about the politicians back home?"

"You worry about your dumb ass, son, and I'll worry about the politicians. And don't forget that we aren't at war here; the ARVN is. Our job is to advise them, not to fight guerillas. If you want to concentrate on something, concentrate on that. And if I catch you running around the boondocks shooting up the jungle again, I'll recommend court-martial. Is that understood?"

"Yes sir."

"Okay, and one more thing. Keep your mouth shut about our strategy and tactics in Vietnam. You're not here to make policy. You're here to carry the policies out. Just do your job and keep your mouth shut. Let me make the decisions. Okay."

"Yes sir.

"Just so we have an understanding: I'll expect never to see your name in combat reports again. You just try to be a good soldier. Keep your nose clean, and we'll get along just fine. For now, that's all. You're dismissed."

CHAPTER SIX

At the Vietnamese paratrooper brigade headquarters the following day, the mood was decidedly more positive. The jump had gone well. The young Vietnamese officers were almost jubilant. They had planned and carried out a complicated combat operation, and it had been a success. They were inclined to give Sandy credit. Everyone seemed to want to shake his hand and slap him on the back. The enlisted troopers grinned as they saluted him, and he soon felt better about his job, in spite of what Old Brick had said. Then a message came from the American embassy. Major Walker was to meet representatives from the embassy on the following Saturday. The meeting place was again to be the Hotel Continental, and the appointment was for five o'clock. The message was not clear as to just who would be the American representatives at the meeting, as if secrecy was needed. Sandy worried it over in his mind. Was it vague because the message might be seen by the wrong eyes as it made its way through military channels? Maybe the writer simply assumed that Sandy would already know who he would be meeting. Nevertheless, Sandy wondered at the imprecision, and on the following Saturday while he walked the few blocks from his billet in the Brinks Hotel, he puzzled over the message, even as he brushed aside he brash boy-pimps on their Vespa motor scooters.

"Great massage for you," they called. "Best looking girls on To Do Street. Two at one time."

He laughed at what American culture had brought to Saigon, sex and money, and he rejected their advances. They soon gave him up to go after other prey, and he went back to considering who he was to look for. Avril? Jon Bourne? Another, perhaps less sympathetic official? At any rate it was out of his control, so he squared his shoulders, took a deep breath, and readied himself for the unexpected. He entered the hotel and headed for the main bard down the marble corridor with its imposing white columns. He ignored the people staring at his cut forehead and black eye. They quickly stepped aside, whispering that the American was a mean-looking man searching for a fight. In the bar, patrons again made way for him, and he surveyed the room. Who wash he to meet?

He need not have worried. Wearing a black au dai with a single strand of white pearls at its high collar, she would have stood out in any crowd. He took another deep breath. She was even more spectacularly beautiful than he had remembered, and he felt the hair stand up on the back of his neck. Jon Bourne was at the bar with her. She was so elegant and Bourne was so cool that Sandy suddenly felt out of place. In slacks and sport shirt, with a badly damaged face, he was tempted to leave. While he hesitated, she saw him and waved. Her warm welcome broke the tension. He relaxed.

"What happened to your face?" she asked.

"Charlie almost got me," he said. "But I'm okay now."

"You don't look okay to me," she said. "Let's buy you a beer and some ice for that eye."

He declined the ice but accepted the beer. Drinks in hand, they made their way through the crowd that parted as they went. Like Moses going through the Red Sea, he thought. In this case, the promised land was a small corner table at the back of the bar. During opening pleasantries, Sandy couldn't keep his eyes away from Avril. How could anyone that elegant and serene have been through what she had? He was hooked on her, and she must have sensed it. Then, Bourne changed the mood.

"I've discussed your views with several of my associates," he said. "I'm afraid they disagree with you."

"How so?" Sandy asked, reluctantly brought back to Saigon and the real world of Vietnamese politics.

"We're in a Cold War with International Communism," Bourne said. "And we can't afford to lose South Vietnam to the North. Ho Chi Minh is an ardent Communist, and there's no way he could ever be our friend in spite of how apprehensive he is about China's intentions toward his country."

"I still think he's a nationalist and we should use him," Sandy said. "Play him against the Chinese."

"Can't be done. Worldwide, Communism is a monolithic block, united against the free world. We can't trust any one of them to join forces with us, no matter how much that might seem to be in their best interests."

"But what about the people?" Avril asked. "The peasants of North Vietnam are just like those South Vietnam. "It was the first time she had entered the discussion, and her interjection startled Sandy.

"She's right, you know," he said. "The peasants up there just want to grow rice, like those down here."

"That may be so," Bourne said. "But because we failed to finish the job in Korea, we can't fail here now. Politically, it would be disastrous."

"I'm not talking about politics," Sandy said. "I'm talking about soldiers' lives. And for that matter, a lot a civilians too. I'd rather give the politicians the black eyes than take more like mine."

"I'm afraid that it's much more than black eyes for the politicians. If we lose South Vietnam, we stand to lose all of Southeast Asian, including Laos, Thailand and Cambodia."

"But the Cambodians hate the Vietnamese Communists," Avril said, breaking in again. "They would take the reunification of Vietnam as a reason to unify themselves and resist aggression. And the people of Thailand are fiercely independent. They would never accept the Vietnamese as their rulers. I don't see that those countries are in any kind of danger from what happens in Vietnam. They're too nationalistic."

"I'm afraid we disagree," Bourne said. "China and a Communist Vietnam would be an immediate threat to Laos; and Cambodia, and Thailand wouldn't be far behind. But the collapse of those countries would never be a possibility if only South Vietnam prevails. That can happen. Diem can be another Ramon Magsaysay, and we can win just as we did in the Philippines."

"Now I know you're nuts," Sandy said. "Magsaysay was one of his people, a Catholic like most of them. The enemy Huks were a minority, mostly Moslem and communist. The people naturally hated them and favored him. That's not the case with Diem."

"If that's true, how do you explain his reception at Tuy Hoa?" Bourne asked. "When Diem flew up there to visit that part of a liberated area on the coast, a hundred thousand people turned out to welcome him as a liberator and leader. That doesn't sound like a loser to me."

"That was five years ago," Avril said. "Freedom was a new hope back then. He hasn't been out of his palace since, and if he went back to Tuy Hoa now, his reception would be much more hostile. The situation today is completely different."

"Listen to the lady," Sandy said. "She makes sense."

"We think you're wrong," Bourne said. "Diem has good ideas. For example, his new strategic hamlet program has great promise. Just as it did in the Philippines, it can cut off the guerrillas and isolate them in the jungles."

"The guerrillas here in Vietnam have lived in the jungles for years, "Sandy said. "What makes you think they can't now? They get all the supplies they need from Cambodia, Laos, and the North. Vietnam isn't at all like the Philippines. The guerrillas here have protected sanctuaries."

"We'll bring in American forces to go into those so called safe areas. We'll fight the main force NVA units in the field and jungle while ARVN provides protection for the villagers. That way, we use the strengths of each of our forces."

"Even if that works," Sandy said, "you'll just push the Communists farther back into Laos and North Vietnam. That won't end the war. They'll just fight on from safe sanctuaries."

"We may eliminate even those safe areas and expand the war to Laos, Cambodia, and North Vietnam," Bourne said.

"That's crazy," Sandy said. "You'll just get bogged down in a wider war in Asia. I told you about that before. And if you start winning it, China will come in just as they did when we went to the Yalu River in Korea. Surely you don't want that."

"He's right," Avril told Bourne. "The French tried to use overwhelming force, and they lost a hundred thousand men. Why would you want to risk that? You said yourself that American politics is involved. What American politician could survive the loss of a hundred thousand of your young men in Vietnam? You're not making any sense."

"Both of you may be too emotionally involved to think clearly," Bourne said. "Ho Chi Minh's ideas of freedom for his people are different than ours. You saw that after the Geneva Accords. When the country was divided, a million people fled the north for sanctuary here, rather than live under Communism."

"Other factors caused that exodus," she said. "Your CIA put out some pretty bad propaganda to make people want to leave. And religion was a major part of it. Catholics didn't want to live under Ho. It wasn't a fair test,"

"Look," he said, "some of our best minds have thought all this out. If Ho Chi Minh wins this fight, fifteen million people in South Vietnam will be enslaved. We can't play the North against China if that means abandoning those people. So what else can we do? Anyway, I'm convinced we're on the right track. My advice is for you to let others worry about these things, people who do it for a living. You're getting all upset over something you can't control. Try to accept it."

With that, Bourne ended the conversation, said goodbye, and left them. As Sandy watched the man make his way through the other bar patrons, he considered the futility of his attempts to influence what America was doing in Vietnam. Based on Bourne's reaction, the State Department was apparently a closed door. As for the military, Newton had proved that nobody there was going to listen to him, much less give him any encouragement. What other avenues were open to him? What was left? Avril interrupted his thoughts.

"Don't feel so bad," she said. "I think you made a pretty good case. The diplomats just don't see it your way right now. They'll remember your arguments, however, and as this fight progresses, things may change."

"For the sake of both our countries, I hope you're right," he said, and then he turned to look at her again. Closer contact hadn't changed his mind about her. She was still stunning, and she was damn intelligent. He didn't want her to leave.

"Will you have supper with me, even as bad as I look?"

"I'll do better than that," she said. "I'll have supper prepared for us at my place, even some cold dressing for your eye. Will you come home with me?"

CHAPTER SEVEN

She lived only five blocks from the Hotel Continental. He offered a rickshaw, but the weather was fine, so she insisted on walking. As they strolled hand in hand from street to street, they gradually left the milling crowds and bright streetlights behind. They met fewer and fewer other strollers, but she seemed unconcerned. As they went, the neighborhood grew darker and the streets more menacing. The streetlights were nonexistent and the sidewalks were empty by the time they approached a particular wrought-iron gate set in a high, stucco wall. She said it was her place, but the soldier in him caused him to look for muggers or even some sort of organized attack. What kind of a situation had he let himself in for? When he saw shadowy figures lurking behind the wall, he tensed in anticipation of an assault. Then she called out to them, and they opened the gate.

"Whore they?" he asked.

"Cousin Ly and his sons," she said. "I'll explain later."

Apprehensively, he moved with her through an unlit garden down a dim path toward a darkened house. Behind the walls and away from the street, he realized that the garden was a perfect place for an ambush. He mentally kicked himself in the butt for putting himself in such a precarious position. What kind of soldier was he? Nobody would ever find his body. The American mission would report him missing in action. Some kind of action: following a mystery woman in a padded au dai. Then, as they approached the porch of the house, a light went on and the front door opened. An old oriental man in a white jacket was holding it wide for them.

"This is Uncle Ba," Avril said, and the old man bowed and smiled as they entered. The foyer led into a typical French colonial home. It had high ceilings, fans in every room, and a clutter of ancient furniture. Knickknacks, cushions, and lace dominated the place, and its hardwood floors were covered with a variety of oriental rugs. Generous windows were well screened, and the place looked lived in. Sandy relaxed; this was not going to be an ambush.

"Uncle Ba and his family live in the back of the house," she said. "They take care of the cleaning and cooking. Cousin Ly and his family tend to the garden and provide security. We have to guard ourselves from bad elements that might seek to harm us. So you're safe here. Uncle Ba has even bought your brand of beer. We've a few moments before supper will be ready. Shall we have a drink?"

"Who are the elements that might harm you?" he asked.

"Saigon has become a dangerous place," she said.

"But you seemed unconcerned as we walked here," he said.

"I have friends who watch over me," she said. "Come, let's relax while Uncle Ba cooks."

They moved to what was apparently the living room, a large, comfortable area with deep chairs and many cushions. Occasional tables were full of pictures, and he saw an old phonograph on one table. Uncle Ba brought Sandy's beer and Avril's white wine, and then she asked Sandy to tell her something about America and his childhood.

"I was raised during what we call the Great Depression," he said. "That was a difficult time for America. My father was an engineer officer, however, a graduate of West Point. So he had a job, and we had food on the table. We didn't have much money, and the Army forced dad to take vacations without pay, but we were much better off than lots of other people. During those hard times, many Americans went without food and shelter. Some died in poverty."

"It was very different for me here," she said. "When I was growing up, the French colonialists were in power. Because of my father, we were a privileged class. We had servants and lots of money. My brothers and I received good educations. One brother even went to France for advanced study. Dad had this house and a vacation villa in the hills around Da Lat. We spent weekends at the beach or at the horse races. It was a good time if you were part of the French colonial system."

"We had a beach too," he said. "It was in a place on the Panhandle Florida coast called Destin. Toward the end of the Depression, federal money started to flow again, and we were able to move there. Some of our best times were at the end of the Thirties."

"It was the opposite for us," she said. "At the end of the Thirties, everything changed for the worst here. That was when the Japanese came. Suddenly Vietnam was a conquered country, and we lived in fear of what the Japanese might do. We had heard of their rape of Nanking, and we were afraid they would repeat that here. It's odd how our fortunes deteriorated as yours improved."

"Well our good times didn't last," he said. "The threat of war caused the Army to send officers and men to the Pacific, to places like the Philippines. We were put on a luxury liner, the *USS Washington*, in New York harbor. The ship was so large that later, when war came, it was converted into an aircraft carrier. In spite of rumors about German submarines, we sailed down the eastern coast of the United States. Then we went through the Panama Canal, and dad gave us lectures on how it had been built. He did the same when we sailed into San Francisco Bay under the recently finished magnificent bay bridge, the Golden Gate they called it. Then we sailed west for five days out to Hawaii. It was a fabulous trip. I'll never forget the millions of stars at sea at night from the top deck."

"While you were admiring the stars," she said, "we were adjusting to Japanese occupation. Vichy France signed an agreement with the enemy that barely averted a formal Japanese invasion. Instead, France agreed to govern for the Japanese if they wouldn't garrison their soldiers throughout the entire nation. Most of the Japanese were in the north, therefore, because the excellent French airfields there were needed to support Japanese efforts against China and the Philippines. Only about eight thousand enemy soldiers initially came down to Saigon and the Mekong Delta. Although that figure gradually increased because of resistance fighting in the area, the French effectively controlled everything where we were. The most worrisome evidence of Japanese control in Saigon was the presence of Japanese agents of the *Kempeitai,* their intelligence agency. They were everywhere. From the beginning of the occupation, they infiltrated

French and Vietnamese organizations looking for resistance fighters. We lived in fear of being accused by them. Just the accusation meant death. Life was bad then."

"Life was good for us in Schofield barracks on Oahu in Hawaii," he said. "The weather was always perfect. We kids went without shoes, and we swam almost daily, most of the time at Waialua, although occasionally at Waianae. Both were great beaches on the coast. At Schofield Barracks, Dad let me join him in training. He had one of his sergeants teach me how to use a walkie-talkie radio. I learned how to fire pistols and rifles. Girls were friendly, and my friends and I began to date. Movies only cost ten cents, so dating wasn't expensive. I learned about American soldiers, good ones and bad. Once, we even came across a deserter out in the woods where we played. It was like that movie, Lancaster. "From Here To Eternity, the one with Frank Sinatra and Burt Lancaster."

"Our movie was more like Casabanca," she said. "French police and enemy spies were everywhere, and the resistance fighters caused all sorts of trouble."

By now, they had moved to the dining room, where Uncle Ba had prepared an excellent meal of fish and rice. She told Sandy that these were Uncle Ba's specialties. And she added that that most evening meals came with an excellent white wine, although on this occasion Sandy's favorite beer was at the table. If the way to a man's heart was through his stomach, he thought, Avril was sure making progress.

"And during all these troubles, what was life like?" he asked. "Were you dating the local boys?"

"We tried very hard for a normal life," she said. "Just like your movies, we had the cinema here. But before and during the war, my brothers were very protective, and they kept me away from other Vietnamese boys. They were stern chaperones when we went to parties and such. After the war, when the French came back, I was older, and my brothers weren't around, so I dated the dashing French paratroop officers."

"You like paratroopers?" he asked.

"*Mai qui, mon cher,*" she answered. "And what kind of girls did you like in Hawaii? Did you date oriental women?"

"I was too young," he said. "And besides, Pearl Harbor came along, and the Japanese attack put an end to enjoyment of our paradise. First, for fear of another attack, mom, sis, and I were crammed into an old school bus and evacuated from Schofield Barracks down to Honolulu. Two months later we were herded like cattle onto a crowded boat and sent home to Florida. Mom didn't like that one bit, but she had to take care of us without dad for the next four years."

"It was the same with us," she said. "The Japanese staged a vicious surprise coup against the French just before the end of the war. They especially targeted the Vichy French governing officials here in Saigon. They sent execution squads to homes and places of business and killed anyone they found there, without trials or any kind of hearings. They just came in and started shooting and stabbing. Our fears of another rape like Nanking were realized, for many women were sexually abused before they were executed. They killed my mother and one of my brothers. Dad and the other two boys barely escaped. I think my brothers joined the resistance, and I believe my father is in France. I haven't seen any of them since 1945. I was devastated by being orphaned suddenly at age fifteen and not knowing what had happened to my parents and brothers or even what my future would be."

"I know only a little of what you must have felt," he said. "Dad stayed out in the Southwest Pacific for four years. We missed him terribly, and it was tough growing up without him, not knowing if we would ever see him again. It was a vacuum. To make up for his being gone, we avidly followed news reports about the war. We learned geography by keeping maps of where the fighting was. And we wanted to serve. Everybody did. I became an Air Raid Warden. I had a white helmet and a flashlight. During air raid drills, I patrolled my sector looking for blackout violations. Because we were living at Destin on the Gulf Coast, we had to keep the lights. We held blackout parties in the basements of our homes, with music on the record players, coke-cola in the fridge, and blankets on the windows."

"Did you have a car?" she asked.

"No. Gas was rationed, but I had a motor scooter. Because of my swimming experience in Hawaii, I had a job as a lifeguard at the Naval Air Station swimming pool. So I had gas rations, and the scooter was my transport. The girls liked to ride behind me on the bike, even reaching around me to steer. And I liked to lean back whenever they did, especially if we were still in our wet bathing suits."

"Men are all the same the world over," she said.

"And aren't you glad of that?"

"No answer, sir. And did you still go to school, all during the war? Here, we frequently had to cancel classes and even close many schools because of the fighting."

"Nothing like that happened in the United States. I went to high school in Pensacola, and then college at West Point. Dad and grandad had gone there, so I wanted to follow them if I could pass the competitive examination. I was lucky enough to qualify and enter the Academy just as the war ended."

"I was in school at Da Lat at that time," She said. "If I had been here in Saigon, the Japanese might have killed me too, or even worse. As it was the only family member the surviving courts could find, and the house became mine. My father also left a trust at his bank for my education, so I had money from him until I became twenty-one and finished the University of Saigon. Then I was on my own and had to take in Uncle Ba and Cousin Ly to make ends meet. I was lucky like you, and I got my job at the American Embassy very soon after I graduated."

"What happened when the Japanese were defeated?"

"First the British came as a part of the peace treaty ending the war. They were strongly anti-Communist and tried to prevent the Viet Minh from raking over. Those were Ho Chi Minh's communist fighters from the north, and they were very cruel. They wanted to take revenge on anyone they even suspected might have cooperated with either the French or the Japanese. The British had great difficulty in stopping chaos and wholesale slaughter. In fear, I stayed hidden in the hills of Da Lat until the British gave up and the French came back a few months later. That was when the Viet Minh began a guerilla war against the French and anyone who cooperated with them. If I had been in Saigon, they would have tried to kill me too. It wasn't until the French finally regained control of Saigon, that I was able to come home and finish my education."

"That's an incredible story," he said. "And while you were suffering through all that, I was at West Point having a great time. Blanchard and Davis led our football team to and undefeated season and a national championship. I started dating the girl I eventually married. Her name was Nancy, and she was from Destin. I had known her in high school. We courted West Point style. That meant mostly by mail, on my limited vacations, or on those few occasions when she was able to come to the Academy. Even with that limited contact, we decided to marry as soon as I graduated. Sometimes when I look back, I think I really never got to know her before we were husband and wife."

"But you had two children?"

"You bet. West Point cadets back then were cooped up most of the time without female companionship. A guy builds up a petty strong sexual drive after four years of that, and Nancy was attractive and willing."

"What went wrong?"

"Korea," he said. "When the North Koreans unexpectedly invaded the south in the summer of 1950, I was in Japan. In the chaos that followed, I was hastily thrown into the line as a forward observer to adjust artillery fire. We were ill trained and poorly equipped, and my unit was quickly overrun. I was missing for almost a month as a few of us worked our way south by night through enemy positions to friendly lines around the port of Pusan. All that time, Nancy thought I was dead. After I recovered in a hospital in Japan, I rejoined my unit and we fought our way north to the Yalu River. We were there when the Chinese unexpectedly joined the war. Again, the communist attack caught us by surprise, and I was almost killed at Chosin Reservoir. When Nancy found out about that, she demanded I resign my commission and find a safer job so she would have a husband and the kids would have a father. The uncertainty was what she couldn't stand. After I came home from Korea, we argued a lot about it, until she gave me an ultimatum: get out of the Army or she would get a divorce. I guess I didn't really believe her, and when I volunteered for parachute duty and then this tour in Vietnam, she went through with her threat. That was pretty bad."

"How did the children take the divorce?"

"At the time, I worried more about them than anything else. Since them, I've learned that the children of an unhappy marriage that stays together for the kid's sake alone may suffer very badly. Whether or not that's correct, I take some solace in the idea. But that's enough about me. What we went through back home was nothing compared to what you described happening to you here in the war."

"Well, the situation got worse. When Japan collapsed, five major groups in Vietnam competing for power: the Cao Dai, the Hoa Hoa, the Trotskyites, the Binh Xuyen, and the Viet Minh. Between them, they had three million followers, of which over fifty thousand were organized as soldiers, guerillas, or gang hit men. Each wanted to gain control over the country. The Cao Dai and Hoa Hoa were religious. The Trotskyites and the Viet Minh were revolutionary, and the Binh Xuyen was a gangster syndicate. Competing mobs roamed the cities, and nobody was safe traveling the roads of the Delta. Anybody who happened to be caught near a fight got murdered. We tried to stay in house as much as possible, and Cousin Ly had to be on guard twenty-four hours a day. The killings didn't cease with the return of French control, moreover, because the new Saigon government supported by the French army waged war on all five of those factions in order to consolidate its own power. Again, that's why we needed Cousin Ly. As street warfare continued, every citizen had to protect his own property, or someone would take it away. During those bad times. Cousin Ly and his sons saved our lives many times. They still watch over me. I won't ever forget them."

Uncle Ba's fish and rice proved to be excellent. Sandy gave up his beer and joined Avril with a glass of wine and discovered that it wasn't half bad. After coffee, they moved back to her living room, and Uncle Ba disappeared. She went to a small table that contained that record player Sandy had noticed earlier. It was not unlike one that Sandy had used at those high school blackout parties during the war back in Destin some twenty years ago. She put on a record and turned to announce:

"My birthday was two days ago, and I bought myself a record as a present. Would you like to dance again?"

She started the player and he went to her. As the music began, she lightly brushed her fingers over his damaged eye, before he took her in his arms. Nestled against his chest, she still fit perfectly. The selection was his favorite, "The Hawaiian Wedding Song." At first, she looked deeply into his eyes. Then as they began to move slowly together in time to the soft strains of that lovely melody, she put her hand on the back of his neck to gently caress him. As she did so, he put his arms around her waist and pulled her to him. She responded eagerly, and he kissed her. Then the soft rhythm of the dance became a hard and intense drive they had to answer. Quickly, she led him to her bedroom, where he learned that her au dai was not padded.

CHAPTER EIGHT

Except for his mother, Sandy hadn't had much luck in his relationships with women. At first, he thought that all women were like her, loving and true. As he matured, however, his perception changed. His first unfortunate experience with a girl had been in the summer of 1942 when he was just sixteen. He met her at the Officers Club pool of the Pensacola Naval Air Station where he was the lifeguard on duty. Her name was Neva, and she was just home on vacation from her first year at Florida State. Maybe two years older than he was, she wore her synthetic blond hair very long. She had a way of looking at him with direct, blue eyes and a big square smile. He immediately noted that she filled out her white bathing suit more than adequately, and it was one of those new two-piece ones that added an element at sensual suggestion. When Sandy came on duty at noon on the day in question, she was at the pool with a group of college friends, but she started flirting with him almost immediately. When she realized he couldn't take his eyes off of her, she stretched her arms and flaunted her body by the water, all the while pretending not to notice him. He responded in kind by showing off in the pool from the diving board. After they dropped the pretense, they spent much of the afternoon teasing each other. At suppertime, people began to leave, and the group of people with Neva yelled to her that they were going home.

"If I stay," she asked him, "will you take me home?"

"As long as you're not afraid to be seen riding behind me on a motor scooter."

"You're on," she said, and she called to her friends that she had a ride.

By the time the pool closed at nine, they were alone. She accompanied him as he went about his closing chores, continuing to flirt as he cleaned the pool and its surrounding deck. When he was done, he turned off the pool lights and focused attention on her. She put her hands on her hips and taunted him. His pentup desire gave him the courage to take her in his arms and kiss her. She didn't resist, and her lips were the softest he had ever tasted. The warmth of her body sent an electric shock through his, and he felt his face turn red and his pulse pound in his head. He picked her up and carried her to the shallow end of the pool, and they sat down on the wide steps leading into the children's section. Half submerged in the tepid water, they lay there embraced. Encouraged by her lack of resistance, he fumbled to take off the top of her suit. When he finally succeeded, she laughed and pulled his face down onto her ample, freed breasts. Overcome with desire, he threw caution aside and began tugging at the rest of her suit. When she pulled away, he thought the had ruined the moment, but she stood up in the shallow water before him and removed the suit herself. Then she posed as she had before during the day, with her hands on her hips. Now, the darkness of her tan contrasted sharply with the whiteness of the areas her suit had covered.

"What do you think?" she asked.

"I think you're the most beautiful woman in the world."

"Then take off your trunks," she said, "so I can tell if you really mean that or are just putting me on,"

When he did as she asked, she could see he was really aroused, and she stepped forward to caress him with both hands as he put his arms around her and felt her firm buttocks. They kissed passionately as his hands explored her eager body. Over the next hour, they made love three times before she indicated she'd had go home while she could still walk straight without wincing. Still, as she rode behind him on the scooter, she hugged him tightly, and he wanted more of her. At her door, however, she said she was going back to college in the morning. She gave him her address and phone number at school. He wrote and called, but she never answered the phone or his letters.

He struggled to understand that evening. Why had she led him on and held him so tightly on the ride home, but now she now longer wanted him? He was confused and hurt, but with his father off winning World War Two, he knew he had nobody to turn to.

He certainly wasn't going to ask his mother, and his sister would have laughed at him. And Neva never returned. He drove by her house several times, but he never saw her again. He felt her rejection deeply. Nobody like her ever showed up at the pool, moreover, and the high school girls he dated for the next two years were neither as experienced nor as willing as she had been. So the hurt lingered and deepened, and he left for West Point in the summer of 1944 without a steady girl friend.

He thought that had changed when he met Helen Cook. New cadets were required by the Academy to undergo at least a minimum of instruction in the social graces, and the Cadet Hostess, a Mrs. Barth, was in charge. She organized ballroom instruction, table etiquette, tea dances, and other less formal gatherings at which new cadets were exposed to the rules of proper behavior. If Mrs. Barth summoned a cadet to one of her gatherings, his attendance was mandatory. On one such occasion at her offices in Grant Hall, Sandy was with a group of other plebes when a busload of young ladies arrived. The cadets called them "Barth Tubs," a name derived from that their Hostess, but they were actually attractive, eager young women from Ladycliff, a women's college in nearby Highland Falls. Helen Cook was one of them.

She was a slender girl with green eyes and bright red hair that tumbled to her shoulders, and she had a casual, easy, sophisticated manner as she handled the many cadet advances launched in her direction. Sandy immediately decided she was worth competing for. Because of his size and rugged good looks, although he was somewhat bruised by his play as a guard on the plebe football team, he stood out among the other cadets. He summoned his courage and walked directly to her. Introducing himself, he asked her name. For a moment, she sized him up, and then she held out a soft hand and murmured "Helen." He seemed to make rapid headway, because she didn't tease him as she did the rest of his surrounding classmates. She soon agreed that they should see each other again, and he took her to movies the following Saturday night, about the only entertainment permitted the Plebes during the academic year. When he walked her to the front gate near the Hotel Thayer, he kissed her goodbye, and they agreed that they should see more of each other. For the next two weeks, she attended his football games down on the North Athletic Field, and each time they went afterwards to the movies. At other times during the week, he found himself thinking more and more about her, and he realized he must have fallen hard. A defining moment occurred after she had come to his third football game.

The Army plebe team had won, but it had been a long, hard contest, and it was dark before Sandy had dressed and come out of the locker room eager to find Helen. She was waiting on the cinder running track near the football field. She was wearing a short fur jacket, buttoned at the neck against the cold, a dark skirt, and high heels. With her beautiful red hair cascading over her coat and a warm welcoming smile, she was lovely. A full moon had risen over the east bank of the Hudson River, and its light created a shimmering path across the wide waters toward them as they stood alone on the track by the great river. He was overcome with emotion at the beauty of the moment, and he wanted to take her in his arms in spite of the rules against cadet public displays of affection. They talked softly about their week, how much they had missed each other, and how painful it was to be apart. Then she took out a cigarette and lit it. The athletic code he had signed prevented him from joining her, and that forbidden pleasure made her even more attractive. In spite of the rules against it, he took her in his arms and kissed her. His hands buried in the softness of her fur coat, and the scent of her Chanel perfume overwhelmed him with desire. He put both hands in her silky hair, gazed into her eyes, and kissed her again. This time, the cigarette aroma and her open, soft lips drove him wild. He wanted to make love, and there was no doubt that she felt the same. Unfortunately, the circumstances of their surroundings and his plebe status prevented satisfaction, but he felt in his heart their time would soon come. They were meant for each other.

The following week, the plebe football team had an away game, against Columbia University in New York. Following the contest, many cadets had agreed to meet at the bar in the Picadilly Hotel just a block off Times Square. By the time Sandy dressed in civilian clothes after the game and reached the hotel, festivities were well underway. As a joke, Sandy had put on false, black, horn-rimmed glasses attached to a large pink nose. Those, plus his changed clothing, considerably altered his appearance, and he was a surprise hit among his friends in the crowded bar. One of them came up to him and because of the noise in the bar almost had to shout in his ear.

"Isn't that your girl over at that corner table with an upperclassman?" he asked.

Through the guys and gals jammed together in the bar, he saw her. Sure enough, Helen was huddled with one of the senior cadets, and they obviously were being more than affectionate.

"They've been there ever since I came in," his buddy said. "I'd say they like each other a lot." As Sandy watched, the cadet with Helen took her hand and kissed it. Then he reached to caress her face. She smiled.

Sandy could see under their table with one foot, she slowly slipped off the other shoe. Then she put her freed toes on her date's leg and ran them as far his trousers would permit. It was a deliberately sensual act that spoke volumes about the relationship between them. Sandy was crushed at the sight. The shock hit him in the stomach like a blow. What had gone wrong? He was about to push his way across the crowded room and confront them, when he saw them rise and disappear through the door leading to the hotel rooms. Like Neva, Helen had led him on and then left him. Once more, the pain of loss was intense, and he had to get out of there. He stumbled from the bar and headed over to Times Square where he had a room at the Hotel Astor, intending to end the evening in the quiet of his room trying to understand what had happened and what he should do. Some of his football buddies on the Astor bar saw him, however and changed his plans.

"Hey Sandy," they called, "come join the party."

Their obvious good will and friendship suddenly appealed to him, and he didn't want to be alone for the rest of that night. He found, moreover, that a group of cadets had rented a suite of rooms upstairs, and a crowd of young people was headed up there. He decided to join them, and together they loudly made their way to the elevators. The suite was on the same floor as his room, and for a moment he almost left them, but then he decided to join the boisterous throng of college kids, men and women jammed into the living room and two bedrooms of their suite. He shoved his way to makeshift bar in the bathroom and poured himself a half glass of bourbon on some rocks. Then he decided that the noise was just too much, and he threaded a path through the chaos into one of the bedrooms that was less crowded. Once there, he saw a windowsill that was free, From it, he could see Times Square. That became his perch, and he spent next thirty minutes sipping sour mash and contemplating his fate, the hurt Helen had caused, and the neon lights below him.

"Hi there, big guy," he heard a feminine voice say, "what's your problem?"

"I'll bet my body it's more than that," she said, and the challenge in her voice made him turn and look at her.

She looked like a high school cheerleader. Bouncy and cheerful, wearing a short skirt, letter sweater, and bobby socks, she was the exact opposite of his sour mood. Her name was Fran Kurtz, and she had short, cropped brown hair, hazel eyes, and an effortless smile. With her saddle loafers, she looked too young to be with this crowd.

"Come on, guy, you can tell me," she said.

"It's not something I'd discuss with a stranger," he said. "Better go back to the party."

"When guys act like you're acting, I'd guess it's a woman every time," she said, and suddenly Sandy began to like her cheerful good humor. It might be just what he needed after the bad scene at the Picadilly.

"Something like that," he said.

"I knew it," she said and took the glass of bourbon from him. Winking at him, she took a sizeable swig.

"Hey, watch out," he said. "That's sour mash. It's pretty strong stuff, and you're too young to be drinking it."

"Appearance isn't always reality," She said. "You'd be surprised at how old I am and what I like to do. Now tell me what this nasty woman did to you."

"She's not a nasty woman," Sandy said. "Or at least I didn't think she was until about an hour ago."

"What happened then?"

"I saw her in the Picadilly bar with another guy. They were making out, and she was enjoying it."

"Why shouldn't she?"

"I though she and I were pretty much of a thing together. I know I had fallen darn hard for her. I thought she liked me too, but I guess I was wrong. I'm beginning to think all women are fickle."

"You've a fallen hard?" she asked. "Poor boy. No use to anyone. How long have you known her?"

He looked sharply at her. Had she really made a joke about an erection? No, he must have been hearing things. He answered:

"About six weeks. She's from Ladycliff, and we met at West Point. We've dated each week since then. She's come to every one of my football games."

"I know those Ladycliff girls. I'm from Marymount College at Tarrytown, and Ladycliff is our chief competition because they are so near to West Point. In spite of that advantage, we do okay. That's because we try harder, but what do you think went wrong with her?"

"I'm bewildered right now, and I can't imagine why she's done this. I thought we had such a good thing going. This is a crash landing."

"Did you have sex?"

The frankness of her question set him back again, and he paused to gain composure and consider her before answering. This time he decided she wasn't kidding. She wanted nothing more than an answer to her question. At first he was tempted to tell her that his sex life was none of her business and to send her back to the party, but for some reason, he decided again to answer her.

"No, we didn't," he said.

"Why not?" she persisted.

"I suppose it was mostly because we never had the right circumstances. We always met at West Point, and we didn't have many places to go where we would be alone. And I'm sure you know that Plebes at West Point don't have a lot of freedom."

"On come on," she said. "You know better than that, Sandy. Time, place, and opportunity are there, even at West Point, if a couple really wants to find them. No, I'm guessing it must have been something else that held you back. Are you shy?

"No, it's not that," he said. "I think I thought she was something special, not just a romp in the hay like I had once before. I thought we were heading for a long-term relationship."

"Take it from me, big guy, for lots of gals like Helen and me, the best long term relationship always include that romp in the hay you're dismissing so lightly, My guess is she wanted that, and she didn't see it coming from you. Presto, she found it in the Picadilly bar with someone who had a convenient hotel room."

"That's pretty harsh," he said. "I'd hate to think all women were like that."

"Don't kid yourself," she said. "As the saying goes, if they drink water, they fuck."

Once more, her language shocked him, and he gave her a long, questioning look. Deliberately, her eyes on his, she took his glass again and sipped the bourbon. This time he had no doubt as to the message, and he suddenly he didn't want to waste the opportunity. He took her hand and quickly led her through the crowd and down the hall to his room. There, they almost attacked each other as they ripped off their clothes and jumped into the waiting queen-sized bed. His pent-up desire and frustration exploded into an athletic night of love far different from his evening with Neva. All night long, Fran never complained about his enthusiasm.

In the morning, as she watched him shave, she ran her hand over his back and told him how good the session had been for her. In turn, he took her in his arms and thanked her for staying with him. It had been great, he said, and it helped him erase the picture of Helen with that guy in the bar. He took her back to her room at the Picadilly Hotel, and they agreed to write and call each other faithfully. It didn't work out that way. Oh, they wrote a few times and called occasionally, but he found no spark there. He guessed he didn't want a long-term relationship with someone who jumped in bed so quickly with stranger. Once, when he saw her with another cadet at a varsity football game at Michie stadium, she waved, but they didn't talk. He decided she had been nothing more than a romp in the hay after all. But at least she had helped him get over the pain Helen's rejection had caused, and he was unattached when he went home to Destin after his plebe year.

He had a month's vacation and the family car, and one of the first places he visited was his old swimming pool. There, he met many of his old friends. Among them was one named Nancy Downs. She had been a year behind him in high school, and they had gone to many of the same parties, but they had never dated. This time, however, he noticed that she had grown up and filled out nicely. She didn't seem like such an awkward little girl any more. Instead, she had become an attractive woman, with long black hair, blue eyes, and a warm smile that seemed to come easily. She was petite but shapely in feminine way. They spent the day together and decided to stop for supper as he drove her home that evening. Over burgers and fries, they chatted easily. For Sandy, it was a thoroughly satisfying time, and he asked to see her the next day. She agreed, and for the next four weeks, they spent the most part of every day together. As the time passed, they grew more and more attached to each other. When his vacation was almost over, therefore, they became desperate for the relationship not to end.

After a late afternoon picnic at the wide, white, Destin gulf beach, they lay on his cadet beach blanket and watched the sun go down. With a half-empty bottle of Chardonnay in the cooler, life was pretty good.

"Don't go back," she said. "Stay here with me."

"You know I can't do that," he said. "But you can change plans. Don't go to Florida State. Come up to Ladycliff so we can be together."

"Maybe I can transfer next semester," she said. "But I'm committed to State now. What can we do?"

"Let's make a commitment to each other," he said. "I'm willing if you are."

"Do you have any doubt?" she asked, and she put her hand inside the front of his trunks.

Although their embraces up to now had been passionate and their kisses had been warm, this was the first time she had been the aggressor. He had explored her body with his hands, but she had not reciprocated. This new caress was different, and it marked a change in their relationship. Spurred to action, he pulled down the top of her suit and kissed her freed breasts. After a few moments, he asked her if she wanted to make love. With wide eyes, she nodded. He quickly pulled off his trunks, and then he watched as she removed her suit.

"God, you're beautiful," he said.

She reached for him, and gently he began to make love to her. Wanting to savor the moment, he took it very slowly. That was a good thing, for this turned out to be her first time, and the act could have been painful. He was sure he had been tender, but when they were finished that first time, and the act could have been painful. He was sure he had been tender, but when they were finished that first time, he discovered she was crying.

"What's wrong, Nancy? Did I hurt you?"

"No, it was wonderful, and I want to do it again."

"But your tears…"

"Happiness," she said. "And the fact that I had always wanted to wait until my wedding night."

"Then let's consider this out wedding night," he said.

She nodded, and the tears were gone. They had little time before he had to go back to West Point, but they made the most of what they had, immersing themselves in the new physical bonds of love that held them. He remained with her as long as he could, and when he left, he swore to write. She promised not only to write, but also to visit him at the Academy. This time, their promises worked out as they planned. He called and wrote frequently, and she responded, always saying how much she missed him. After she wrote that she couldn't stand being alone any longer, she spent some of her savings to come to West Point and see him. He took her to Flirtation Walk across from Constitution Island. This was just off the great parade ground overlooking the Hudson River and beautiful Trophy Point. This was the exact spot where, on a beautiful summer day many years before, his grandfather had met Kate, his future grandmother. His father had also told him the story of how he had proposed to Penny, Sandy's mother, on Flirtation Walk under Kissing Rock. Now it was

Sandy's turn, so after he had taken her out to the great parade ground and showed her the monuments on the Point and the upstream view of the mighty Hudson, he led her to the same path down Flirtation Walk and then to Kissing Rock. There, he showed her a miniature version of his cadet class ring. Then he knelt on one knee and formally proposed marriage. In tears again, she accepted.

At Christmas that year, she came again to West Point, and he took her to his mother's family home in Westchester County.

Sandy had not seen his father since 1942 when Andy Walker took his engineer battalion to the Fiji Islands and Penny took Sandy and his sister, Kathleen, home from the war, and he, Penny, and Kathleen had come north to spend Christmas at Penny's father's home. He was Patrick Nugent, a prominent New York corporate attorney, and his home was more sumptuous than Sandy had ever seen. Nothing like it ever existed on an Army base.

The joyous reunion was made more festive by Sandy's happy announcement of his engagement to Nancy. For several days, the celebration continued, and at first Sandy was content to be with his family and lover and share the family's joy. Gradually he began to note, however that relations between his father and mother were strained. Penny was critical of Andy, and her repeated caustic remarks gave Sandy pause. And his father was drinking too much. Something he had never done in Sandy's presence before. When he had a chance to be alone with father, therefore, Sandy asked what was wrong. Instead of an explanation of what had happened between him and Penny, Andy started a rambling discourse about nuclear tests in the Marshall Islands and the dropping of atomic bombs on Hiroshima and Nagasaki. None of that made much sense to Sandy, and he ended up attributing the nonsense to Andy's generous use of bourbon, so he saw no need to press for more of an explanation. When he mentioned the session to Nancy, moreover, she said she was too much in love to care. So he forgot it.

They married just after his graduation in June of 1948 and headed first to Fort Sill for basic officer's training and then to Fort Hood to start life as an army family. Sandy immersed himself in learning the esoteric arts of the armored artillery, and Nancy became a full-time army wife. Life was good. Walter was born in 1948, and Sara in 1950, and Nancy had her hands full. When Sandy was ordered to Korea that year, therefore, Nancy went home to Destin so that her family could help take care of the kids while he was gone. His absence was supposed to be for just a year, but the North Korean attack in the summer of 1950 changed all that. Sandy was missing in action twice, and the reports of his absence so unnerved Nancy that she wanted change. When he finally came home safely three years later, she demanded that he never leave her again, and the arguments began. The conflict between what Sandy thought was his duty to his county and the needs of his family soured their marriage, Lesser women would have put up with him, but Nancy came from stronger steel, and she would not bend. In the end, she decided to leave him, in spite of the bonds that Walter and Sara mean to them both. Thus once more he had failed with a woman. This time it had happened in spite of their shaper overwhelming need to nurture their children, and even Nancy had left him. Neva may have simply used him for her own pleasure, and Helen may have wanted more than he was prepared to give. Fran had probably been nothing more than a convenient reaction to what he saw as Helen's infidelity, but Nancy probably had had good reasons to leave. Whatever the various explanations might have been, Sandy had failed them all. In every instance, one thing was clear: he had never been able to maintain a relationship with a woman for any length of time.

Would Avril be any different?

CHAPTER NINE

For the next five months, Sandy welcomed Avril's positive insight to what he saw every day in the field as he worked with the Vietnamese. She listened patiently as he pointed out that the Communist forces in the Delta seemed to be growing stronger. He complained that the insurgents were surrounding Saigon in an ever-tightening circle, and the commander of the paratroopers he was working with had ignored his repeated recommendations to mount offensive operations against the guerrillas. Instead, the airborne soldiers had remained in camp, limiting themselves to sending relief forces when and where the guerrillas attacked. Those tactics surrendered the tactical initiative to the enemy, and the insurgents took full advantage of it. Even occasional setbacks did not deter them. In April, Communist forces attacked Ben Cat just north of Saigon, for example, and in response President Diem quickly sent a paratroop battalion with other ARVN units as a reaction force. The engagement unfolded so suddenly that Sandy didn't have time to join them. Furthermore, at Ben Cat, the ARVN relief force acted so quickly that they killed more than a hundred guerillas and repulsed the attack. Basking in his success, President Diem told his American advisors that this was the correct way to use his forces. For him, to mount major offensive operations was too risky, he declared His staff forecast that the enemy would soon tire of attacking and suffering so many casualties.

"Is he right?" Avril asked.

"Casualties have never stopped the Communists before," he said. "They have an apparently inexhaustible supply of warm bodies, and they don't care how many die."

Their discussions continued for three more months, as the same pattern of conflict continued. Then in mid-July, amidst the bloodiest battle since the French armistice in 1954, the Vietnamese Communists, now beginning to be called contemptuously the "Viet Cong" by the media, mounted another major attack, their largest to date. The target was in the Plain of Jars, just west of Saigon. Upon receiving word of a developing major battle, Diem quickly dispatched several airborne battalions and other ARVN units to the scene. This time, Sandy could not stand to hold back, and he accompanied the brigade headquarters, although he had sense enough not to lead any combat patrols. The paratroopers didn't need him, however, and in fierce fighting the South Vietnamese killed over one hundred and fifty enemy soldiers. President Diem was ecstatic, and in the glow of success, Brick Newton did not dare censure Sandy for violating the Colonel's orders against any American advisor going on a combat mission.

"What happened out there?" Avril asked him.

"Good training paid off," Sandy said. "The other side got careless and ambitious, and we caught them out in the open."

"Doesn't that mean Diem's defensive policy is a good one?"

"On the contrary," he said. "What he doesn't understand is that these operations are simply training grounds for the enemy. As such, they reveal a continuing increase in the size and intensity of the Viet Cong operations. That in turn means the VC are growing stronger, better, and bolder."

"But he says the Plain of Jars was a great victory."

"And he's ignoring the fact that the VC are more and more able to mount ever stronger operations. Instead, he's taking their losses in expendable soldiers as proof of the wisdom of his tactics. Like many leaders with extreme power, his mind is set, and he won't listen to objections."

Restrictions continued on the use of the airborne soldiers. They were to act only in reaction to enemy actions. Their inactivity had a plus side for Sandy. He was left with little to do besides training and planning, because Colonel Newton's warning kept him from joining the few combat operations that did take place. Thus he had more and more time to spend his evenings and many weekends with Avril in Saigon. He took the sweet with the bitter and did not object.

In their long talks alone, she wanted to know more about him and the United States. She repeatedly questioned him about the motives of the United States for sending more money and men to Southeast Asia.

"North Vietnamese propaganda says that your country seeks to replace France as the colonial power in Indochina," she said. "They emphasize that you want us to be just another territory of the United States, like the Philippines. Is that true?"

"Of course not," he said. "That's absurd."

"Then, other than because you are a soldier under orders, why are you here?"

"Let's make it very simple," he said. "The last three American Presidents created this situation. First, President Truman decided to appease France so it would join us in the defense of Europe against the Soviet Union. That was why he gave the French a green light to return to Indochina. That brought on the first French-Indochina War. Then, the State department convinced President Eisenhower that America's disappointing stalemate with Communist forces in Korea meant the free world couldn't afford to fail in Indochina. That was when he decided to drastically increase monetary aid to the French. And now, President Kennedy has concluded that his narrow victory over Nixon means he must show strength against International Communism. So he has escalated out manpower involvement here. Those explanations may actually be too simplistic, but in a nutshell, that is how we arrived at the situation we're in today."

"Do you really believe International Communism is the reason?" she asked. "It's possible that money and trade might be involved. Indochina would be great financial asset to your country."

"I really believe that financial assets have little to do with why we're here. It may sound trite and simplistic again, but I believe we're fighting in your country to preserve your freedom and defeat a worldwide Communist triumph, even though we may be going about it poorly."

"But if you're going about it poorly, how on earth did your Presidents come to make the decisions that got you in this mess? Who advised them? Surely they didn't act on their own."

"In each case, they made what was primarily a political decision, recommended by their Security Councils and tempered by the advice of the State Department. The American military made many recommendations that differed with the State Department, but our Joint Chiefs of Staff were schooled that civilian authority must be have the ultimate control of what our country does. The Chiefs could recommend, but they couldn't bring themselves to object once a President had made a decision."

"But I heard that the generals and admirals had actually supported those Presidential decisions."

"In some instances, you're correct," he said. "First, Admiral Radford, the Chairman of the Joint Staff recommended that we come to the aid of the French and even use atomic weapons at Dien Bien Phu. Then, Generals Paul Harkins and Maxwell Taylor successively advocated escalation, because they though we could do a better job than the French did. They said we could win in Indochina. And General MacArthur once told President Truman that all the French needed to defeat the Vietnamese was an aggressive general."

"And now you have doubts?"

"Doubts? Sure," he said. "If we continue down the path Diem is taking, we'll lose South Vietnam and waste a lot of lives in the process."

"Does anybody else in the military agree with you?"

"In the past, two great soldiers have spoken out against our involvement in Indochina: Generals Mathew Ridgeway and Lightning Joe Collins. They warned President Eisenhower about getting involved in Southeast Asia, told him to get out before being pulled too deeply into a quagmire. They were overruled and silenced."

"So what will happen?" she asked.

"A lot of people will die."

"Dying doesn't sound too good," she said.

"No doubt about that," he said. "I'm against death. He and I go back a long way."

"How so?" she asked.

"Let me tell you a story," he said. "When I was just nine years old, my family was at Fort Sill. Charlie was my age, a friend of mine, and we used to play at swimming hole just east of the fort's housing area. We called one of our favorite games 'Life on the Mississippi.' I was Huck and Charlie was Jim. I vividly recall a particular day when we ran with special enthusiasm through the woods out to the pond, because we were almost finished with a raft we were building. I had a roll of light rope and a knife, and Charlie had an axe. That day, we intended to complete the raft and launch it for an initial voyage. The weather was hot and dry, and the country was in the terrible Depression I told you about, but we were lucky and happy because we had a place to play and a roof over our heads. A lot of people didn't have houses or food, and we had an icebox to keep the milk fresh, fans to stir the air, and screens to keep out the Oklahoma flies.

"The woods were thicker along the creek coming from the swimming hole, and there we pulled aside some branches and leaves to uncover our almost-finished treasure. It consisted of four ten-foot boards laid out in a rectangle, across which we had tied various branches and small logs. Charlie set to cutting more logs, while I used bits of rope to tie them to the boards. In less than an hour, we were ready to launch our raft into the creek, but the damn thing had become to heavy. We pushed, shoved, and tugged, but try as we would, the contraption just wouldn't budge.

"Then three high school boys came out of the woods where they had been hiding. The bigger ones pushed us aside and grabbed hold of the raft. With a few grunts, they had it in the little creek We watched helplessly as those three goons shoved our prize toward the swimming hole. There, they clamored aboard and lay on the logs, attempting to paddle into deeper waters. The little craft would not support their weight, however, and it soon sank below the surface and rolled over, throwing the boys off. As it turned over, a log struck one of them on the head, and he disappeared under the surface.

"When the two surviving boys realized their buddy had not surfaced with them, they stripped off their shoes and shirts and dove again and again into the swimming hole after him. Charlie and I ran for the houses to find help. In less than thirty minutes, a fire department truck and an ambulance arrived, but they were too late.

Two hours later, they found the body. Water had filled his boots and dragged him under. That was my first experience with death."

"And it must have been terrible for a young boy," she said. "But I meant in the war, as a soldier?"

"Well, when I came to Korea in the spring of 1950," he said. "I had no idea what I was in for. You see, since 1947, the United States had been steadily withdrawing its forces from Korea. First, the 6th Infantry Division at Pusan was deactivated in December of 1948. Then, in 1949, the 7th Infantry Division was transferred to Japan, leaving only a few hundred Americans as the Korean Military Assistance Group (KMAG). I was one of those advisors.

"The Soviets and the North Koreans had watched President Truman make drastic cuts in American defense spending, and they concluded that his Secretary of Defense, Louis Jordan, was a gutless peace monger. Kim Il Sung, the leader-for-life of North Korea, had observed with interest the withdrawal of U.S. forces from the south, as well as the lack of money being spent to build up the South Korean forces. The final sign came when Secretary of State Dean Acheson announced in a speech in early 1950 that Korea was outside of the United States' sphere of influence and defense perimeter in the Far East.

"Kim Il Sung needed no further encouragement. He sought and received blessings from Mao Tse Tung in China and Josef Stalin of the Soviet Union. Thus he went all out to prepare an attack. In mid-summer, he was able to mount a major surprise offensive. I happened to be on a mission in Japan when his forces swarmed south, and that saved my life. The forces I had been with were quickly overrun. In response, General MacArthur hastily threw the Twenty-Fourth Infantry Division from Japan into the teeth of the advancing North Koreans, and I was ordered to join the Seventh Cavalry Regiment, part of the First Cavalry Division, as a forward observer. In less than three weeks, the North Koreans had chewed up and destroyed the Twenty-Fourth Division, killing over fifty percent of its soldiers, and the Seventh Cavalry and I had to be committed into the battle to replace them.

"The Seventh Cavalry was General Custer's outfit at the Little Big Horn in 1876, near where my great-grandfather had fought at the Rosebud the week before that famous Sioux victory. The Seventh was also the unit that caught Big Foot and his Sioux followers near Wounded Knee Creek in December of 1890. Wounded Knee effectively avenged Custer and ended America's wars against the Plains Indians. The Seventh Cav was a proud unit with a great history, but it wasn't ready for the North Koreans. Its only strength was its noncommissioned offices. They were combat veterans of World War Two, and they were ready and able to lead again in Korea. Unfortunately, they were furnished only green soldiers, draftees with just weeks of service, and their junior officers had had little training. The Seventh was also equipped with outmodel material, light reconnaissance tanks armed with low velocity weapons that were no match for the heavier Russian tanks and weapons the North Koreans had. Our troops also had an anti-tank rocket launcher that wouldn't even dent those Russians heavy tanks, and because of defense cutbacks the Cav's radios didn't work. The Cav lacked spare parts and were undermanned, but all their shortcomings had to be ignored. The Twenty-Fourth was no longer an effective fighting unit, and the Seventh Cavalry had to be thrown into combat to gain time, no matter what the consequences. I was assigned to one of their squadrons as a forward observer.

"We landed at Pusan and immediately rushed forward to fill the breech left by the decimated Twenty- Fourth Division. Three days later, we were in the line to the east of Yongdong about halfway to Seoul. The highway from Yongdong to Hwanggan was crowded with refugees fleeing from advancing North Koreans. Men, women and children streamed south down the road, mostly on foot and carrying what they could of their life's possessions. That first night, we set up a perimeter a few hundred yards south of the road and prepared defenses, knowing that the enemy was only a few miles away. All went well until an apparent refugee came into out position. Before we could stop him, he threw three grenades, killing one of our guys and wounding several more. Those first casualties sobered us all, and the squadron commander quickly passed word to keep all refugees out of our lines, using all necessary means to do so, including lethal force. That order restored morale.

"The next day, we sent patrols north along the road to set up forward warning posts. Some fire came from among the refugees, and the patrols had to return fire to prevent any approach to their positions. At one point, our men received automatic weapons fire from under a railway trestle near the hamlet of No Gun Ri, and one of our posts returned fire. It was a chaotic situation in which green troops had no way to tell the difference between the enemy and fleeing South Koreans. In desperation, they had to fire in self-defense. Our fire didn't stop the North Koreans. Soon our forward listening posts come under intense pressure, and they had to withdraw to our main position.

"Just after midnight, we were hit by an overwhelming force. Heavy tanks accompanied by large numbers of infantry swarmed at us. I called in artillery fire, but our batteries were short of guns and ammunition. Soon, we too were overrun, and the enemy was all around us. In the darkness, we couldn't tell who was who. When we lost all contact with the rest of our squadron, my radio operator and I joined the troop lieutenant and another sergeant, and the four of us slipped away toward the east hoping to locate our reserve elements. All we found was two frightened American soldiers, and together we headed deeper into the rugged hills to put distance between us and move farther away from the advancing enemy on the road below us.

"The six of us were in barren terrain, and we had no way to communicate with friendly forces. When morning came, we huddled hidden among the boulders on a mountaintop and surveyed our situation. With no way to notify other units, we were on our own. We had little ammunition and almost no food, so we couldn't last long and there was no way we would survive a face to face fire fight with the enemy. We decided to stay hidden in the hills, living off the land and making our way south during the night. We risked drinking water from the little mountain streams, and we chewed leaves and ate whatever bugs we could find. That was when I discovered that a starving man will eat almost anything to stay alive.

"After three weeks of this, we descended from the hills and worked our way to the banks of the Naktong River. On the other bank lay safety, but crossing would be hazardous at best. If either side spotted us, we would be fired on. We waited until the moon was down, therefore, and then entered the water. Weak from fatigue and lack of food, our crossing was a close call, but nobody spotted us, and we made it. We were exhausted and near starvation. I had lost thirty-five pounds, and I was in the hospital for three weeks. Death had been close, but I escaped."

"Now I know why Nancy wanted you to resign," she said. "Did you go home then?"

"No such luck," he said. "I stayed there two more years."

"What happened?" she asked.

"The war changed?" she asked.

"The war changed when MacArthur made a brilliant landing at Inchon behind enemy lines. His success with that maneuver let us take the offensive, and the North Koreans fled in a rout. When I got out of the hospital, I was quickly assigned to the Seventh Infantry Division. Back in August, it had been stripped of its officers and key noncommissioned officers to beef up the first three Divisions sent into the line to hold back the advancing North Koreans. As a result, the Seventh badly needed leaders, and I joined them at the end of October just as the boarded ships to flank the enemy by landing at Iwon on the northeast coast of Korea. The objective was to establish a bridgehead well behind enemy lines and drive inland to cut off North Koreans retreating from the MacArthur's invasion farther south. The operation succeeded, and elements of my Tenth Corps soon reached the Yalu River. We thought we had won the war and would soon be going home, but we were badly mistaken.

"In the first part of November, thirty Chinese Infantry Divisions crossed the Yalu and took up positions in the hills surrounding us. As brilliant as MacArthur had been at Inchon, he failed now. He refused to believe Intelligence reports that three hundred thousand Chinese soldiers were in Korea, and he neither gave us warning, nor prepared a response. At the end of the Month, the enemy attacked in overwhelming force. They were hardened combat veterans of the long war against the Chinese Nationalists. We had air support during the day, so the enemy had to attack at night. They came at us in great waves of soldiers, shouting, blowing whistles and bugles, and banging tin cans together. We killed great numbers of them, but they had a limitless supply of men, and the situation soon turned against us. Nighttime temperatures dropped to thirty degrees below zero, and out ammunition supplies ran low. We had to retreat. We moved in daylight, so that navy and air force planes could cover us. Unfortunately, clouds came in, and our air support disappeared. The Chinese closed in for the kill, and I was overrun again. The infantry platoon I was with lost its commander, and I was the only officer left. We were on our own and taking intense fire from the hills around us. For three days, we crawled, wiggled, and crept south. Finally, we were surrounded on the three sides with the reservoir at our backs. That night, we set out across the frozen ice, hoping to find Marines, not Chinese, on the other side. Luck was with us, and we joined elements of the First marine Division, themselves straggling south and under intense assault. We struggled for a week more and finally reached the perimeter the Marines had set up at Wonson. Although the Seventh Division had been overrun and its men scattered, my little group had stayed together. Over fifty percent of the Division's Infantry were casualties, but eighteen of the twenty-four men I was with survived. All of us suffered from some degree of frostbite, and ten of us were wounded, but we were alive. We were soon evacuated from Wonson and sent south, and I spent two more years in Korea before the Army took pity on me and sent me home."

"Thank God," she said. "Hearing that, I now completely agree with Nancy. You should have quit the Army right then. And today, you should resign. Your luck could run out at any time."

"It's not the same here," he said. "Vietnam is a guerilla war, nothing like Korea."

"VC bullets still can kill you," she said.

"Good point," said. "But there aren't as many of them."

"But your army has never fought a war like this one."

"Sure we have," he said. "During the last century, we fought many similar battles against the Indians on our western plains. We did the same against Aguinaldo's Filipinos for three years in the Philippine Insurrection after the Spanish-American War. Those campaigns were much like Vietnam in many ways."

"You think we're Indians?" she asked.

"Of course not," he said. "But the stories my father told me about the Indian Wars show lots of similarities. On the Great Plains of the American west, our soldiers went through day after day of endless boredom that at any time might erupt in sudden savage violence, just like here. The army controlled the roads and villages, as we do now, but the Indians could mass for an attack almost anywhere, as the VC have done."

"Did all the Indians fight you?"

"No, just the warlike ones: notably the Apaches, Cheyenne, and Sioux. For years, the Apaches in the American southwest fought successfully against the invasion of Mexicans and Americans into Apache territory before gold was discovered in California. After that, the steam fortune hunters was too overwhelming."

"Like the Chinese and the French coming into Cochin China," she said. "We fought their invasions for a thousand years."

"It only took fifty years in the case of the Apaches. From the discovery of Californian gold in 1848 until their final defeat, three leaders led them in a hopeless cause: Mangas, Cochise, and Geronimo. They had few warriors, and the Americans had artillery and thousand of soldiers. Even so, the Apaches held out until finally Geronimo had less than fifty warriors left. His cause was hopeless. Nelson Miles, the general who captured Chief Joseph and eventually led the forces at Wounded Knee, had five thousand men chasing those few renegades. Even so, Geronimo escaped for months until he could hold out no longer, and he had to surrender. For his success, General Miles became the Army Chief of Staff. But some comparisons are interesting. Miles had five thousand men, and Geronimo less than fifty. If the same ratio of forces held here in Vietnam, the Unites States would need more than five hundred thousand men to eliminate today's twelve thousand VC, and the campaign would take fifty years,"

"But isn't it possible that the Apaches were an isolated case?" she asked.

"Not really," he said. "Other major battles against the Sioux and Cheyenne on our Great Plains took almost the same amount of time, forty years, and during that period, we had overwhelming superiority in weapons and numbers. And the conditions along the Bozeman and Oregon Trails there were similar to Routes One and Four here in Vietnam. As we do here, soldiers in the Old West controlled the roads and villages during the day, but the Indians took over at night."

"Why did it take so long?" she asked.

"Like today, politics got involved, and like the Viet Cong, the Indians were resisting what they saw as our invasion of their homeland. National Indian pride was involved, and they fought until disease, treachery, and overwhelming force did them in. The end was marked by a massacre at a place called Wounded Knee, as it was in the Philippines."

"The Philippines?"

"Sure. In 1899 in the Philippines, we began the same kind of irregular Indian warfare, this time against the Moros, who were fierce Filipino guerillas. For years, they just wouldn't give up. Finally, in 1906, the Philippine Constabulary led by American General Leonard Wood trapped most of the remaining Moro men, women, and children at the bottom of an extinct volcanic crater on Jolo Island. For three days, the constabulary fired artillery into that crater until all nine hundred insurgents were dead, and he declared victory. But he was wrong. The Filipino guerrillas weren't really defeated. Just recently, fifty years after that massacre, they are in the news again. This time they call themselves. Huks, but they are really Moslem Communists who are direct descendants of the Moros. Colonel Lansdale and the CIA like to point out our apparent success against those Huks these last few years, and Lansdale has now apparently persuaded Diem to use the same techniques here in Vietnam. That's where Diem to use the same techniques here in Vietnam. That's where Diem got the idea for his new strategic hamlet program. But the point is that the Moro guerillas had really never given up. The descendents of the Moros General Wood thought he had defeated fifty years ago are still fighting today. There's a lesson in that. Since the Joint Chiefs and the State Department have agreed that the United States would never invade North Vietnam, the best we can hope for here is another stalemate like Korea. If the Indian Wars, the Philippines and Korea are precedents, that stalemate might drag on for forty years. And to prevent the rise of another insurgency during that time, America would have to maintain a military presence here in Vietnam for a very long time."

"Would the people the United States accept that?"

"Not on your life."

CHAPTER TEN

In the summer of 1961, Sandy received orders sending him home. He was to leave in August, and before then he had to write a review of his year in Vietnam. He summarized the capabilities and activities of his Vietnamese airborne battalions to bring out their decrease in offensive operations and recommend a change in that strategy. He explained that the paratroopers were well trained and ready to seize the initiative and perform wider duties, but that they were not being allowed to do so. His analysis of the unfolding situation in South Vietnam was even harsher. He was pessimistic, and his conclusions were foregone. In his opinion, far from moving in a positive direction, the outlook for President Diem had deteriorated. Intelligence reports showed that the Viet Cong now had twice the number of organized followers in the south as they had when Diem had taken over, and indications were that they were growing stronger every day. And Hanoi had just announced the formation of the National Front the Liberation of the South, soon to be known as the National Liberation Front, or NLF. Furthermore, Soviet Premier, Nikita Khruschev had announced his support for Ho Chi Minh by declaring that the Soviet Union would support all valid wars of national liberation, worldwide. That had dire implications for South Vietnam, because President Diem and the ARVN were clearly not winning the heats and minds of the rural Vietnamese. In reaction to that and to meet a rising concern at home, Vice President Johnson had visited South Vietnam in May to assess the situation. When he returned and reported to President Kennedy, he gave glowing, unqualified support to Diem, calling the little man the hope for freedom in Southeast Asia, Johnson further recommended that the United States send more men, money, and material to South Vietnam. The only alternative, according to Johnson, would be retreat to the coastal shores of the United States and become "Fortress America." To adopt the latte course of action would be to admit defeat by Communism worldwide, and that would result in the loss of freedom for millions of people around the world. President Kennedy had no choice. The Vice President's report had given him a blueprint and a mandate for escalation in South Vietnam.

In a resulting press conference, Kennedy announced that the United States was considering the use of American ground forces in Southeast Asia. In the furor over such a change in strategy, the President immediately authorized American Special Forces and the CIA to expand their training of South Vietnamese Special Forces for operations in the highlands against North Vietnam, Laos, and the growing supply route from the north. ARVN itself was given permission to double the size of its army to sixty thousand men, and President Kennedy mandated that America would be responsible for their training. Fifteen thousand United States advisors were to be sent immediately to Vietnam for that purpose, he said, and the direct infusion of American combat units into the conflict there was imminent.

At the same time, Diem was growing weaker. He had alienated the religious sects that in the normal order of events would have been supporting his government against the insurgents, and out in the villages and rice paddies of the Delta, disaffected peasants were either supporting the communists or at least condoning them. The Viet Cong now controlled more than half of the southern part of South Vietnam, especially the rice-rich Delta, and were surrounding Saigon in an ever-tightening circle. To Sandy, these developments clearly mandated a change in the policies of the United States in Southeast Asia, and he said so in his report.

"The future here is chaos." Sandy told Avril as he was preparing to leave. "Come home with me."

"I wish I could," she said. "You have to know that, but I can't leave. I must stay."

"Why on earth?"

"This is my country," she said, "I can't abandon it."

"These never-ending wars in this unfortunate land have killed almost everybody you love," he said. "You've no family left except Cousin Ly and Uncle Ba. Come with me. We'll build a better future in a better place."

"But this is my home," she said, looking around the room. "There are memories here, and I don't want to leave them. And I've got a job that has grown to be meaningful. Moe and more I see where I can help improve things."

"What kind of things?"

"Much good comes out of the American Embassy," she said, after hesitation. "The Cultural Attaché is a powerful force for change, positive change that can improve people's lives."

"Is that what you really want?" he asked. "I mean really, really want, and I mean you, not the embassy or anybody else. What do you really want?"

"I want the war to stop," she said. "This version has been going on for twenty years now, and I want it to end."

"Avril, it's been going on for much longer than that," he said. "Warfare has been a way of life here for thousands of years. Think back. How long have your people been fighting the Chinese? It never stops."

"Thousands of years, yes and my people never gave up," she said. "If I leave now, I'd be abandoning that tradition. I'd be a traitor, letting them down. I'd be giving up."

"If the war were to stop tomorrow," he said, "your life would never be what it was like when you were growing up. You were a part of Colonial France back then, with all that that entailed. The French exploited your people, and your father was a part of what happened. You can't want to return to that."

"Of course not," she said. "I don't want to go back to my childhood, no matter what your amateur psychiatrists might say. I just want a future without fear. And I want to have children, but not if I have to have raise them in this chaos."

"In the United States," he said, "you could do exactly that. We'll have ten kids if you want."

"My father told my mother exactly the same thing," she said. "But she stayed here, where she had family, position, and an honorable place in the scheme of things. She said that in France, she would have been a homeless nobody. At least here she was somebody, and so she wouldn't leave."

"And the Japanese killed her," he said. "That could happen to you. In the States, you'd have stability, some sort of certainty, a future. Here, you've none of those."

"Vietnam used to be what you describe," she said. "It could be again, a place where Uncle Ba can start a restaurant and Cousin Ly can rest at night, instead of guarding my house. If I desert them before that happens, I will have betrayed them. My life will have been wasted."

"But don't you want to be with someone you love?" he asked. "With someone who loves you very much? Come with me."

She burst into tears, and he held her tightly until she calmed. And then they made love with an intensity he had not known before. It was as if they knew they would never be together again and they wanted the memory of that final act of passion to sustain them for the rest of their lives. In the morning, she held him tightly, but she would not leave her country.

CHAPTER ELEVEN

After that last night with Avril, sad and frustrating, yet marked by a driving passion that remained with him, Sandy was thrust into a whirlwind of final activities. He had to turn over his duties to his successor and render final reports. Then he had to say goodbye to the many officers and men, both American and Vietnamese, who had served with him. It was a sad, time-consuming time, and it kept him busy until his final moments. In a way, he was happy for that, because he had no opportunity to see her again, and he thus avoided another painful farewell. When he finally left Vietnam without seeing her, outwardly he radiated success and confidence. In one sense, Vietnam had been easier on him than Korea had been ten years earlier. He had been involved in only minor combat operations, had not been hospitalized for wounds, and had never been overrun by a charging enemy.

To the casual observer, Sandy looked great in his starched khakis with all those ribbons. He was tan, trim, and impressive. Inwardly, he felt far less confident. He was really disheartened over leaving Avril, and he was discouraged over what had been happening to the United States in Vietnam. He desperately needed a change of pace. Given thirty days vacation to recover before reporting to Fort Sill again, he therefore immediately went to Destin to see Walter and Sara. Walter was now thirteen, and Sara eleven. Nancy had rented a small house near her mother and father across the bay from Pensacola, and she had earned a real estate license so she could start a new career and become more independent. She told him that her life was on track, and that their kids were apparently happy.

On several occasions during his vacation, Sandy took the kids over to see his father, who had retired from the Army to his small cottage directly on the wide white beach where Sandy and Nancy had first made love. On one particularly hot August day while the kids ran and swam under the bright sun, Sandy rested with a cold beer under a beach umbrella, contentedly watching them and trying to remember the love that had first brought Nancy and him to that place. Andy remained in his little cottage, as was his habit, apparently drinking and watching television. Occasionally the kids would race out of the water from some cold Coke Cola and more suntan lotion. Once, while Sandy was rubbing lotion on Walter's back, the boy asked about Vietnam. At first, Sandy was reluctant to talk about the tortured country. He wanted to leave it behind, but Walter persisted. He knew that grandfather Andy had fought the Japanese for three years in the Pacific. And great-grandfather Walker had fought Aguinaldo's guerillas for more than two years in the Philippines, and great-great-grandfather Joseph had battled against the Plains Indians for twenty-five years. Walter had always been fascinated with Sandy's stories about those men. Now, the developing situation in Southeast Asia had caught his attention.

"Maybe I should be a soldier too," he said. "When it's my turn to serve, Vietnam might be my war. What's Vietnam like?"

"It's a bad place to fight," Sandy said. "But then, there aren't many good places."

"Do you think I'll have to go there?"

"Maybe," Sandy said. "If our country doesn't change its direction pretty soon, a lot of guys like you will go. But you've always said you wanted to be a lawyer, not a solder. Have you changed your mind?"

"Naw. I'd still rather be a lawyer," Walter said. "But if I had to, I'd fight like all the Walkers."

"What about West Point?"

"No, I don't think I could be a cadet."

"You don't want to be an officer?"

"I don't care if I'm an officer or not," Walter said. "You always said that serving is what matter."

"But you're a natural leader. You're smart. People like you. You could contribute much more as an officer."

"I don't think I'm cut out for that," Walter said. "I couldn't tell guys what to do and then see them hurt or killed. That would be gross, a really bad scene. Besides, you've always told me that the individual soldier is the most important thing an army can have. I think I'd rather be one of them."

"Four generations of your family before you have been commissioned," Sandy said," and they met the challenges of command you describe. It may be in your blood."

"Maybe," Walter said. "But mom says command didn't always work out too good for us. She says both my great-granddad and his father died early, and the memories of their military service as officers might have been part of the reason they did. She also says grandad and grandma don't live together because of the war. He drinks a lot. I don't think I'd want to end up like him."

"Grandpa has a lot on his mind," Sandy said. "He worries about things over which he has no control. That's not good, but it wasn't because he was on officer."

The conversation was the longest Sandy and Walter had ever had on such a serious subject, and it must have been to much for the boy, for he suddenly ended the talks by running to join a beach football game. Sandy was left thinking over what Walter had said. Nancy must have filled the kid with negative stories about him, his family, and the profession of arms. What she had told him must have been pretty bad, he guessed, for Walter to feel so strongly. Sandy had to admit that whatever good the military life had in it, and there was much, had to be weighted against other relationship. Too many moves and separations caused stress on a marriage and damaged a child's self esteem. No wonder that Andy and Penny were struggling to keep their marriage from Sandy and Nancy end that way? No, she had gone a step farther than Penny and had actually gotten a divorce. And she wasn't trying too hard to get back together. And on his part, Sandy had too many memories of Avril, and they weren't fading fast. Nancy had to come to hate the Army. She had had to date him at long distance while he was at the Academy, and the first place he had taken her after West Point had been dry, hot, dusty Lawton, Oklahoma. She was already pregnant, and because Fort Sill had no room for them, they had to rent a small place in downtown Lawton. Pregnant and morning sick in small-town Oklahoma was a poor way for Nancy to start her marriage. And after the basic officer's course, they had gone to Fort Hood, down in Texas, and that fort had been even hotter, dryer, and dustier than Fort Sill. She'd become pregnant again, just as he'd received orders to go to Korea, and she had to go home to Destin to have the baby without Sandy. When he came back from Korea, alive and in one piece, he'd been ordered back to Fort Sill, and Nancy hadn't liked that one bit. Their arguments had begun then, and he couldn't blame her. When he volunteered for parachute training and Special Forces, she really let him have it. She deplored the dangers of airborne training and the risks of Special Forces operations. That was when she went back to Destin to start all over. She told Sandy she would be there when he came to his senses. Would he ever do that? Old dog learns new tricks? The chances were getting slimmer by the day.

His thoughts were interrupted by Sara's arrival. She too wanted a back rub. But Sara wasn't like Walter. A year ago, she had been nervous and afraid because he was going to Southeast Asia. She hadn't wanted him to leave them, and now that he was safely back, she hated the idea that Walter might eventually have to go fight in the same dangerous place.

"Why do we want to fight there?" she asked.

"We don't want to," he said.

"But you went there, and now Walter says he's going to go too. And it's so far away. What do we care about it?"

"We care about the people there," he said. "Fifteen million of them. They're just like us. They want and deserve their freedom, and we want to help them find it."

"But Walter could get hurt," she said. "And mommy said you were wounded again. Were you?"

"Not badly," he said. "I'm okay now,"

"But if you go again," she said, "you could get hurt again, and maybe then it would be really bad. Couldn't you?"

"Yes, I, suppose I could. But that's my job. I'm soldier, and soldiers take risks for the good of their country."

"Mommy says you've taken too many risks already. She says that's why you don't live with us any more. Is that true?"

"I suppose it's one reason," he said.

"I hate soldiers," she said.

"Do you hate me?" he asked.

"No, of course not," she said. "But don't go."

"I have to," he said.

She paused for a minute and then took a chain from around her neck and gave it to him.

"Will you wear this?" she asked, tears in her eyes.

"What is it?"

"It's religious medal. Saint Christopher. It's supposed to keep you safe while you travel. Please wear it. I really don't care if you have to be a soldier. I just want you to come home safely."

He slipped the chain over his head. The little emblem hung securely on his chest. He took between his fingers and felt the reassuring engraving.

"I'll bring it home to you," he said.

She hugged him tightly, wiped her eyes, and went back to her friends. He wanted to talk more with her, to change her mind about soldering, but he knew it wouldn't do any good. She was just echoing what Nancy must have said to her so many times before. Military like had to many risks for Nancy, and Sara had been listening to her mother for a long time. It was on his mind when he next saw Nancy.

"Are you poising my daughter's mind against me?" he asked when they were alone later that evening.

"What do you mean? Nancy asked.

"She says she hates solders" he said.

"That's just girl talk," Nancy said. "Girls use the word 'hate' too easily. She certainly doesn't hate you. Actually, she loves you a lot, and she wants to see more of you. She misses you. Walter does too. It's a price you and they pay because you are what you are."

"Other families pay that price," he said," and they manage to stay together."

"Well, get it through your thick head, Sandy," she said. "This family isn't just any other family. We're not waiting around until you come home in a body bag. Go ahead and do what you think you have to. That won't be anything new, but don't try to drag us with you. We're building a new life, and waiting around to see if you're going to come back from the grave again is not going to be a part of it."

Thoroughly rebuffed, and admitting Nancy had a point, Sandy gave up any additional attempts to bridge the gap between them. He tried to keep communication with Sara and Walter open, but he kept remembering what Walter had said about Andy. The guy was really drinking too much and spending most of his time alone in that little cottage. Sandy looked for and found a quiet moment to ask his father what was going on.

"Where are you and Penny headed?" he asked.

"She's up in New York," Andy said. "Lives with her father, and works at his law firm. She used to write now and then, but not much and not recently."

"How long since you've seen her?"

"More than ten years now," Andy said, "I think she's dating again, that guy Harrison we knew in the Army. You remember what I told you about him. Trash."

"But what's wrong?" Sandy asked. "Why did she leave?"

"A lot of things, I suppose. After World War Two, I was ordered to duty here in Pensacola, and she wanted to leave Florida. Been here too long, she said."

"Did you guys talk about it before she left?"

"Not really," Andy said. "My mind was on other things, and she thought I was obsessed with them."

"What other things?"

"I guess I had become too concerned about the nuclear tests in the Pacific."

"What about them?"

"I think that as a country, conducting those tests, we're heading down the wrong path. We don't need to … "

"But all we're doing is testing weapons," Sandy said.

"No, it's much more than that," Andy said. "We didn't have to use those bombs against Japan. They were already beaten. A demonstration atomic bombing of some uninhabited desert island would have been enough to make them surrender. Instead, we killed all those women and children."

"Wars are bad," Sandy said. "People die. Soldiers try to prevent wars, but we have to win 'em if we're in 'em. As for the atomic bombs, they might have been a blessing. I sure didn't want you killed invading Japan."

"And I understand that," Andy said. "It's just the way we went about it. First President Roosevelt said we wouldn't bomb enemy cities from the air, but then we changed our minds and targeted all those places in Germany, like Cologne where we destroyed everything, and all those people died. And we killed a hundred thousand people by fire bombing Japanese cities in March of 1945, even before we dropped the atom bombs on Hiroshima and Nagasaki. And do you know why we used them against Japan and not Germany?

"I've got a feeling you're going to tell me."

"Because the Germans in those cities had blue eyes, blonde hair, and lots of relatives in the States. The Japanese didn't.

"You think our government is racist?

"What's going on in Alabama right now would seem to indicate that. Why else would we have to have federal troops at the entrances of public schools in our cities?"

"But dad, just because some people are deeply prejudiced." Sandy said, "that doesn't mean our government is."

"How 'bout the treatment of the Japanese-Americans on our west coast after Pearl Harbor? We not only shipped a hundred thousand of them off to concentration camps, but we stole their money and property in the process. And remember the nine hundred Filipinos who died in that crater in Philippine Islands back in 1906. And don't forget the deaths of more than two hundred Indian women and kids at Wounded Knee sixteen years before that. It goes back a long way."

"But we were talking about the atomic testing out in the Pacific," Sandy said. "How'd we get around to the massacre at Wounded Knee?"

"It's all the same thing," Andy said. "Whether you're talking about the treatment of the Marshall Islanders today or the American

Indians a hundred years ago, we're the ones who are taking land, killing children, bombarding women with radioactive fall-out, or slaughtering Muslims in an abandoned Philippine crater. These are racist crimes based on racist hate, and I fear for the future of our country if we as a nation can't get over what seems to be our deep, inbred prejudices."

"And this kind of talk was what sent Mom away?"

"Naw, it was probably much more than that," Andy said. Anyway, she's happy now, anyway, and I've got old sour mash."

Andy went back to his bourbon, and the discussion was over. Sandy little more than he did when it started, but he realized that his father was deeply troubled about something, and he knew his parents would not soon reconcile. He also knew that the poor record of the Walker men with their women would not end with Andy, for Avril had answered none of Sandy's letters. Whenever he thought about her, late in the middle of some sleepless night, the old hurt returned with a vengeance.

CHAPTER TWELVE

After his frustrating and too brief vacation in Florida with Sara and Walter, Sandy headed west to Fort Sill once more. The Artillery School there wanted him to write a report setting forth his experiences during his year in Vietnam with the ARVN paratroopers. In particular, it requested his conclusions and recommendations concerning the use of artillery in the conflict with guerrillas in Southeast Asia. As the United States became more involved in South Vietnam, Fort Sill needed to insure that all future students of the Artillery School could study his and other such reports in order to be better prepared to serve in that theater of operations. The experience if the Army of Korea, where green officers had been thrown into combat only to be sacrificed without proper training, was not to be repeated. In Vietnam or other combat environments of the future, the Army wanted experienced, qualified leaders. Their men deserved no less. Thus Sandy's first duty was to write a detailed report about what he had seen and done in Southeast Asia. Following that, he was to draw conclusions and make recommendations concerning what was to be taught at The Artillery School. In early September, he began.

Counting his childhood at Fort Sill and his basic officer training there after graduating from West Point, this was his third visit to venerable old fort. Established in 1869 by Major Phil Sheridan, Fort Sill had for many years been a major base for the Army's campaigns against the Comanche and Apache Indian tribes. Near the end of the century, Famed Chiricahua Chief Geronimo had been imprisoned there for almost ten almost ten years.

Sandy's father had told him many stories about Geronimo and other famous Indian leaders like Mangas Coloradas, Cochise, and Natachez. Sandy remembered how those chiefs had frustrated and eluded a hundred times their numbers of American soldiers for forty-five years. In doing so, they frustrated the best leaders the Army of the Southwest sent against them. The American generals were fine commanders, men like George Crook, soon to be famous as an Indian fighter in the Dakotas, and Nelson Miles, who would be the Army Chief of Staff in the Spanish-American War. They led thousands of soldiers in many fruitless chases after the Apaches through the Arizona and Mexican badlands. Finally, Captain Henry Lawton, Medal of Honor winner from the Civil War, for whom the Oklahoma town is named, wore the Apaches down. Geronimo was their last great chief, and he was captured and taken to Fort Sill in 1894, never to return to his hunting lands before his death in 1909.

Once Andy had taken Sandy to see the small, concrete-block building that had been Geronimo's cell for such a long time at Fort Sill. It was a small blockhouse, so small that Sandy knew how confining it must have been for the great chief. After a life roaming the great expanse of America's southwest, Geronimo must have been traumatized by his confinement to the dark cell. Indeed, Andy showed him a depression in the wall, telling that Geronimo had dug it with his fingernails in an attempt to regain his freedom. Freedom was so important, then and now. Thinking about Andy's many stories of the Indian Wars, Sandy was struck by similarity of their battles to what was happening in Vietnam, and those thoughts influenced the writing of his report. Among other tales Andy had told him was also a legend that held that if a person ever came to the hills around Fort Sill, he would return for three more visits. Andy had instilled a great faith in those Indian legends, so Sandy knew he still had one more visit waiting for him.

After two months work, he submitted what he considered to be a good draft report. The idea was for the school faculty to review his conclusions and recommendations. Then he would be asked to elaborate or defend his submission. He waited for three weeks until he was summoned to the office of a senior colonel on the school's faculty. From the colonel's opening remarks, Sandy knew he was in trouble.

"You question our instruction about massed artillery fires," the colonel said. "On what basis?"

"Lack of targets," Andy said. "The ARVN.

"Wait a minute," the colonel interrupted. "If there are no targets, who are we fighting?"

"Individual terrorists, small groups of guerrillas, and only occasionally a company of Viet Cong. When attacks occur..

"Hold it. Can't artillery be used against VC companies?"

"Only occasionally. Most engagements are isolated attacks or chance meetings that are widely dispersed or out of artillery range, some in areas where artillery fire of any kind wouldn't be appropriate or would.

"Wait a minute. That doesn't make sense. Why wouldn't artillery fire be appropriate?"

"We can't fire into the Vietnamese villages that are being overrun. In addition, ARVN has a large area to defend and many isolated posts are out of range of their artillery. Those posts, and many are small, have to defend on their own until help arrives. The VC can select the time and place of any attack. Much of the time, small ARVN units stand the chance of being overrun by superior forces before help arrives."

"I don't follow you. If the VC wants the support of the people, why do they attack their villages?"

"Many reasons, but right now, they want to kill the village leaders. You see, when President Diem took power, he stopped the popular election of local village officials. Then he appointed his own people to fill those posts. The Viet Cong wants to kill Diem's henchmen. Thus they are now systematically assassinating village leaders, many time with the assistance of the villagers themselves. These are isolated actions where artillery either is out of range or not registered to fire in defense. Even if in range, the guns would have to fire into the villages where most attacks occur, and that would result in many innocent villagers being killed."

"Why doesn't ARVN put forward observers at those posts and position artillery in order to support them?"

"Too many villages and not enough observers or artillery units. ARVN is too small. It would have to.

"Hold it. That means we need to train more observers for them and send them more artillery. But in your report, you don't recommend more advisors or artillery units. Why not?"

"Those steps would be very close to a violation of the Geneva Agreement of 1954," Sandy said. "But even if we could get ARVN more forward observers and weapons, the emphasis here at the school would still have to change to focus more on training for small unit actions, rather than massed artillery fires against hard targets. That's what I wanted to.

"But it's obvious that ARVN should take the initiative and go out after the Viet Cong, rather than sit back and wait to be attacked. And it would have to go out in substantial force with more artillery. Why doesn't it?"

"Two reasons," Sandy said. "First, ARVN is too small. It has just recently been allowed to increase to about 150,000 men. If it were to attempt massive offensive operations, it would need more than twice that number, and there is no way they could raise that many. Secondly, the French tried to do what you suggest. They called those operations 'search and destroy,' and they lost a lot of men conducting them. The Viet Minh could see those larger units coming and decide to either ambush them or melt away into the jungle or tunnels. When the French had passed through, the Viets just came out of hiding and continued as they…"

"You've got a negative attitude, Walker," the colonel said. "Are you telling me that artillery is of no use in operations against guerrillas? I find that hard to accept. There must be a way to use that firepower. In Korea, we learned to use massive fires as a way to counter Chinese human wave attacks. That way, we saved American lives and made the Chinese pay dearly."

"Vietnam isn't Korea," Sandy said. "In Korea, the Chinese used mass attacks. ARVN is fighting in a war of small, isolated units that need ways to defend themselves until help arrives. That's why I'm recommending we put much more emphasis on the old 4.2inch mortars. The ARVN now has a few, but they need many more. They're cheap and easy to use. And they pack a big punch. Every isolated post could have a mortar squad, and they'd be better able to hold out until help arrived. But the Artillery School doesn't teach the mortar any more."

"That's because those old mortars are outdated," the colonel said. "There must be a better way."

"If you want to go modern," Sandy said, "think about choppers and parachute units. They have mobility and plenty of firepower. They can stay on alert, move quickly to the battle, and catch the VC in the open. ARVN just needs to have enough firepower, like the heavy 4.2inch mortars, in place so they can hold out until such reaction forces get to them. I agree that where possible, ARVN artillery units should be positioned so as to fire in defense of the smaller ARVN units, but massed battalions of artillery would be wasted and out of the question. Instead, artillery pieces may have to be used individually or in pairs and be placed in key villages to defend themselves by lowering their tubes and using direct fire. I realize that if you break up artillery units like that, you are violating normal rules of employment, but the situation over there is different. We need to…"

Wait a minute. Surely the ARVN has artillery," the colonel said. "How do they use it?"

"They have very little," Sandy said.

"But how do they control those they have?"

"They're trying the Strategic Hamlet program," Sandy said. "President Diem is moving all the rice farmers into fortified villages, as the British did in Malaya and the Filipinos did against the Huks. The entire countryside outside of the villages is a free fire zone. Anybody in those areas is assumed to be VC. But it isn't working, because many South Vietnamese villagers are reluctant to cooperate and vacate those zones. Their families have lived on that land for generations, and they have roots in the soil. So ARVN ends up either displacing angry villagers so it can fire at suspected VC or killing a lot of bystanders and alienating many more by firing into occupied areas. Massed artillery tends to be counterproductive because ARVN uses heavy handed tactics, like air bombardment or long range artillery rather than putting its infantry on the ground to fight with the bayonet."

"If that's true, what are American advisors doing over there? Maybe better, what should they be doing?"

"American advisors can help ARVN develop appropriate small unit tactics. If it weren't for the Geneva Agreement, we could use more advisors at every level, down to and including squads. What I'm hearing, however, is that Washington is not leaning in that direction. Instead, the President's military advisor, General Taylor, has recommended the introduction of American combat units. In my report, I say that's a mistake. ARVN should be the ones to carry this fight to the VC, not American combat units. The French learned that lesson at great cost. They lost one hundred thousand men doing it their way. We should profit from their mistakes, not repeat them. If the ARVN can't be trained to do this job, we'll lose. And I mean more than men."

Sandy's initial recommendations apparently did not set well with the Artillery School. He was not asked to amplify on the changes he advocated. Instead, he spent three more months in a vain attempt to reconcile his report with current artillery doctrine and defend his conclusions to the school's faculty. He made little headway. Official United States theory maintained that the United States was in a Cold War with the Soviet Union, and war was most likely to come in Europe, where massed Americans artillery would be essential in defending against great numbers of Soviet tanks advancing in places like the Fulda Gap. It was only natural for institutions like the Artillery School to emphasize the importance of Europe's higher profile conflict and America's overriding need to support NATO. Sandy's only hope was that some people in the Kennedy Administration would recognize the need to change doctrine and tactics to meet the challenge of small, "brushfire" wars.

Soon he had at least some satisfaction. He learned that someone at the highest levels of the Army must have held similar views concerning small unit tactics and shared his opinion of the inertia in the Army and at the Artillery School, for President Kennedy soon approved the formation of the Fifth Special Forces Group. The new unit was to be stationed at Fort Bragg, North Carolina, where the Special Warfare Center was to be given a greatly expanded mission. Because of a sharp increase in the number of Special Forces advisors in Vietnam, the new Fifth Special Forces Group was to take full responsibility for irregular warfare in Southeast Asia. Sandy was elated, and he wanted to be a part of that new operation. He therefore applied for a transfer to the new Special Warfare Center. Because of his experience in Vietnam, or maybe just to get him away from the feathers he had ruffled at the Artillery School, Washington quickly approved his request, and in 1963 he received orders sending him to North Carolina.

CHAPTER THIRTEEN

The Army Special Forces had a long history. Before the United States became a nation, in the French and Indian War, those guerrilla fighters were known as Rogers Rangers. Those men used the roughest terrain and darkest nights to infiltrate French lines and strike behind the enemy when they were least expected. In the American Revolution, Francis Marion, the American Swamp Fox, continued the Ranger tradition for two years as he harassed the British in the Carolinas, tying up thousands of British regulars who were needed elsewhere. In the Civil War, Moseby's raiders of Virginia struck terror in the minds of the Union soldiers they surprised, and won the hearts of the people as they did it, exemplifying a tenet of how to live off the land. Finally, early in World War Two, the First Special Service Force was formed at Fort William Henry Harrison in Montana. Ironically, the new fort was located in the same country where Sandy's great-grandfather had fought the Sioux and Cheyenne for control of the Bozeman Trail. The First Special Service fought in Italy and France, while an offshoot, Merrill's Marauders, campaigned in Burma. Another unit with a similar mission was the Office of Strategic Services, the famed OSS. General Wild Bill Donovan formed the OSS with two goals in mind: First and second to develop intelligence fight behind enemy lines. The OSS dropped be and Axis fronts in Europe and Burma and gained the respect of friend and foe alike. Based on this unit's notable success and wanting to expand on its principal missions, President Harry two Truman created two organizations: the Central Intelligence Agency in 1947 and the Army Special Forces in 1952.

Near the end of World War Two, OSS operatives had contacted Ho Chi Minh and furnished him arms to fight the Japanese in what had been the northern part of French Indochina. During that relationship, in furtherance of their mission, the OSS also gave Ho assurances that when the war was over, the United States would support the Vietnamese in their bid for freedom and independence from France. President Truman's failure to live up to that promise after World War Two led to the war of the Vietnamese against the returning French colonialists. Now, America seemed to be headed into the same morass that had resulted in the defeat of the best of the French Foreign Legion at Dien Dien Phu.

When Sandy reported to the Special Warfare School on Smoke Bomb Hill at Fort Bragg, he found that school to be in the midst of a dynamic expansion. President Kennedy had directed that the school be granted greatly increased funding and also be given the new designation of Special Warfare Center. Its mission was to train soldiers to fight in places like Vietnam, and its importance was underlined by its being named after the President himself. A new Special Forces Group, the Fifth, had also been created to have sole responsibility for operations in Southeast Asia. The Fifth was to be organized into small teams, each member of which was cross trained in small unit weapons, medicine, engineering, and communications. All were to be given instruction in the Vietnamese language. Their mission was to go into the most rugged terrain of Vietnam, win the hearts and minds of the natives, and turn them against the Viet Cong. In contrast to the Artillery School, the Fifth Special Forces welcomed Sandy and his report.

"How can we improve?" they asked him.

"You're teaching the right things," Sandy Said. "But the South Vietnamese aren't practicing what you teach."

"How so?" they asked him.

"In the battle for the hearts and minds of the people, President Diem isn't competing for the loyalty of the Vietnamese peasants. He doesn't trust them, and they know it. His soldiers have adopted French tactics of sweep and destroy, rather than taking and holding. ARVN treats the villagers with contempt, and the villagers resent President Diem's soldiers. That makes the task of the VC much easier."

"Is ARVN any good at all?" they asked.

"ARVN soldiers will fight when they are well led and armed. They do especially well if American soldiers accompany them."

"And how would you evaluate their leadership?"

"Not so good," Sandy said. "They really need your training and example. As of now, they treat their own people almost as badly as the enemy. They routinely use torture in violation of the Geneva accords or the rules of land warfare."

"And you think the war goes badly?"

"The VC is growing stronger every day," Sandy said. "The guerrillas now control over fifty percent of the rural land in South Vietnam, and they are moving closer to Saigon. Instead of building alliances, President Diem is destroying infrastructure that he thinks might eventually be a threat to him. He should be attempting to convert it to his side."

"What can the Fifth Special Forces do?" they asked.

"I know that you are training to conduct special operations in Laos and Cambodia, but you ought to find a way to train ARVN simultaneously. I know that isn't your mission, but if ARVN is going to expand first to one hundred and fifty thousand men and then to three hundred thousand, as I believe it will eventually need to, it is going to need all the training it can get. I realize we're going to send ten thousand more logistic advisors to help ARVN, but all of those new advisors ought to be trained here."

"We don't have the capacity to train that many," they told him. "We have a mission in the hills adjacent to Cambodia and Laos, and we can't dilute that by training people down in the Delta. Conventional army force will have to do that."

"And that's the problem," Sandy said. "Conventional soldiers will want to train for and then fight a conventional war. and Vietnam isn't that kind of a fight. President Diem is rounding up his citizens and putting them into eleven thousand fortified villages he calls Strategic Hamlets. If he insists on doing that, then we ought to put a Special Forces team in each of those villages. Those teams could train the locals to defend themselves. They would soon win the hearts and minds of those villagers by dispersing medicine, building wells, and providing good communications support. If we are indeed sending ten thousand logistic advisors to Vietnam, and violating the Geneva Accords as we do it, we should send more Special Forces soldiers instead of logistic personnel."

"We can't do that," they said. "We would need more than sixty thousand new Special Forces soldiers. That would mean several additional Groups. Even if the Administration would approve the men and money, we couldn't train that many new men in time to help. And I doubt the Regular Army would give up their role in Vietnam without a fight. No, we probably have to stick to our mission, which is to interdict North Vietnam's supplies on the Ho Chi Minh Trail. But what would you have us change out there?"

"Special Forces personnel need to stay in place after they train their in-country counterparts. You need to occupy ground rather than train people and move on. Occasional raids into Laos and Cambodia aren't as productive as occupying and holding ground in South Vietnam. You need to work with the ARVN to set up quick reaction forces, like airborne and helicopter units, to come to the aid of villages and Special Forces camps that are targeted by VC and NVA units."

"We realize the need for quick reaction forces," they said. "In fact, eighty helicopters and their pilots are on their way to Vietnam as we speak."

"But that's a major violation of the Accords," Sandy said.

"Evidently the decision has been made at the highest level to ignore the Accords. The violations will be selective at first and done gradually, but the United States is well on its way to the introduction of conventional forces."

Although the discussions went on for months, Sandy never convinced anyone at the Center that they should become involved in training personnel to serve with ARVN in places like the Delta. The Army preferred conventional forces for that task. The Fifth Special Forces adhered to its original mission, and they did it well. They won the hearts and minds of the Montagnards and others in the hills of Laos, Cambodia, and Vietnam. Then they formed those primitive tribesmen into an efficient army of sixty thousand men and used that force with great success. They concentrated on attacking the Ho Chi

Minh Trail, and the North Vietnamese had to divert thousands of soldiers in order to defend its supply lines. That mission kept those soldiers from moving south and attacking the Americans and their allies in South Vietnam.

In November of 1963, President Kennedy was assassinated in Dallas, and that changed everything, especially what he was trying to do in Vietnam. Earlier that same month, ARVN officers had staged a coup and murdered President Diem, and the CIA may have been involved. When they learned of Diem's death, peasants throughout Vietnam spontaneously rioted and set about destroying the hated strategic hamlets.

Sandy did not join the Fifth Special Forces in the hill country of Vietnam and Cambodia. Instead, he received news that newly installed President Johnson had decided to introduce American combat units into Vietnam. The 101" Airborne Division, the Screaming Eagles, at Fort Campbell, Kentucky, was gearing up to go to Southeast Asia. Seeing an opportunity to serve with paratroopers again, he requested to join them. In doing so, he made no attempt to reconcile that decision with his reservations about the use of conventional forces in Vietnam. He only knew he wanted to return to that tormented land and to Avril. And because of his experience with the Vietnamese airborne brigade, he knew he would be a perfect fit. The Army apparently agreed, for it approved his request. After less than two years at Fort Bragg, Sandy was ordered back to conventional airborne duty. By the time he reported to Fort Campbell, Kentucky, the First Brigade of the Screaming Eagles was headed for Vietnam. A new phase of the war there was about to begin.

CHAPTER FOURTEEN

Sandy was delighted to be with the troopers of an Airborne Division once again. They were outstanding soldiers in an elite outfit, and they had a specific mission. Washington had told the 101" to prepare for imminent deployment to Southeast Asia, and the Division was focused on its new assignment. For Sandy, the highly qualified and motivated troopers would be a pleasure to work with. He was not disappointed. Morale, enthusiasm, and professionalism reached a new high as word came that the First Brigade of the Screaming Eagles would be the first unit of the 101" Airborne Division to go. Sandy volunteered to be Operations Officer of the direct support artillery battalion that was to accompany the brigade, but he was turned down. Disappointed, he went to the Division Artillery Commander to find out why he had been rejected.

"We have other plans for you," the colonel said.

"Plans?" Sandy asked. "What could be better than...."

"How 'bout a promotion and command?" the colonel asked.

"What on earth...?"

"You had combat experience in Korea, and you spent a year in Vietnam," the colonel said. "You're qualified and we're going to promote you to lieutenant colonel and give you a battalion command over there."

"With the First Brigade of the 101st?"

"No such luck. You've got to go to Staff College at Fort Leavenworth first. Get through that, and then we'll see about your battalion."

That's the way it happened. In the summer of 1965, Sandy went to the Army Staff Command and College at Fort Leavenworth, Kansas. He was thus at that historic fort at Christmas of that year, exactly 100 years from the time his great-grandfather, Joseph, had been there. The following spring, Joseph had moved west on the old Oregon Trail to fight the Plains Indians, just as Sandy would be flying west to Vietnam.

The similarities were striking. Like Sandy, Joseph had been preparing to deploy to a little known but decidedly hostile land and a dangerous battlefield. He was also a unit commander, and he was to lead the men of his regiment as they marched west along the Platte River and across the Great Plains. They were headed for battle with the Sioux and Cheyenne Indian tribes in Wyoming and Montana. It would be a prolonged and difficult campaign. On that march, his bride, Ida, was the only woman accompanying his command. As such, she was allowed to ride in the supply wagon. Everybody else walked. They moved at an average pace of three miles an hour. Breaking camp before daybreak every day except Sunday, when they rested, they marched for six or seven hours, before stopping to prepare camp and defenses for the night. Ida and Joseph had a tent for sleeping quarters, a cow for milk, and chickens for eggs. Aside from the danger of attack during darkness, the chief drawbacks for Ida were the lack of privacy and the presence of a large number of rattlesnakes. To prevent those reptiles from entering her tent, soldiers used rolled buffalo hides to form a ring around her sleeping quarters, in the belief that the snakes would not cross the coarse hides. She wasn't sure that the snakes would be thus inhibited. She only knew that in those difficult times, she was able to rest in comparative safety.

As Sandy thought of those and many other stories his father had told him about Joseph and the Indians, he compared them with his own experiences in Vietnam. The Sioux fought much like the Viet Cong, using hit and run tactics, mostly at night. Because of their knowledge of the terrain, they could move freely through the badlands, while the soldiers stuck mostly to well established trails like the Bozeman and Oregon. Again such tactics compared well with the Viet Cong and their use of the jungles, while the Americans moved mostly on the major highways like Route Four to My Tho and Route One to Tay Ninh. The Sioux were known for torturing and mutilating their captives, much as the guerrillas habitually did in Vietnam.

Sandy's War

Both the Viet Cong and the Indians controlled the local inhabitants by a combination of terror and persuasion, and the soldiers did not know whom they could trust. The movement of the Army of the West on the Great Plains was just like that that of the French in the Vietnam Delta. The Indians moved aside when the soldiers marched against them, only to return when the soldiers were gone. The little forts the Army set up along trails like the Bozeman were much like Diem's strategic hamlets. Soldiers and travelers were relatively safe inside, but the Indians were a threat to anyone outside the confines of the walls. Officers and men endured days of boring duty, only to be shocked by sudden, terrorizing attacks. Those who were caught outside the forts with their guard down were exposed to torture and a horrible death. In that hostile environment, only the professionals survived. Sandy's memories were indeed lessons any commander about to lead men to battle in Vietnam would do well to consider carefully.

He pondered those similarities as he completed the Staff College, and he wrote a thesis on the subject. It disappeared into the school's archives, probably never to be seen again. Then, just before he graduated, he received his promotion and orders to join the Twenty-Fifth Infantry Division in Vietnam. He was delighted to be going to such an historic outfit, for some of its units traced their heraldry back to the American Revolution. He was ready to go, but before he had to report to San Francisco for his flight over the Pacific, he was granted thirty days leave. He immediately went down to Destin to see Walter and Sara, wondering and almost dreading what their reactions might be.

Walter was fascinated. He was seventeen, and he was torn between volunteering for service and waiting to be drafted when he turned eighteen. Sandy was alarmed at Walter's attitude. The boy had to be restrained.

"If I were you," Sandy told the eager teenager, "I'd get myself a commission."

"But I don't want to go to West Point," Walter said.

"Then go to Officer Candidate School," Sandy said. "You'd get better training, and you'd have some control over your assignment and your unit in Vietnam. Those are big positives when you serve in combat."

"But if I went to OCS, I'd have to agree to stay in for a longer time," Walter said. "I'd rather volunteer to go over for a year, do my duty, and get out."

"You may have to wait anyway," Sandy Said. "Regulations say that you can't go until I come back. There's some sort of rule about both of us being in a combat zone at the same time. It has to do with several members of a family being killed or badly injured at the same time. The restriction goes back to World War Two when six brothers of the same family all died in the same action. Their parents were obviously sickened by that tragedy. So now that I'm going over, you'll have to wait at least a year anyway."

"But I'd rather get it over with," Walter said.

"Rules are rules," Sandy said. "And if you have to wait for me to come home in any case, why not use the time to get some rank. The experience would serve you well no matter what kind of work you do later on, even as an attorney."

"But if I have to go, I'd rather go with the guys I know. Everybody in school is either volunteering or being drafted. I'd just as soon go with them. And my girlfriend, Cathy, says if I'm going to go, I should go with them."

"Don't be in too much of a hurry to get shot," Sandy said. "My father was just like you back before World War One. He tried to enlist when he was just fifteen. Luckily, he got caught. The experience gave him a chance to reconsider, and he ended up at West Point. He never regretted it. Think about it. War is not some kind of a glorious charge up a hill. It's a deadly, dirty business, and you'd do better to wait a while until you're older and things calm down."

In the end, Walter stopped offering objections, and Sandy thought that just maybe the boy might change his mind while he waited a year and matured a bit. Walter needed to temper his exuberance and learn some patience. He'd appreciate that and more in Vietnam, no matter how much he wanted to fight for his country. Maybe the boy would consider taking a commission if he thought about it while he waited to go. Right now, he was too enthusiastic for his own good. On the other hand, Sara was a different matter. She was clearly disgusted at the whole Vietnam thing, and she hated even the thought of Sandy's returning to Southeast Asia. "Why on earth are you going back there?" she asked. "You've already been. Why again?"

"I have to go," Sandy said. "It's what I've been trained to do. I'm a soldier, and soldiers march toward the sound of the guns. I think I can do some good."

"What good is all that killing?" she asked. "Everybody dying. All those people being burned and their homes blown up. What good is that?"

"I'll feel better if we can stop the killing," Sandy said. "And I have no intention of being killed myself."

"But Vietnam is so far away. And what business is it of ours if they want to be independent? Why do we want to interfere in their affairs?"

"Interference isn't what I want to do." Sandy said. "I want to protect those unfortunate people from some pretty bad things happening to… "

"What could be worse than being killed?"

"I'm not trying to kill them," Sandy said.

"But lots of them are dying," she said. "And our bombs are doing most of the killing. And burning things! I hate that."

"We're in a war," Sandy said. "People get hurt when wars are fought. I'd rather not kill, but some things are worth fighting for. Freedom is a…."

"Freedom is living. We have no business fighting over there," she said. "If Walter is drafted and goes over, he'll be hurt. I just know it, and I hate it. And all the guys from school are being drafted and sent over there. It's no good."

Sandy couldn't get past that "hate" word again, no matter how much he tried to explain to her. She was opposed to our fighting in Vietnam, and she was too emotionally involved to listen to his reasoning. She confused him because she so obviously loved her brother, yet Walter was so eager to fight for his country. She was so opposed to war, even though Walter was volunteering for just that. It was a paradox. Finally he saw that he couldn't penetrate her resistance, and that was where he had to leave the discussion. So he turned to Nancy. Even though he wasn't having much success with women, he had to at least say goodbye to her.

"When are you going to grow up and stop jumping out of planes?" she asked.

"I won't be jumping out of planes with the Twenty-Fifth in Vietnam," he said. "It's a ground assignment."

"Don't play word games," she said. "You know what I mean."

"I hope to command a battalion," he said.

"So go do it. Why come here?" she asked.

"To see Sara and Walter," he said.

"You're just making it harder for her. She didn't need to see you go off and be killed. She had enough pain from you the first time you went."

"That's pretty harsh, isn't it?

"It's the truth," she said. "And you're leading Walter down that same path. He wants to go with you."

"Not so. I just talked him out of volunteering."

"Maybe, we'll see. You stand a real chance of losing your son in some Vietnamese rice paddy and your daughter to the Peace Movement. Is that what you really want?"

"I want Walter to get a commission," he said. "And I'm asking you to help me with that. You can talk to that girl of his. What's her name, Cathy? Get her to help you. He'll have a better chance of surviving if he gets that extra training."

"I'd never encourage him to take up the life you've chosen. He'll have to do that on his own. I don't want him to end up like your father."

"What about my father?" he asked.

"He's a drunk," she said. "All he does is sit in that little cottage with his bourbon and babble on about some Indians and a nuclear war."

"What're you talking about?"

"Go see for yourself."

And so the following day, Sandy went over to the place on the beach to see his father. Andy looked terrible. He was unshaven, and he smelled like he hadn't bathed in a week. His pasty complexion indicated he hadn't been out in the sun for some time, and from the fat around his waist, Sandy guessed that he was at least forty pounds overweight. It was midday, and he had a rocks glass of sour mash bourbon in his hand.

"What's wrong, dad?" Sandy asked.

"What's right," Andy answered.

"Come on, dad. What's worrying you?"

"Everything," Andy said. "The Army is sending you off to fight where our country has no business fighting. And Walter will probably follow you. War with the Vietnamese! For what? We killed a hundred thousand Asian women and children at Hiroshima and Nagasaki, and you'd have thought that would have taught us a lesson. Not on your life. Because of that testing, we're still killing all those Marshall Islanders out in the Pacific. We will be for years. It's crazy."

"But we stopped those tests back in 1958," Sandy said. "You'll see. We can never stop the effects of those tests. Doctors are now finding all sorts of cancers in the natives and their children. Even our own people who were out there are full of tumors and dying. It's absurd."

"It was new technology," Sandy said. "Back then, nobody knew what to expect from radioactive fallout. And anyway, you had no responsibility for any of that. Why does it concern you so much?"

"I think everybody ought to be concerned," Andy said. "Our government has a history of acting this way. We used to call it manifest destiny or the White Man's burden. It's really a form of exploitation. And you know what the worst part is? Our family has been involved at least back to your great-grandfather and the Indian Wars."

"Joseph?" Sandy asked. "What has he to do with all this?"

"He fought the Sioux for twenty-five years. And in the end, the great Sioux Medicine Man Sitting Bull was so angered at the White Man's invasion of Indian lands that he confronted Joseph and cursed him and all his children to die violently. And right after that, we killed that senile old Indian, and you know what? That murder resulted in the tragedy of Wounded Knee."

"Wait a minute," Sandy said. "I've studied the reports of that battle and the subsequent trial. Nobody was found at blame for what happened at Wounded Knee."

"I know what the official record says, but I also know that we had over five hundred soldiers with artillery surrounding three hundred Indians, two hundred and fifty of whom were women and little children. No matter what the court martial found, the soldiers could have avoided killing all those women if they had had competent leadership."

"So Sitting Bull put a curse on Joseph?"

"That's what I said. He cursed our family. We are guilty, and condemned to die violently. Joseph killed himself, and Junior was so sickened by it that he died of a stroke. Now you and I are heading for exactly the same end. Mark my words, you are tempting more than fate to go back to Vietnam, and if Walter is drafted, he'll be in great danger too."

"You're not making a great deal of sense, dad. I've got to go back to Vietnam. We're fighting a war there, and experienced leaders are needed. There's a battalion waiting for me. You commanded one in World War Two, and you survived. Now it's my turn. I've been waiting for this opportunity."

"I survived all right, but I learned a few things in New Guinea. First of all, the jungle is a terrible place to fight, and Vietnam is full of jungle. Secondly, Asia has too many people and is too big for us to conquer, and Vietnam is most decidedly Asia. And really, a pretty good argument can be made that we shouldn't be there at all. Sara isn't all wrong to hate it, and I would understand if Walter went to Canada rather than be drafted and go over there."

Andy rambled on all day. At times he talked about that massacre of hundreds of Moros in a place called The Crater. Then he would shift to the tragedy of the Buffalo Soldiers in Houston in World War One. And then the atomic bombs in Japan. Always he talked about people of color. He didn't make a lot of sense, and Sandy feared for his father's sanity. He seemed to be possessed by some sort of interior demon that Sandy couldn't comprehend. At dusk, Sandy gave up and left the man to his sour mash in the little cabin by the white beach on the Gulf.

Sandy departed the following week for the Far East to command an artillery battalion in the Twenty-Fifth Infantry Division. He had not made many good farewells. His ex-wife was contemptuous of what he was doing. His son was about to make a major mistake that might cost the boy his life. His daughter hated the profession he had chosen. And his father sounded like a raving drunk. It was an ominous start of what might be a difficult period in his life. And through it all, as he looked in the mirror late at night when no one was around, he wondered if he was going back to Vietnam to command a battalion or to find someone he couldn't get out of his mind, a mystery woman with a French name.

<<pic>>

President Ngo Dinh Diem

<<pic>>

Above: Grunts in the Rice Paddies

Below: Tracks in the Delta

<<pic>>

<<pic>>

Above: Grunts in the jungle dry season.

Below: Grunts in the jungle wet season.

<<pic>>

<<pic>>

Above: Artillery ARVN training

Below: ARVN Artillery in the field.

<<pic>>

<<pic>>

Above: ARVN Village Parade.

Below: ARVN clears the highway.

<<pic>>

<<pic>>

Above: Saigon ARVN victory parade

Below: Saigon women in their Au Dai

<<pic>>

CHAPTER FIFTEEN

Sandy was to lead the Third Battalion of the Thirteenth Artillery Regiment. It was a unit of the historic Twenty-Fifth Infantry Division, one of America's great fighting outfits that traced part of its lineage back to the War of 1812. In that war, one of the Army's recently formed units was the Twenty-Seventh Infantry Regiment, eventually to be nicknamed the Wolfhounds. That regiment came into being just as the Regular Army of the United States began to take shape. After honorable service against England in 1812 and in the Civil War, the Twenty-Seventh became a part of the Ninth Infantry, the same regiment that Joseph Walker joined in 1865 at Fort Leavenworth. They were with him as he moved west on the old Oregon Trail to fight the Plains Indians. In 1901, the regiment separated from the Ninth Infantry so as to participate in the Philippine Insurrection, and Joseph commanded those Wolfhounds for two years of that campaign. Afterwards they became a part of the Hawaiian Division. Just before the Japanese attacked Pearl Harbor in 1941, the Hawaiians were broken into two Infantry Divisions: the Twenty-Fourth and Twenty- Fifth. Those numbers were the old Buffalo Soldier regimental designations, and the Wolfhounds were assigned to the Twenty-Fifth Infantry Division. That Division fought for three years as a part of General Krueger's Sixth Army from Guadalcanal to Luzon. It was in Japan in 1950 when the North Koreans attacked, and shortly thereafter it landed at Inchon with General MacArthur to rout the North Koreans and drive them back to the Yalu River. It was during the Korean War that Sandy's new battalion, the Third of the Thirteenth, earned its nickname, The Clan. That name came about because the battalion stuck together like a large family, taking care of its own and fighting so well as a unit.

In August of 1966, after a long flight from San Francisco by way of Alaska, Sandy arrived at the United States base at Long Binh. The Division Artillery Executive Officer met him and expedited his processing. In less than three hours, they were on a chopper heading for Division Headquarters at Cu Chi. Sandy was going back to one of the first places he had been sent during his first tour in Vietnam. He was there training ARVN artillery when his paratroopers attempted a coup against President Diem back in Saigon. It would be an artillery old home week, about twenty miles west of Saigon. Sure enough, three days later, Sandy assumed command of The Clan. To his surprise and delight, his Sergeant-Major was a full blooded Sioux Indian. Naturally, the men called him Chief. Sandy discovered that the man had extensive combat experience in the Korean War, and after just a short period of working together, Sandy knew the sergeant could be trusted to lead the enlisted men of the battalion and keep their loyalty. In addition, the skills that a soldier needed to survive in Vietnam's irregular warfare seemed to be ingrained in Chief. Sandy wondered how many of the fellow's skills came from his Native American background. At any rate, he knew he could rely on his Sergeant-Major for significant assistance in leading the battalion. That knowledge was confirmed after a month of field training, briefing, and planning. The two of them pronounced the battalion ready, and they moved out on one of the first major combat operations of the Vietnam war: Attleboro.

The operation was named after the home of the 196th Light Infantry Brigade in Massachusetts. That brigade was originally assigned to duty in the Caribbean, but at the last minute it had been diverted to Southeast Asia because of the sudden buildup of United States combat units in Vietnam. New in country, it had nevertheless been selected to be the spearhead of an operation in War Zone C north of Tay Ninh, west of Sandy's base at Cu Chi. The 196th began Attleboro quietly on September 14th, but as it approached the Cambodian border, the brigade gradually ran into stiff resistance. As the intensity of the contact grew, the brigade had to send out calls for reinforcements, and Sandy's Twenty-Fifth Infantry Division was ordered to send two units to reinforce it: Joseph's former Twenty-

Seventh Infantry and a battery of Sandy's artillery from The Clan. The 196th needed Sandy's guns because Sandy's medium howitzers had longer range and greater punch than the light artillery attached to their brigade. Eventually, it would become common practice to send the heavier guns of The Clan to back up the lighter direct-support weapons of the infantry. Occasionally, the "Grunts" as the men of the infantry were affectionately called would even ask for individual 8-inch howitzers to blast enemy bunkers with direct fire. In the case of Attleboro, however, they wanted a full battery of his 155mm howitzers. That meant Sandy would lose control of four of his self-propelled guns and their support, because the entire battery would be attached to the 196th for the time being. To make matters more complicated for the Clan, Sandy was simultaneously directed to take his two others medium batteries to another fire support base on another mission. He was thus prevented from accompanying his detached battery to Tay Ninh and seeing after its welfare. That responsibility fell to the infantry officer commanding the base his detached battery was to join. The result was a catastrophe.

After a road march of some twenty miles from Cu Chi toward Tay Ninh on Route one, Sandy's howitzers turned north and west of the Don Dien Michelin rubber plantation to join a 196th fire support base late in the afternoon. Then the confusion began. When Sandy's guns arrived, the infantry commander at the base ordered the battery commander to place them on the northwest side of the temporary perimeter of the new base and to dig in for the night. The situation reminded Sandy of Joseph and the Ninth Infantry on the Oregon Trail. Sandy's battery had to be ready for a night attack, but the order given by the base commander was ambiguous. The weak point was who controlled a tree line some two hundred yards in front of the howitzers. The Clan thought the infantry of the 196th had outposts there, but such was not the case. Unknown to Sandy's artillery, the NVA occupied that critical position. The ambiguity offered the enemy conditions ripe for a major American tragedy.

Just after midnight, an NVA company staged a diversionary attack on the eastern side of the base. When the 196th committed its reserve to reinforce against that attack, the guerrillas launched their main effort against Sandy's undefended howitzers, always a prime target of any attackers. Before the Americans could react, an NVA battalion destroyed one of the four guns and severely damaged another. Eleven of Sandy's men died in the effort to defend the remaining guns. Many more were wounded. The attackers left four men on the battlefield. Weapons and other evidence found on the field indicated that the attackers had paid a severe price for their success, but that was no consolation for Sandy's lost men and the destruction of a howitzer. On the following morning, Sandy received a report of the attack, and he immediately flew by chopper to the scene, leaving his Executive Officer in command of the rest of his battalion. Enraged and saddened by the deaths, damage, and destruction, Sandy demanded an explanation from the infantry battalion commander. The man's weak response did not satisfy him. The battle for Attleboro was growing, however, and Sandy had no time to pursue the matter. His experience as a battalion commander had not begun well.

Attleboro had begun as a sweep to the north and east of Tay Ninh, about thirty-five miles west of Cu Chi. That sweep was to be a shakedown operation for the newly arrived 196th. Because the brigade had been training for deployment to the Caribbean, and at the last minute Washington had diverted it to Vietnam, it needed time to accustom itself to Vietnam's vastly different environment and to work out new tactics and techniques. After a welcome six weeks of uneventful patrolling, however, the brigade uncovered a large VC supply area between the Don Dien Michelin rubber plantation and Dau Tieng to the south. They also found evidence that the 101" NVA Regiment intended to attack a Special Forces base at Suoi Da, northeast of Tay Ninh. Receiving the Twenty-Seventh Infantry Regiment as reinforcements from the Twenty-Fifth Division, the 196th moved by helicopter to a landing zone west of the Don Dien plantation. In dense jungle, the Wolfhounds ran into fierce, well-planned resistance. Both the 9th Viet Cong Division and the NVA 101" Regiment were waiting at the landing zone, and the 196th suffered severe losses as it landed. At that point, the battle dramatically expanded as Saigon rushed units in to exploit what the 196th had found. Quickly, Sandy had to move his remaining two medium batteries from a position south of Cu Chi some thirty miles up Highway One, where he went north to set up another fire base. His mission was to fire in support of the now greatly expanded battle for control of Tay Ninh. In this effort, two light artillery batteries and an infantry battalion joined him on the new fire support base.

For the next three weeks, more units from the Twenty-Fifth Infantry entered the battle, and Field Force headquarters in Saigon added elements of the Fourth Infantry Division and the 173rd Airborne Brigade. At the height of Attleboro, some 22,000 American soldiers were committed to battle in the jungles north- east of Tay Ninh. Before that could happen, however, the Wolf- hounds led another assault. Massing his helicopters, its battalion commander led his first company into another landing zone selected to cut off the VC and the NVA from supplies they had positioned near the rubber plantation. The first company of the Wolfhounds landed without incident, and thus the battalion commander radioed for the second company to land. As they did, however, guerrillas waiting in the tree line on the northern side of the landing zone met this second wave of incoming choppers with a withering fire. It was an elaborate ambush. The Wolfhound battalion commander was wounded, but he refused to leave his unit and be evacuated from the landing zone. All day long, the battle raged, and it was not until nightfall that the entire Twenty-Seventh was able to land and establish a strong position. When morning came, the VC had disappeared, and the Wolfhounds set out in pursuit along deep jungle paths. They immediately ran into another carefully set ambush, this time even more effective because of the narrow trails in the thickest kind of triple-canopy jungle. In the heat, confusion, and heavy weapons fire, the survival of the Wolfhounds was initially in doubt. Finally, reinforcements arrived, and the VC retreated again. The brave Wolfhounds paid a high price, but their final success led to the eventual defeat of the 9th VC Division, and Attleboro was added to the long history of valor in combat on the part of Joseph's old unit.

The Wolfhounds were not the only ones to hold off a major attack by elements of the 9th VC Division. When Sandy had arrived at his firing position northeast of Tay Ninh, he found an infantry battalion had preceded him to that area. The new base was roughly circular. The infantry had responsibility for the northern half, and Sandy the southern. He placed his two light batteries on the perimeter and his two medium units behind them. Then he and Chief toured the entire perimeter assigning fields of fire and responsibility for outpost security. They and the battery commanders positioned each howitzer for direct fire at a specific sector in defense of the perimeter. Where needed, Sandy and Chief showed the men how fields of fire were to be cleared. Every gun was to have a generous supply of the new "bee hive" rounds, previously classified top secret. Each round carried eight thousand steel flechettes an inch long. Those vicious little arrows would soon prove to be a major defense against the mass attacks of the VC and NVA. That done, he went to the medium howitzers and had each one pointed in a specific direction so they too would be ready to fire in defense of the base. The medium guns were to have a ready supply of time fuzes that when put on a minimum setting would explode high explosives just outside the base perimeter in the air above any attacking enemy. Finally he had every officer brief his men to expect mass attacks supported by mortar fire and rocket-propelled grenades, the famed RPG the VC were using more and more frequently. Every man was to have a fighting position, while Sandy and Chief would be responsible for a small reaction force. The Clan was ready.

They were none too soon. For the next three days as his guns were firing in support of Attleboro, Sandy received more and more reports from his outposts of enemy activity on his perimeter. Scouts told of seeing Viet Cong officers with binoculars studying the fire support base, and scraps of paper found on the few VC soldiers killed nearby showed crude diagrams of Sandy's positions. Thus alerted, Sandy and Chief passed word to the batteries to maintain special vigilance. Every man was to sleep with his boots on and his loaded weapon at his side.

The expected attack began just after midnight on the third night when a volley of incoming mortar fire hit the base. The infantry then reported an attack on the northern perimeter. That effort seemed to be a diversionary attack designed to draw base reserves away from Sandy's guns. Sandy told his men to stand in place and be ready for a mass attack. It was not long in coming. Sandy's listening posts reported numerous men in black pajamas moving through the darkness toward his barbed wire. Soon, trip flares began illuminating Viet Cong soldiers rushing toward the defenses in front of the howitzers, and mortar rounds began landing among his guns. On their knees and wearing flak jackets, his gun crews responded by firing the bee hive rounds in defense of their sectors. The VC attack seemed to falter at first, but then one of the howitzers fell silent, and the enemy began to breach the wire in that sector. It was time for The Clan's reaction force to move. Sandy, Chief, and ten men ran doubled over to the threatened area. There, they found the silent howitzer had a jammed round in its chamber. Chief positioned his men to fire at the VC on the barbed wire, while Sandy checked the silent gun and its crew. The gun chief was inexperienced and didn't know how to free the jammed round. Quickly, Sandy showed the sergeant how to position a shell casing in the breach so as not to hit the primer of the jammed round. Then, while holding the casing in place, he had the crew chief hit it hard with a sledgehammer. The quick fix worked, and the jammed shell went in. The howitzer was back in action. With the threatened sector restored, Sandy and his men ran back to his command post to see how the battle was going. The VC had more men than Sandy, but they had a major weakness, and it worked against them. Because they lacked battlefield communication and flexibility, they could not change their plan of attack once they were engaged. All they could do was continue fruitless assaults against Sandy's guns. The result was a slaughter. When the charges ceased and morning finally arrived, Sandy found ninety-seven pajama clad bodies in front of his guns. Not a single soldier of The Clan died that night.

Sandy's success in defense of his base was an indication of things to come. The expected NVA attack against the Special Forces camp at Suoi Da never materialized. Instead, the 9th VC Division retreated back to the northwest seeking sanctuary across the Cambodian border. Before Attleboro ended in November, moreover, more than eleven hundred dead Viet Cong soldiers were counted. Although the

Americans lost one hundred and fifty-three men, vast VC supplies were destroyed, and a major enemy base was eliminated. The battle became a model for future operations. From then on, when light patrols were sent out, reaction forces had to be held in readiness for immediate action. When the initial patrols encountered significant enemy resistance, the ready rapid reaction forces immediately came to the aid of the endangered soldiers. Initially, air and artillery fired in support. If the need arose, reinforcements waiting on alert were quickly dispatched to the battle by helicopters. Finally, other major headquarters were tasked to have larger units ready to move on short notice when the chance encounters escalated into larger battles. The combat techniques proved in Attleboro were invaluable models, and made it one of the crucial battles of the Vietnam War.

CHAPTER SIXTEEN

After two months of combat, Operation Attleboro ended and War Zone C quieted down. The Viet Cong and main force NVA units were nowhere to be found. Apparently exhausted by the violent and extended battle, they seemed to have given up the field, and American intelligence indicated they had withdrawn either to Cambodia or the deepest jungles along the border. Analysts concluded that the insurgents would need at least a month to rest, recover, rearm, and regroup before they would be able to resume offensive operations. Because of that analysis, Field Force Headquarters in Saigon began pulling American units back to locations nearer the city. Sandy's battalion gradually filtered back to Cu Chi, one battery at a time. By the week before Christmas, they were all together at their home base, and Division Artillery ordered Sandy to spend the next two weeks in recovery from the damages suffered during the just completed months of fighting. After a welcome week of rest, maintenance, and repair, The Clan was well on its way to renewal, and Sandy himself was due a break. On the Saturday before Christmas, therefore, he and Chief headed for Saigon in Sandy's Jeep. The Sergeant Major and the driver, a boy from New Jersey named Jeff, were to scrounge up some needed supplies, while Sandy would be on a mission of his own. The plan was for them to go their separate ways and meet Sunday morning at Sandy's former bachelor officers quarters, the Brinks Hotel, near the now expanded MACV headquarters compound.

They left Cu Chi about ten o'clock, after an ARVN cavalry squadron had checked Route One for ambushes and mines. By then, the road was full of the normal bustling commercial traffic that filled all the major roads near Saigon, especially on Saturday market days. Route One reminded Sandy of his last trip on Route Four to My

Tho some five years before. Although this new morning scene looked just as peaceful, Sandy and Chief took no chances. They were well armed. Jeff had an M-16 slung beside him on the Jeep. Sandy had his holstered pistol and another M-16 slung on his side. Chief had an M-60 machinegun and a grenade launcher. They felt they were prepared for anything they might meet on the trip. Because the road was so crowded, however, they had to drive more slowly than they would have wanted, and their deliberate speed made them easy targets for an ambush. A village just east of Cu Chi, the one locals called the Watch-tower, made them especially nervous, because the villagers clustered closely around the slowly moving Jeep. With their weapons at the ready, Sandy and Chief studied the faces around them for signs of trouble, but none appeared, and the Watchtower was soon behind them. The next choke point was the village of Hoc Mon, just west of Saigon. It was notorious as being sympathetic to the VC, and its bridge was a known ambush point. The villagers glowered sullenly at the Jeep as it passed, but the crowds stepped aside to let the Americans through safely. The twenty miles to Saigon had taken them almost two hours, but they were finally again in the capital.

Saigon looked like a city at peace. Sandy could find no signs to the contrary. He noted that the Renault taxis he remembered had been joined by a few more Citroens, and the Lambretta motorbikes now had competition from Vespa scooters. But ancient trucks overloaded with people, chickens, and produce still filled the streets, and the sidewalks were crowded with shoppers, pimps, and onlookers. Had they not known that a guerrilla war was in progress, onlookers would have described the place as a normal metropolitan area of the Far East. Sandy told Jeff where to turn into the French residential area and then onto Avril's street. It was several blocks off the main thoroughfare, and the crowds there were not as thick, but it looked exactly as he remembered it. He showed Jeff the gate to her walled compound. Would anybody be there? And would they recognize him in jungle fatigues? More importantly would they know where Avril was?

Jeff stopped the Jeep directly in front of the house, and Sandy took a deep breath and dismounted. Leaving his M-16 with the vehicle, he approached the gate. It was closed and locked, and he could see no one inside. A rope was attached to a small bell above the gate, however, and he pulled on it. For what seemed an eternity, nothing happened, and Sandy feared the worst. When he rang again, however, a young Vietnamese boy came out of the small guesthouse near the gate and approached Sandy timidly, eyeing him nervously.

"English?" Sandy asked.

The boy shook his head.

"Avril?" Sandy Asked. "Avril de Castries?"

Again, the boy shook his head.

"Cousin Ly?" Sandy said. "Ly, Ly, Ly."

This time, the boy hesitated. Finally, holding up his hand as a signal for Sandy to remain there, he turned and hurried back into the gatehouse. After a short wait, Cousin Ly appeared. He stared at Sandy with a puzzled expression, as if he were trying to figure what to do.

"Avril?" Sandy then asked. "De Castries?"

Cousin Ly finally smiled and nodded. Holding up one finger he turned, scurried toward the big house, scampered up the steps, and disappeared inside.

Anxiously, Sandy waited, and then Avril appeared on the porch. She stared at Sandy with her hand over her mouth as if she were in shock. Then she laughed with joy, ran to open the gate, and threw herself into his arms. Sandy didn't hear Chief call out that his Cu Chi express would leave at ten the next morning, nor did he hear the Jeep drive away. He was lost in the arms he had missed so much. Who said you can't go home again?

Cousin Ly and his boys watched as the two of them, arms around each other's waists, moved to the house, up the steps, and into the wide foyer. There, to his surprise, Sandy found a beautiful little girl staring at him. She was a miniature Avril dressed in black slippers and a plain white silk au dai with a high, choker neck. Her black hair was pulled back and braided into a ponytail that reached halfway down her back.

"This is your daughter," Avril said. "Her name is Joy.

Sandy hardly heard Avril. He knelt in front of the exquisite little girl and stared at her in wonderment. His daughter? What did Avril mean?

"Do you speak English?" he asked the child.

The perfect little creature in front of him solemnly nodded, never changing the serious expression on her face.

"Who taught you?" he asked.

She shyly pointed to Avril, her eyes never leaving Sandy.

"She speaks French and Vietnamese too," Avril said.

"Do you know who I am?" he asked.

She nodded slowly.

"Will you shake hands?" Sandy asked.

For an agonizing moment, Joy didn't respond. Then she shyly held out her hand, and he took it slowly and softly. Her gentle touch sent a shiver through him.

"I'm Sandy," he said.

"I know," she spoke so softly he could hardly hear her. "I'm Joy."

"May I pick you up?" he asked.

He held out both hands to her. Solemnly, she nodded again, and he gently put his hands under her arms, stood up, and slowly brought her to his chest. It was a critical moment for both of them. Suddenly, she smiled and threw her arms around his neck. He had to blink to hold back the moisture in his eyes. Then, with the little girl still hugging him fiercely, he looked at Avril. She was now even more beautiful than he remembered.

"My daughter?" he asked.

"Yes," Avril said. "She's been waiting for you."

From then on, Joy acted as if a dam that had burst inside her. She chattered on and on, showing off her English. She hurried to bring Sandy her toys and tell him about each one. She took him to her little room to show him her bed and brag how she always cleaned up after herself. The three of them spent the afternoon making up for lost years, until it was time for one of the women to bathe Joy and prepare her for supper. When Uncle Ba brought hors d'oeuvres and wine at five o'clock, Avril and Sandy were finally alone. "Why didn't you write?" he asked her.

"I tried," she said, "but I couldn't."

"Why not? If only to tell me about Joy."

"She was part of it, part of why I couldn't write."

"What does that mean?"

"It's hard to explain. I just…"

"Try harder," he said. "You had to have a reason. Is there, was there another man?"

"No. It was because I didn't know if you'd be coming back."

"And that was why you couldn't write?"

"If you weren't coming back, I didn't want to get my hopes up. I had to forget about you and try to break the link between us. And I didn't want to beg you. I knew I would if I wrote."

"But how about Joy? You should have told me about her."

"That would have been blackmail to bring you back. I didn't want to use her to have you again."

"But she's my child."

"That's right, she's your child. And if you never came back, I'd have her, a part of you."

"But you told her about me. And you taught her English. That doesn't sound like you were breaking any ties. It sounds like you were holding on for dear life."

"And I suppose I knew in my heart I was. I just couldn't face it. I think, if you hadn't come back by the time she grew up, I'd have sent her to you. I just didn't know what else to do. Anyway, you're here now. Please forgive me."

"But I thought you didn't want to have children in the middle of this war," he said. "What made you change your mind?"

"You were leaving," she said. "I wanted something of you to stay here with me. It happened that last, wonderful night we had together. Say you'll forgive me. Please."

Before he could answer, Joy returned to join them for supper. Fresh and clean, smelling of some wonderful soap, she climbed into Sandy's lap and heart. When Uncle Ba brought fish and rice to the dining room, Sandy carried her to the table. In her high chair, she struggled to act like her mother and eat like a lady, and Sandy was charmed all over again. On her best behavior, she named the eating utensils in English, French, and Vietnamese. Spilling just a little now and then, she showed she could hold her knife and fork in both the American and European fashion. It was a heart-warming performance, and Sandy was disappointed when it was over. Afterwards, she played in the living room for just a little while, until Avril told her that bedtime was near, and she left to wash her face, brush her teeth, and put on her nightclothes. When she returned to say goodnight, Sandy picked her up for one last kiss and warm hug. Then she was gone.

"She's a beautiful child," he told Avril. "You've done well. I'm proud of both of you."

"She's got good genes," Avril said. "Now tell me about the United States. I read your letters. I still have them. You saw Sara and Walter. Tell me about them."

"Sara hates the war, but Walter wants to be a soldier like the Walkers before him."

"And your wife, how does she feel?"

"You mean my 'ex,'" he said. "She still wants me to leave the Army, and she's pretty uncompromising about it. She says I'm going to lose the kids, Sara to the peace movement, Walter to the war over here."

"And how does that make you feel?"

"Puzzled," he said. "I want Sara to think for herself, but I'm not happy with the results. I'm proud that Walter wants to be a soldier, but I'd prefer he be an officer. And I don't understand what made Nancy so bitter."

"They all feel the same way," she said. "The women love you still, even Nancy, and they don't want you to be killed. Walter just wants to be like you, without making a lifetime career out of the military. I can understand all this. Can't you?"

"I suppose so," he said, "but if understanding is to be a part of all this, I'd hope for more from them. Surely they know that soldiering is what I do."

"And I would hope you'd understand about my not writing to you these last few years."

"I guess I do," he said. "But tell me about you, your pregnancy and her."

"Uncle Ba and his women took care of me," she said, "and I had an easy time of it. Afterwards, Cousin Ly did his part by keeping the war away from us so we could protect her. I decided early on to keep the dream alive by teaching her to speak English. And I told her about you. Either you were coming back for her, or she would go to America when she grew up. Except for your absence, she's had a happy childhood."

They had years to catch up on, and they talked for an hour. They were still deeply engaged after their third glass of wine, but then she rose to put a record on that same old player. She turned and smiled as the strains of "Harbor Lights" filled the room once more, and he rose to take her in his arms again. She put her arms around his neck and they clung hard to each other, barely swaying back and forth to the music. He realized that she was the reason he had come back to Vietnam.

"I forgive you," he whispered.

She nodded as the tears came, and when the song ended, she took his hand and led him to her bed. They still had much more to make up for.

CHAPTER SEVENTEEN

He awoke in silence. Her room was so peaceful, and the tension that had driven him over the last few years was gone. A great lassitude swept over him, and the stress of the last few months had melted away. The war seemed to be a nightmare of the distant past, another world. Her wonderful bed was incredibly soft, not at all like an air mattress thrown on the floor of the jungle in the heart of War Zone C. Last night, after they had exhausted each other's bodies, he had fallen into a deep, dreamless sleep that left him completely relaxed. He now lay there limply, wanting to stay forever, until she came into the room. God, she was gorgeous. Like an angel, she floated toward him. Serene in a white morning gown, she sat on the side of the bed and put a hand on his cheek.

"You have to go, my love," she said. "Your chariot will soon be here, and the war will not wait much longer for you to return. You have responsibilities."

He tried to pull her down onto the bed, but she broke away laughing. He gave up and rose to find that Uncle Ba had cleaned and pressed his jungle fatigues and shined his combat boots until they matched the best dress jump boots of a Screaming Eagle. As he shaved, Avril stayed with him, asking little questions, making small talk. She had a glow about her, and he knew he reflected the same. If this wasn't love, it was infatuation of the highest order. She and the child were a future worth fighting for, and he resolved that when this war was finally over they would come home with him to the United States, to a better life.

He went with her to the dining room table to find Joy and Uncle Ba's version of breakfast waiting. Hot coffee, a fresh croissant, and some fruit were just what he wanted, but even more, he wanted to share more time with the lovely little girl. With big eyes that stared at him, she was alert and smiling, a perfect little doll. He couldn't remember such happiness. Then with childlike innocence, she punctured his balloon.

"Do you have to leave?" she asked.

"I'm afraid so," he answered.

"When?" she asked.

"Very soon," he hated to reply.

"Will you come again?" she asked.

"Of course," he said.

"When?" she persisted.

"I'm afraid that depends on the war," he said. "Your mother just reminded me that I have responsibilities. Men depend on me. I can't let them down. They mean very much to me." She considered his words for a moment, as if evaluating a difficult concept. Then she resumed questioning.

"Do mommy and I mean very much to you?"

"More than you'll ever know," he said.

"As much as your soldiers?" she asked.

"In a different way, yes," he said. "Even more." "Then you'll you come back real soon?" she asked.

"As soon as I can," he said.

"And when you do," Avril came to his rescue, "we'll be here waiting. Don't be too long."

The moment was too good to last. Sure enough, shattering the mood, Cousin Ly came to the front door and announced that Sandy's Jeep had arrived.

In the foyer, when Sandy again lifted little Joy to kiss her goodbye, she hugged him fiercely. Her embrace was so intense that he had to blink back tears again. At that moment, he wondered who c created the rule that said men shouldn't cry. He put her down, and slipped Sara's Saint Christopher medal chain over his head. He showed it to Joy and let her touch it. Then he put it around her neck.

"Promise me you'll wear it always," he said. "It will watch over you wherever you go."

"What is it?" she asked.

"A guardian angel," he said.

She fingered the medal and nodded seriously.

He turned to Avril, and she took his hand. Together, they walked to the gate and looked back. Uncle Ba's woman cradled Joy on the porch. Stopping just inside the entrance, Avril turned and kissed him long and deeply. Then she put her arms around his neck and whispered in his ear.

"As you go to Cu Chi, you must be very alert and careful. The roads out there are not as safe as they were when we met at My Tho. There is much more danger now, and it will come when you least expect it."

She pulled away and gazed intently at him for a moment, as if to see if he had heard what she said. Satisfied, she ran her fingers over his cheek as if memorizing his face. Finally, she hugged him one more time, turned, and hurried back to the house without looking back.

"Congratulations, Colonel," Chief said. "You just went way up on the SAS. That's the Sioux approval scale. I underestimated you. Don't know what tribe she's from, but she can share my teepee any time. She's damn near perfect in my book."

"You brave Indian warriors have good taste, Chief," Sandy said. "But we were supposed to meet at the Brinks Hotel. What changed the plan?"

"It's not here any more," Chief said.

"Not there?"

"Nope, the Gooks blew it up a year ago."

"What happened?"

"A sapper got into the garage and set off a charge."

"Any dead?"

"Nine Americans and the sapper."

"Poor guys," Sandy said. "A couple of years before, I'd have been in a body bag, just like Nancy said I would. How long will my luck hold?"

"You never see the one that gets you," Chief said. "It's better that way," Sandy said. "Okay, the break's over. Time, war and death wait for no one. Let's get back to the battalion."

CHAPTER EIGHTEEN

They drove in silence through the semi-quiet Sunday city streets toward the west and Cu Chi. Out on Route One, more of the usual commercial and family traffic built up, but Sandy paid little attention. He let his mind drift. A dull ache came over him, like Johnny Cash's Sunday morning coming down. He tried to put a good light on it and thought back to Avril and Joy, wondering at his good fortune. He didn't know how long he had been day dreaming, but near the Hoc Mon Bridge, Chief interrupted his reverie and brought him back to reality.

"Where're all the villagers?" Chief asked.

"You've got me," Sandy said, as he looked around at the suddenly empty streets, far more deserted than a normal Sunday morning would have dictated. "I've never seen it like this."

Where was everybody, Sandy wondered. Then, as they emerged on the western side of the village, Chief spoke again.

"And look at that deserted highway," he said. "Not a single vehicle or farmer. What gives?"

"Damned if I know," Sandy said. "I don't like it. This is too quiet. Sometimes villagers hide when they know a battle's about to happen. Jeff, hold her here a second while we radio home base. Maybe the Division's on some kind of alert."

Jeff pulled up, and Chief began working the radio. It was then that Sandy suddenly remembered the intensity of Avril's whispered warning as she said goodbye. Danger on the road, she had said. Something was very wrong, and it wasn't an alert. He yelled at Jeff.

"Pedal to the metal, man, real hard. Get us out of here, and I mean quick."

Sandy grabbed his M-16. Jeff jammed the accelerator down and the Jeep lurched violently forward. As it did, a mine or a rocket grenade exploded in the road just behind them. The blast stunned Jeff, and the Jeep swerved into the right-hand ditch, throwing the three of them out into the rice paddy. Dazed, with his ears ringing, Sandy barely had time to shake the cobwebs from his head when he looked up to see men clad in black pajamas and the conical hats of the Viet Cong coming from the woods on the other side of the rice paddy. As they ran at him, by reflex, he raised his M-16 and began snapping off bursts of three rounds. Chief already had the M-60 working, and Jeff had begun to fire. The three of them took a toll on the guerrillas, but there were too many of them. They seemed to be coming at the Jeep from all directions. Suddenly, Jeff took a hit and fell. Chief moved to check him and see how badly he was hurt, and the VC used that opportunity to rapidly reduce the distance between them. Sandy had to reload, and the guerrillas charged to close the final gap. Just as they came within grenade range and the end seemed near, Sandy heard the heavy, slower, deeper thump of 50-caliber machinegun fire. The guerrillas began falling, and their survivors suddenly broke off the attack. Soon, the field was quiet, and Sandy stood up. Chief resumed his work on Jeff, while Sandy scanned the field for wounded enemy soldiers that might still be a threat.

As he looked around, still dazed by the suddenness and ferocity of the attack, he saw three ARVN armored personnel carriers on the road behind him. They must have been the sources of the heavy machinegun fire. Around him, friendly ARVN security forces were spreading slowly out into the fields searching for more enemy soldiers. An ARVN lieutenant approached him and saluted crisply.

"Sir, is your driver badly hurt?" the Lieutenant asked.

"Not too bad," Chief called. "I think he'll be okay, but we need to get him to the base hospital at Cu Chi fast."

"We'll take you there right now," the Lieutenant said, and he called to his sergeant to have Jeff put on a stretcher and loaded into a personnel carrier.

"There was some sort of explosion," Sandy said. "It almost got us. The VC must have been waiting for our Jeep, and they were pretty aggressive. Lucky for us you guys were nearby."

"It was not luck, Colonel," the lieutenant said. "And the explosion was a radio controlled mine. Your Jeep accelerated just in time to make the mine operator miss you. Just a short time ago, we had been ordered to follow you. I'm sorry we were delayed. We were almost too late."

"Ordered to follow us? Why?" Sandy asked.

"Our intelligence passed word that you had been targeted for a Viet Cong ambush," he said. "The Hoc Mon VC are hard core terrorists, skillful and hard to find. We were to follow you in hopes of catching them out in the open for once. Please accept my apologies for using you as bait."

"But who told you we were targeted?" Sandy asked.

"Sir, I regret that I have to be the one to tell you, but for some time now, our intelligence service has been watching the woman you were with last night. After you arrived yesterday, she sent word through her gate guards that she would keep you with her overnight, but that you would be leaving for Cu Chi this morning, probably on Route One. Her guards are Viet Cong sympathizers, and they passed the word to the Communist cell in Hoc Mon. We monitored that call and set up this response team. A short time after you left Saigon, we intercepted another call to Hoc Mon. The ambush was just about to take place, so we moved out after you. While the VC guerrillas were setting up the ambush, we were trying to catch up with you."

"But the woman you're talking about is Avril de Castries," Sandy said. "She works at the American Embassy. Why would she have VC sympathizers as guards?"

"She is a North Vietnamese agent.

CHAPTER NINETEEN

His Jeep out of action, Sandy sat stunned in the tracked ARVN personnel carrier as it rumbled all too slowly toward the military hospital at Cu Chi. Almost deafened by the roaring engine and clanking tracks, and imprisoned inside the carrier, he tried to concentrate on what had happened. He kept telling himself that the ARVN lieutenant was wrong, making up a story, repeating rumors. After all, the man wasn't an intelligence officer. There was no way he could know anything definitive about her. She was an embassy employee, had been for more than ten years. She had a security clearance, was an insider at the embassy, and everybody knew her. The man simply couldn't know what he was talking about. And as soon as Sandy could talk to her, he would straighten everything out. It was simply a matter of getting Jeff to the hospital and finding a phone to call her in Saigon. He would clear up the matter and request that the ARVN officer be made to stop spreading false rumors.

A hollow feeling in his gut reminded him that sometimes where there's smoke, there just might be a fire. He tried to dismiss the idea, but could not. Oh my God, he thought, what if the man was right? Disbelief that he could even consider the idea caused him to shake his head. It just couldn't be true. Then he remembered her whispered warning as they said goodbye. What had she said? The roads were more dangerous now. Be alert. Anything could happen. Was she trying to tell him about the ambush? No, that couldn't be, because it would mean she knew about the planned attack, and that she really was an agent. But if she were really an agent, why would she warn him. Then the same sharp pain hit him in the stomach, just as it had hit him when he saw Helen with that guy in the Picadilly bar. Now it had happened again: betrayal. He bent over in agony. The pain would not quit, and by the time they dropped Jeff at the hospital and reached his own headquarters, his hands were shaking.

"Get her on the phone," he told Chief.

As he waited, he tried to look at the stack of battalion reports and other papers he needed to sign, but he couldn't concentrate. For what seemed like an eternity, he sat there in frustration and anxiety like a mouse in a maze, banging his head against walls of confusion, pain, and disbelief.

"No answer," Chief called from the outer office. "I'm getting dumb messages about the phone being disconnected or something. But that's not unusual, Colonel. It happens all the time here. Phone system around these parts isn't much good. I wouldn't put much stock in it. They'll probably fix it soon. I'll keep trying."

Without success. For the next week, Chief attempted several times a day to call her, but he never got through. The question of Avril's loyalty overrode everything else, and he couldn't shake it. Then, almost thankfully, new orders forced Sandy to shift his attention to the battalion and concentrate on operations. Field Forces wanted his guns repositioned so as to provide interdiction fires along known Viet Cong infiltration routes leading from Cambodia to Saigon. To accomplish that, Sandy had to set up three separate fire support bases in War Zone C north of the Cu Chi, Tay Ninh line. That meant providing security for his medium batteries as they moved men, guns, and ammunition through dangerous areas. Then each new base had to be organized to defend its own perimeters. This was dangerous work. and he had to be in the field much of the time. He worked from dawn to dusk each day, and thus he didn't have much opportunity to think about her. The nights were a far different matter.

He slept poorly, if at all. He found himself grinding his teeth in frustration as he kept going over what had happened that Sunday. Then he began to recall her many questions about his battalion. What had prompted them? Was she interested in him, or was she digging for intelligence about his guns? For him to consider that question caused more pain, because it meant that he was considering the possibility she was an agent. The answer meant everything to him. And she had wanted to know when he would return. Was that because his return would mean the guns had been pulled back from the border, or because she wanted to see him again? Night after night, he tossed and turned as he worried the questions around in his mind. Then gradually he began to blame himself for failing with another woman, as he had with Helen and Nancy. And his frustration grew. Until he had his units safely in their new positions, he couldn't leave his guns and go to her. The agony threatened to consume him, and he had to concentrate even harder to avoid making a fatal error out in the jungle. After three weeks, his batteries were finally established on secure fire support bases, each with the equivalent of an infantry battalion as additional defense. Only when his guns were finally set up and engaged in firing routine interdiction missions did he feel able to free himself from daily operations. First, he went to the hospital at Long Binh, east of Saigon, to see how Jeff was doing.

"Good news and bad, Colonel," Jeff said weakly from his bed. "The good news is I'm going home alive. The bad news is that I'm all messed up inside. They're going to have to operate again. They say I'm be okay, but what the hell happened back there in Hoc Mon?"

Sandy told the boy about the ambush and how the Jeep's quick acceleration had caused a radio-controlled mine to miss them. He described the following attack by the Viet Cong and the timely ARVN rescue, carefully omitting anything about Avril. Still under heavy medication for pain, Jeff fell asleep as Sandy was talking. Sandy checked with Jeff's doctor and learned that Jeff was out of danger and would be well cared for. Only then did he feel free to head for Saigon.

As he entered the city, the streets seemed normal. Like him, outwardly the capital was calm. But on the inside, he churned with apprehension. When he finally reached her house, his worst fears were realized. Everything had changed. ARVN soldiers were guarding the compound. They told him they had been in place for several weeks, that no one was inside, and the house had been stripped bare. They wouldn't let him see the wreckage for himself, so he continued down the street to MACV headquarters. There, he asked for the intelligence section and was routed to the duty officer. Shortly thereafter, he found himself in the office of a sympathetic major who carefully wrote down Sandy's description of the ambush and his relationship with Avril. Then, asking Sandy to wait, he went off to check some files. In about fifteen minutes, he reappeared with a stack of papers. "American Intelligence had no record of any spy named Avril de Castries," he said.

"Then where should I check further?" Sandy asked.

"I haven't the slightest idea," the man said.

"I find that hard to believe," Sandy said. "Somebody's hiding something. Let me talk to your boss."

The major hesitated and then told Sandy to follow him. They walked to the next floor and into the office of the Deputy Chief of Staff, Brigadier General Robert Newton.

"Well, well, if it isn't Colonel Walker," Newton said after Sandy reported. "And from what I read in your report, you're in hot water as usual. Tell me, why you aren't out in the field with your battalion?"

"I had business at Long Binh." Sandy said. "My driver's been hurt. And if I can get any answers from your staff, I'll be back with my men by nightfall."

"I'm sure you care about your men," Newton said. "Yet your driver in the Long Binh hospital is there unnecessarily, just because you put him in harm's way."

"We're all in harm's way here in Vietnam, General," Sandy said. "I'd like some answers so I can avoid more of it."

"What answers?"

"I'd like any information you have on an embassy employee named Avril de Castries."

"I'm sure you would, but I can't help you."

"As I told your Intelligence guy back there," Sandy said, "I find that very difficult to believe."

"Walker, you remember the story about the squirrel walking on the railroad track? When the train came, he was too slow jumping off the rails. The train's wheels nipped off just the tip of his tail. When he looked back to see what had happened, the wheels cut off his head. The moral to that story is never to lose your head over a piece of tail. You get me?"

"You're talking about the mother of my child," Sandy said, feeling the blood rush to his face.

"But she's evidently not your wife," Newton said. "And she's also a woman we know nothing about here at headquarters."

Realizing he was at a dead end, Sandy wheeled and left. He had one more chance, and he took it. At the front desk of the American Embassy, he asked for Avril. When he was told that she didn't work there any more, he asked to see someone who could explain. The officer on duty hesitated and then made a phone call. Hanging up, he told Sandy an officer would be down shortly, and he directed Sandy to a nearby waiting area. After about ten minutes, Sandy was surprised to see Jon Bourne appear. Jon greeted him enthusiastically and led him to a small, nearby conference room that Sandy assumed was bugged.

"You're still here?" Sandy asked.

"I've got lifetime tenure," Bourne said.

"Then you must know what happened to Avril," Sandy said.

"I'll tell you as much as I know," Bourne said. "First of all, her arrest was a complete shock to all of us here. We had no idea she was in any way compromised, and all of us are uniformly sorry, embarrassed, and saddened."

"Are you saying she was really an agent?"

"Apparently she was," Bourne said.

"How could that be?" Sandy asked. "The embassy must have checked her background for a security clearance. She worked here for more than ten years.

"Until this recent military buildup, security checks were pretty cursory in Saigon. But now, the new Administration has started a complete overhaul. Everybody is going through the process again, only this time the checks are much more thorough. Lot's of questions are being raised about many people. As a result of the volume of new activity, it is taking considerable time to check everything out. Evidently during those checks, we found that she had some questionable roots."

"What roots?"

"Two brothers in the VC, for starters," Bourne said. "But back when she was in school, she must have said some pretty strong things about independence and freedom for Vietnam. And since then, some of her contacts have turned out to be bad apples. I guess that was why South Vietnamese authorities began tapping her phone calls. Lucky for you, they did."

"Jon, I find all this very confusing," Sandy said. "You're not describing the woman I know. There must be more to it than what you're telling me. I'd like to hear her side of the story. Let me see her."

"I'm afraid that won't be possible," Bourne said.

"Why not?" Sandy asked. "At least let me see her attorney ." "I'm sorry, but I've got some really bad news for you, Sandy," Bourne said. "At the same time you were being ambushed, an ARVN strike force went over the walls around her house. Two of her men were killed and the rest were taken prisoner. Avril and daughter were not harmed in any way, but they were taken to her ARVN security area. Two days later, Avril was tried by a summary court and found guilty of treason."

"Treason?" Sandy asked. "In two days. What kind of trial was that? What's that mean? What about an appeal?"

"This is wartime," Bourne said. "The Viets are pretty tough on treason. Trials are quite summary, and there is no such thing as an appeal. The day after the trial, she was shot."

Sandy was stunned. Pain almost caused him to bend over.

"No appeal?" he asked, still not comprehending. "None," Bourne said. "While Vietnam is at war, its military courts have almost unlimited powers."

"But why didn't the embassy intervene?"

"She was a Vietnamese national, and we had no authority."

"May I see the body?"

"Cremated."

"Where is the grave?"

"The ashes were scattered."

It was too much. She was completely gone. In shock and denial, Sandy sat there, his head hung in his hands. His future was lost. It couldn't be true, none of it. He was having a bad dream, and he would soon wake up. Suddenly he thought of Joy.

"The little girl, what happened to her?"

"We're not quite sure," Bourne said. "We think she's been sent to some sort of indoctrination camp somewhere in the Delta, but the Vietnamese authorities won't talk about it."

"She's my daughter, Jon."

"Avril never confirmed who the father was, but I always thought you might be. I'm sorry."

"But the embassy now has a legal interest in what happens to the girl. She's the daughter of an American citizen. You have to follow up, press them. I want to take custody of my daughter and send her to the States."

"We'll do our best," Bourne said. "You have my word. I promise to explore every avenue possible. I'll let you know anything we find, but you'll have to sign some papers for me."

"I'll sign anything you need," Sandy said. "Just get going on it fast. Find her and take custody. No telling what they're doing to her."

"You can be assured that we'll redouble our efforts right away," Bourne said, and then he left Sandy, soon to reappear with a secretary and some papers needing signature. She took Sandy's statement, and then explained that the forms would be used to establish Sandy's claim of custody. That done, Bourne showed Sandy out, repeating his promises that the embassy would make every effort to find Joy.

Having been rebuffed by both the military and the State Department, Sandy had no other avenues to turn to. At least Jon had been more sympathetic than Brick Newton, but after all, Bourne was a diplomat. Saddened, dispirited, and at a loss for anything else he could do, Sandy headed back to Cu Chi.

CHAPTER TWENTY

Plenty of work awaited him. MACV headquarters had decided to eliminate the proximate insurgent threat to Saigon. To that end, Sandy's guns were to be ready to support operations in the Iron Triangle. This was a VC jungle and tunnel complex in Binh Duong Province just to the north and west of the city. The Iron Triangle had a fearsome reputation. It was reputed to be the headquarters for all military and terrorist activity in the capitol area. Because of its strong fortifications and extensive underground complex, it had not been attacked by ARVN in years. MACV had decided to change all that, and it had assembled a strong force for the attack. The 1st Infantry Division was to move into the Iron Triangle from the north, and at the same time the 25th Infantry Division would attack from the south. Before the operation, Sandy had to shift his artillery again so as to be able to support both efforts. The new operation was called Cedar Falls, and by the 8th of January, everything was in place. When the two American Divisions moved out, they expected stiff resistance. To their great surprise and disappointment, the VC elected not to fight. It gave up the ground with only a minimum of resistance. As a consolation, the Americans uncovered great stores of supplies and killed about seven hundred and fifty guerrillas, while suffering only minor casualties. Sandy's guns had an easy time of it, undergoing no attacks and firing only occasionally at light VC resistance.

A major, well-publicized result of the operation, however, was the elimination of an entire village named Ben Suc. For years, this particular village had been an established Viet Cong area, and it had continually provided men and supplies to the insurgents. To eliminate such support in the future, ARVN and the Big Red One forcibly evacuated all six thousand villagers to other secure locations, and the village was destroyed. The action recalled to Sandy the many American operations in the Philippines after the Spanish American War. Indeed, the destruction of the village had been patterned on the experience of the United States against the Filipinos. In both cases, the media published heart rendering stories of the forcible displacements that aroused respective Peace Movements to new heights of fury and gave them visible examples of what they called the abuses of American power. Sandy had less than a week after Cedar Falls before the start of MACV's next major operation: Junction City. Because Cedar Falls had reduced the immediate threat to Saigon, MACV now wanted the major North Vietnamese infiltration routes from the Ho Chi Minh Trail into War Zone C to be attacked. Junction City was to do that. Four United States Divisions were to move in a coordinated operation to the Cambodian borders in that area and clear out any North Vietnamese found. It was to be a major effort, requiring Sandy's guns first to move west up Route 1 to Tay Ninh and then north to the Cambodian border. The complexity of the operation gave Sandy little opportunity to talk to Bourne at the embassy, especially since Jon didn't return calls from either Sandy or Chief. The absence of news about Joy kept him in a continuing state of anxiety, but there was nothing he could do about it while he was operating in the field. Junction City was far different from Cedar Falls. In this case, the North Vietnamese evidently decided to defend, for they prepared carefully. By now, they had plenty of experience in fighting the Americans, and they put that experience to good use. To overcome the American advantages in aviation, the NVA developed special machinegun tactics for use against helicopters and low flying planes. Because artillery observers in small aircraft directed the devastating American heavy artillery, those light planes were also special targets that received concentrated, heavy fire. In addition, the North Vietnamese in the area had built up supplies of 60mm and 82mm mortars and recoilless rifles to attack any fire support bases that might be set up, and they had plenty of men for humanwave attacks. To counter American mobility by air, they worked out ways to mine and defend logical helicopter landing zones. Finally, they could choose the times and places they wanted to attack. They did so with a ferocity and intensity that was a warning for the future. In three places, Ap Bau Bang, Ap Gu, and Fire Support Base Gold, they mounted efforts that showed signs of thorough planning and coordinated efforts. In each case, intensive mortar barrages and recoilless rifle fire preceded coordinated waves of fanatical soldiers that swarmed over American defenses. If American helicopters or artillery observer in spotter planes came too close to the ground in defense against these attacks, they came under withering fire, and ground forces moving to relieve beleaguered bases were ambushed by well-organized traps.

All three major battles were touch and go. Only the bravery of the grunts on the ground and the effectiveness of the new beehive rounds of the artillery saved the day. Sandy's bases came under attack several times, but his men acquitted themselves well, and finally the NVA moved back across the Cambodian border, having lost more than three thousand men in the various battles of Operation Junction City. Sandy could take little satisfaction in the result, however, because he knew that the enemy had gained experience and could recover and regroup in the safety of their Cambodian sanctuary, only to attack again at a time of their choosing. The fierce opposition the Americans encountered in Junction City proved that the enemy was wage a long war in Southeast Asia. ready and willing to Sandy had little time to reflect, moreover, for he had to move back from the Cambodian border to join the American 9th Division in an attempt to clear out VC areas to the west and south of Saigon. The logistic problems were immense and the fighting was intense, and so it was May before he could take a break and return to the American Embassy seeking news of Joy. What he heard was not good.

"She's nowhere to be found," Bourne said. "At least that's what the Vietnamese say."

"But I refuse to believe she's dead," Sandy said. "She has to be somewhere."

"I agree with you, Sandy. And we know they're probably lying. We just can't do anything about it. I give you my word, however, that we won't stop trying to find her. And when we do, we'll get them to send her to you. I'll keep pushing them. You can count on it."

"But what's their problem?" Sandy asked.

"My guess, and it's only a guess," Bourne said, "is that the idea of a Vietnamese spy in the American Embassy is a source of great embarrassment to them. They act as if the whole thing is a very sensitive subject."

After an hour of protest and discussion, Sandy realized he was getting nowhere, and he had to give up and return to his battalion. The final month and a half of his command reflected a decrease in operational missions and an absence of guerrilla activity. The Clan won Presidential Unit Citations for its efforts in Attleboro, Cedar Falls and Junction City. Then, in June, Sandy received orders to return to the United States and report to the Pentagon. At first, he was determined to refuse to leave Vietnam without Joy, and he prepared papers requesting he be permitted to stay in country for another year, but Bourne convinced him that the embassy would continue its efforts to find her and send her to him. Other embassy officers pointed out that at the Pentagon, Sandy might be in a better position to search for answers. There, he might find someone in authority who would press his case for him. In July of 1967, therefore, Sandy reluctantly complied with his orders and left Vietnam. In spite of The Clan's outstanding combat record and the American embassy's assurance that Joy would be found and sent to him, he was a sad and frustrated soldier.

CHAPTER TWENTY-ONE

A terse letter from Nancy, necessitated by the terms of their divorce agreement, had told him she and the kids had moved to a place in South Carolina called Sea Pines on Hilton Head Island. She said Kathleen and her husband, Dan, had set up their real estate business there, at a newly established planned community that was doing fairly well. Evidently this Hilton Head was a coastal island between Savannah and Charleston, and fresh money was developing it into a promising resort. Kathleen and Dan had thus seized the opportunity to get in at the start of the new development, and because of their high school friendship and Nancy's success in Destin real estate, they had asked her to join them. After some reluctance in leaving her parents, she had decided the opportunity was too good to resist, and she had taken them up on the offer. Reading between the lines, Sandy could tell Nancy really wanted to leave Destin, his father, and her painful memories behind. At any rate, he headed there to see the kids. He would visit his father later.

The Army flew him and about two hundred other returning soldiers in a civilian chartered jet from Tan Son Nhut Airport near Saigon to Anchorage, Alaska, and then on to Travis Air Force Base in California. There, he was given a ticket to Atlanta on Delta, with connections to Savannah. During the twenty-four hours of flight, as he tried to put Vietnam behind him, he realized that he wanted desperately to see Sara and Walter again, Somehow, the loss of Avril and Joy made that need even stronger. He didn't want to be alone, and the kids were now at ages where they would be se changing so quickly that, after a year's absence, he didn't know what to expect. Nancy had not said if Walter had been drafted, just as she had omitted any personal details about Sara. The children themselves had not written, and in the thirty days leave granted him, he needed to catch up with and be a part of their lives.

In her letter, Nancy had told him that she had bought a small house in the new Sea Pines community, actually in something she referred to as a plantation. He immediately thought of something like a grand plantation home, but she really had about two thousand square feet in a ranch style home with three bedrooms. It was on a cul-de-sac and bordered a small inlet. She had a small dock and a rowboat for fishing the waters of Calibogue Sound, a part of the Inland Waterway. Surrounded by tropical trees and plants, her place had a little, Bermuda grass lawn. She sounded content. When he looked up her number and called her from the Savannah airport, she was only momentarily taken aback. Then she told him he could find a room at the William Hilton Inn or the new Seacrest Motel on the Atlantic side of the island, outside the gates to Sea Pines Plantation. When he was established there. he was to give her a call so that she could call the gate to let him in. The possibility of his staying at her house never came up.

Hilton Head proved to be about an hour north and east of the Savannah Airport. A recently completed bridge from the mainland across the Inland Waterway took him to Highway 278, evidently the island's major access road. Hilton Head was shaped like a human foot with its toe pointing left and the bridge from the mainland as the ankle. Sea Pines Plantation, where Nancy lived, was the ball and toes of the foot. Other plantations made up the rest of the island. Port Royal Plantation was the heel, and Palmetto Dunes was the instep. The access highway split the island and ended at the gates of Sea Pines Plantation. As Sandy came onto the island, he was immediately taken with the beauty of the place. Great expanse of water mixed with a lush green landscape. It was a semi-tropical paradise, and not a single red light marred his ten-mile trip to Sea Pines.

Sandy's motel was down an exterior road to the Atlantic beach just outside of Sea Pines. In his room, he examined his reflection in the mirror. He had left about fifteen extra pounds in Vietnam, and he was trim and tan in golf shirt and slacks, with no visible wounds. Interior injury was another matter. He knew he carried mental scars.

No matter, he thought, the poet said that time heals all wounds. So he shaved and then called Nancy. She invited him to join them at her place just before supper. A pass would be waiting for him at the Sea Pines gate. He found her house easily, and there she, Sara, and Walter were waiting. Nancy was trim and efficient looking, the picture of an effective real estate agent, and she welcomed him with a firm, businesslike handshake. Walter was more enthusiastic. Not content with a manly handshake, he added a bear hug. Sara was just the opposite of Walter. Withdrawn and reserved, she barely nodded in acknowledgement of Andy's hello. Nancy offered a beer, and they all moved to the family room that shared space with the kitchen. Awkwardly, they gathered around the little coffee table, where he learned that Kathleen's real estate business was doing very well indeed and that he was expected at their place for supper the following evening. He also discovered that Sara was in her last year of high school, and Walter had already been drafted. In return, Sandy told them a little about Vietnam, his command of a battalion, and his upcoming assignment to the Pentagon. He omitted any reference to Avril or Joy, for he could think of no way Joy's existence and Avril's death would not provoke an extreme response. More than ever before, he felt like a stranger in his own family. If relations were to continue as they were, Nancy would be correct: he would be in danger of losing his kids. He resolved to change that, but Nancy was evasive as to any future contact. She said he was welcome to drop by whenever he wanted, but she asked that he call first to insure that she could get him a pass through the Sea Pines security gate. Walter was much more outgoing. He said he was finished with basic and advanced individual training at Fort Jackson near Columbia, and he was due to ship out soon to join the 4th Infantry Division in Vietnam. Sandy winced when he said that he wanted to pick Sandy's brains about "Nam," as he called it. Sara reluctantly agreed that she too might want to talk sometime, but she was noticeably ambiguous about the details of any meeting. Taking what he could, Sandy asked Walter to come over to the motel for supper the next afternoon. They would talk.

At five o'clock the following day, therefore, they met at the Seacrest Motel and went down the street to the Hofbrau, a German restaurant that Walter said had a great chef. Over a beer in a frozen mug, they exchanged small talk as they waited for the Wiener Schnitzel special. As advertised, the food was excellent. Through the glow of his second mug of brew, Sandy realized just how far he had come from the jungles of War Zone C. The thought that Walter would soon be in danger over there sobered him, however, for the boy remained far too enthusiastic.

"I was really good on the M-60, dad," he said. "I'm gonna carry a machinegun." "That's an important job," Sandy said. "But it's also a dangerous one. You'll be a prime target."

"Why's that?"

"In the rice paddies, Machine gunners and radio operators draw the first and most VC fire." "Because they're important," Walter said. "I like that."

"Important is not good if you're dead," Sandy said. "Ah come on, dad, what's it really like over there?"

"Well, I meant what I said about its being no good if you're dead. And death is more than likely to happen to a machine-gunner than a cook. But there are ways to make Vietnam less dangerous. The first and most important rule is to take care of your buddy. That's because when you're out in the jungle and the bad guys are swarming at your wires, you fight to protect your own. Some call it loyalty, but it's also self-preservation. You want your buddy to be around to take care of you. In the jungle, men don't fight to save the world from communism. They fight to survive, and that means not letting their buddies down. Nothing else counts as much. When picking buddies, however, it's a good idea not to pick one braver than you are. The really brave ones are more likely to start a fight you won't be comfortable with."

"And that's the key to survival?"

"Your buddies are the best insurance you've got," he said. "There are other keys, lots of them, too many to remember. Part of survival, therefore, is instinct built up over the years. That's why good sergeants can help a lot. They made their rank by surviving, and in doing so they've built up a reservoir of knowledge they can pass on. So try to stay near them. They're professionals, and professionals are predictable. Unfortunately, in the jungle, the ranks are also full of amateurs. So, listen to the your squad leader, not some loud mouth private who's a dummy who thinks he knows it all."

"Point well made," Walter said. "Any others?"

"Well, I'd say that the important things are simple, but the simple things are hard. For example, you should never start a firefight with someone who has more ammunition than you do. But in a fight and in doubt, it's best to fire everything you've got. And clean your weapon every chance you get, 'cause the jungle is a dirty place and if your rifle is dirty, it will always jam just when you need it most."

"Were you in the jungle a lot?"

"More than I wanted to be. And it wasn't a lot of fun. Anything you do there can get you killed, including doing nothing. Some things you should remember: The easy way is always mined, and mines don't have feelings. They are equal opportunity killers. And don't get too close to the radio operator. He's a prime target for snipers, and poor snipers might miss him and hit you. Try to look inconspicuous yourself, 'cause the enemy may be short of ammunition and he'll want to pick the best targets. Most of all, when the going is easy and everything is working the way the platoon leader said it would, you're about to be ambushed." "You're talking about fighting in the jungle," Walter said. "Didn't you ride helicopters a lot?"

"Sure. And helicopters are better than personnel carriers, which are better than walking, which in turn is better than crawling. All of these are better than being shoved into the medevac chopper on a stretcher, even if that is indeed a form of flying. Remember, you're a grunt, and helicopters were sent to Vietnam to help the grunts. Unfortunately, someone always forgets that, and the grunts are left on their own, on the ground in the bushes with the bugs. When that happens, it's important to win the fight. Then it's too late to decide if being in Vietnam is a good idea or even fair. Because being fair doesn't count. All that counts is winning, not losing. And that's because the winners get to make up the rules and wear the medals. Finally, on that subject, I'll tell you that medals are okay, but having all your body parts is better."

"What's night in the bushes like?"

"Hot, wet, and filled with red ants," Sandy said. "One leaf can hold thousands of them little critters, and if you shake that leaf, they'll all spill all over you and start biting. Every bite burns like hell, so you end up looking like you have the measles. And when you stop every afternoon, you can't rest until you're ready for an attack, 'cause it will come every time you're not dug in. Dig in deep, too, because all incoming fire has the right of way. And when you set up the defense of your position, remember that your Claymore mine has a label that reads 'this side toward enemy' for a very good reason. But when you can't remember which way the Claymore is pointed, it's always pointed toward you. Finally, at night, you have the right to remain silent, and that is an excellent idea."

"Were you ever afraid, dad?"

"Every now and then, everybody is, but not a lot. After all, the enemy can only kill you. I was more afraid of the reporters who came clustering around when we got back to base camp after an operation, 'cause they can twist what happened until they take away your reputation, and you can't live without that. Eat when you can. Sleep when you can. Pee when you can. The next opportunity may be long in coming. And most of all, because your M-60 machinegun was made by the lowest bidder, you might try a little prayer. Prayer may not help, but it can't do any harm."

By the time supper was over, Sandy felt he had established a bond with the boy. That was when Walter summed up his courage and made his announcement.

"My girl friend, Cathy, and I are going to be married."

"That's great," Sandy said. "When?"

"We want to do it before I go overseas," Walter said. "Mom's against it, but we want to do it next week. What do you think?"

"I'm all for it," Sandy said. "Maybe nobody ever told you, but both my aunts did the same thing back in World War One. They married their guys so if the men didn't come back, the girls would at least have good memories. You're just following a family tradition."

"Then I want you to be my Best Man."

CHAPTER TWENTY-TWO

Walter and Cathy were married the following week in the island's Episcopal church, and Sandy was the Best Man. To his surprise, and in something of a reversal, Nancy didn't put up much of a fight either over the wedding or Sandy's role. The kids were too obviously in love for her to object. More notably for Sandy, Sara also reluctantly overcame her misgivings about Walter's marrying and then going to Vietnam. She joined the ceremony as Maid of Honor. As he watched the youngsters join hands and kiss at the altar, Sandy felt the loss of Avril slowly dissipate. The kids were so young, so much in love, and their lives were right before them. Their commitment seemed to bring him some sort of closure, and he was ready to move on. And too, the ceremony had made everybody seem much closer together, and a week after the wedding, Sara agreed to meet him and talk. They went to the same German restaurant that Walter had chosen. At first Sara was subdued, and she barely responded to his attempts at small talk. But after an excellent meal, she really opened up on him.

"I still hate us being in Vietnam," she said. "Tell me why," he said.

"It's unfair," she said.

"What's unfair?" he asked.

"We're drafting young Black men to be killed," she said.

"Sara," he said, "the Army keeps very accurate records of such things. The statistics show that fewer than eleven percent of those who have served in Vietnam thus far have been Blacks. The entire American population is about thirteen percent Black, so it seems to me that neither the Army nor the government is singling them out unfairly."

"But we give them the dirty jobs and they get killed," she said. "That's the unfair part."

"Actually, thirty-four percent of Blacks who have entered the service during this period have volunteered for combat. The record shows that about twelve percent of the deaths in Vietnam are Blacks. That just about matches their proportionate numbers of the population, and so it seems to me that if we must fight, the risk is pretty fairly distributed."

"But all my friends are being drafted and killed."

"Actually, if you really look at the figures, Sara, about ten percent of your generation is serving over there," Sandy said. "But only twenty-five percent of the soldiers in Vietnam are draftees. The rest are Regular Army, National Guard, Reservists, or enlisted volunteers. So not just those drafted are being killed."

"But only the poor boys get sent over," she said.

"There may be a small bit of truth in that," he said. "But only a small bit. In reality, about a quarter of the men sent to Vietnam come from families where the father has a managerial, professional, or technological job. Three-quarters come from families with incomes above the poverty levels. And eighty percent of those serving have a high school education. In World War Two, only forty-five percent of serving American soldiers had finished high school." "But it's my generation that's getting killed."

"On that, I can agree with you. The burden of the Vietnam War is falling mostly on the young, but that happens in any war.

Young men have always been soldiers. They have the stamina and strength to do it. Thus, it's true that in Vietnam our records show that sixty percent of those who have been killed so far have been twenty-one or younger. So your point is well made: If war is indeed unfair to anyone, it is unfair to the young."

"That's what I mean," she said. "And Walter's young, and you're letting him go over there."

"I don't think I could stop him if I tried."

"Well you should try," she said.

"I've done my best, Sara, but he seems determined."

"I'll hate it if he's hurt," she said.

"Believe me, I will too," Sandy said.

When Sara left him, he knew he hadn't changed her mind one small bit. She was thinking with her heart, and no amount of his reasoning was going to alter her mind set. He left their supper knowing that he hadn't established with her the bond he had felt so strongly with Walter. That especially hurt, because he wanted so much for her to love him the way he loved her. Fathers and daughters usually have a special relationship, but she seemed to have rejected theirs. He took that rejection very much to heart and blamed himself for it. He knew that every father has to face losing his daughter sooner or later, but Sandy had lost Sara far too soon. In addition, he realized that he was still batting zero with the ladies. He had to face reality: he remained a hopeless dunce in his dealings with the fairer sex.

CHAPTER TWENTY- THREE

Walter and Cathy were away on their honeymoon in Bermuda, and Sara remained aloof, when the time came, too soon, for Sandy to move on to the Pentagon. Telling himself he would soon return to the island, he left Hilton Head reluctantly, and drove up Interstate 95 to Washington and the Pentagon. Threading his way through that five-sided maze, he found a desk that had his assignment. He was to be in an office with a grand title: The Assistant Chief of Staff for Force Development, "Axe Four" as it was called in that labyrinth of halls housing the best military minds America could muster. When he eventually found the Axe Four personnel department, he discovered that he was to be part of a section that was responsible for seeing that the Army would always have the finest artillery possible. There, because of his command experience in Vietnam, he was given his first mission: Examine the current use of artillery in Southeast Asia. Based on his command of a battalion over there, the Army Staff wanted an evaluation of artillery tactics and techniques, as well as any recommendations for changes. In particular, the Staff had an interest in knowing if it would make sense for artillery shells to be guided to their targets by new computer technology just coming on line.

Sandy's report took months to write, and that was only the first draft. Every item had to be coordinated with any member of the staff who might possibly have an interest, from the money people to the logisticians and then to the tacticians. He even had to obtain input and comments from the Artillery School in Oklahoma. After walking the halls of the Pentagon for months, and visiting Fort Sill twice, he fulfilled the Indian legend that forecast his many returns to Oklahoma. At the end of three months, however, he thought he had a good draft report. He also had a better understanding of why the Pentagon had so many critics. The importance of a project was directly proportional to the number of offices and agencies that had an interest in it. To get anything done at all required a massive effort and many compromises. He also learned the truth of the axiom that a camel was a horse made by a committee. Every office he visited wanted changes. In spite of the need to compromise, however, he fought against the most inane suggestions and at the end of that trial period, he had what he thought was an acceptable draft that was ready to be circulated for formal comment and approving signatures.

Many of his observations remained unchanged from his first tour in Vietnam. He reiterated his major recommendation: In Southeast Asia, current doctrine concerning the need to mass fires from many weapons on a single target needed to be reconsidered. This time, however, he had more ammunition in support of his position. First of all, no targets of a size that merited such concentrations had ever appeared in Vietnam. Secondly, the war in Vietnam was too dispersed to permit the massing of the guns of two or more Divisions Artilleries and their supporting Corps Artillery weapons. And even if a giant target suddenly materialized, the necessary survey to connect them all on the same grid just did not exist. The current infantry doctrine in Vietnam was to use vigorous patrolling to ferret out the enemy and then to shift men and weapons to meet the new threat. That meant the artillery war in Southeast Asia boiled down to targets of opportunity. Complicated fire support plans and massive attack fire preparations had been made obsolete by an elusive enemy in the jungle. As for the project investigating the use of guided artillery shells, he reported that they were simply too expensive to expend in great numbers on ill-defined targets.

On the other hand, some concepts remained as important as ever. The artillery still had to be able to do three things: shoot, move, and communicate. To shoot accurately and quickly, commanders had to be able to locate themselves and their targets from maps and registration fires. Some sort of method of locating one's unit in the jungle had to be developed. Just as importantly, the artillery had to move massive amounts of ammunition to rapidly changing firing positions. That was because, to his amazement, he found that statistics now revealed that the artillery in Vietnam was firing more than it did in either Korea or World War Two. Thus the science of moving weapons and ammunition quickly on dangerous roads to be able to fire on new targets almost every day took on added importance. Finally, communication needed to be reliable and secure in an extremely hostile environment. Most of this part of Sandy's report was acceptable to everyone.

He ran into trouble when he began to discuss the nature of the war itself. He first raised the issue of defense of the fire support bases. Artillery training and doctrine had always cited the need for artillery units to defend their own positions, but such training had never envisioned the kind of war being waged in Vietnam. Because of the absence of organized front lines, the enemy was just as likely to attack an artillery battery as it was to attack an infantry battalion. Sandy's own experience confirmed that. He therefore recommended that either artillery units be assigned more men for defense against ground attacks, or the infantry or armor be tasked that responsibility. He knew that such diversion of strength to defense would mean that fewer soldiers would be available for offensive operations. Defense is never as popular as offense, and thus his observations met firm resistance. Even less popular was his detailed conclusion that the Americanization of the war was not proving a success. In his view, current doctrine and operations were as wasteful and futile as that of the previous French attempts. He recommended change, and that got him in trouble.

It came from the Office of the Vice Chief of Staff. About a month after Axe Four had sent his paper up the line for comment, Sandy was instructed to report to Brigadier General Robert Newton, back from Vietnam and working with the Vice Chief on Army concepts for the future.

"We meet again, Walker," Newton said, motioning Sandy to take a seat at a small conference table. There, Sandy found a copy of his report.

"I don't have a problem with all this nickel and dime stuff in here," Newton said, holding up the paper. "That's for the piss ants to figure out. What bothers me are your comments on how we're running the war. You haven't absorbed much since we talked about it seven years ago. You a slow learner?"

"That's the question, isn't it?" Sandy said. "Who's the slow learner, the Army or me?"

"Don't get wise with me, Walker," Newton said. "I'll kick you out of the Army so fast you won't know what hit you. Now, you've said in your report that we ought to change what we're doing over there. I'd like you to explain that. I want to hear it hear it directly from you. Do it right, you hear. You got just one more chance."

"Okay, General," Sandy said, "here it is: From what I can tell, the effectiveness of current American tactics is the real question. We could argue about that for a long time. As a matter of fact, the Army Staff has already done that, and I've listened to most of it. Well meaning, thoroughly professional soldiers disagree, and I accept that, but I would ask you to think about just one statistic. It involves the buildup of American combat force in Vietnam and just what that buildup has or hasn't accomplished. We know that early on, General Westmoreland asked President Johnson for permission to deploy five hundred thousand men over there. Back in 1961, the Special Military Advisor to the President, General Maxwell Taylor, had cited that exact figure to President Kennedy, and the President's response was one of incredulity. Kennedy told Taylor that the recommendation was out of the question, because the American people would never accept sending so many of our young men to fight in the jungles of Southeast Asia. Yet we have almost that that many in Vietnam now, and more may be required. In addition, as you and I know, seven of the Army's eighteen active Divisions are now deployed to Vietnam. Forget about the cost and our ability to respond to trouble elsewhere in the world, maybe in the Fulda Gap of West Germany or in Korea. Focus just on Vietnam. Remember when you and I first met. That was before the buildup started. Based on what happened to the French when they tried the same thing, I told you then that any large increase in American conventional forces would be a bad idea. Back then, intelligence reports told us that the VC had about six thousand men in the south. What has happened since we built up our force from five hundred to five hundred thousand men? The

VC has grown even stronger. Instead of being defeated in the field and retreating to North Vietnam, the VC and NVA now have well over a hundred thousand men in the south. That's up from just six thousand in a little over five years. I can think of no other statistic that better proves that we are going about this in the wrong way."

"Assuming for the moment that I accept your argument," Newton said, "And I assure you that I don't, just what is it you would have us do?"

"Well, as I see it, we have about four alternatives. First, we could declare war and invade North Vietnam."

"You can damn well forget that dumb idea," Newton said. "The Chinese would come in and we'd have World War Three, And the American people wouldn't permit it."

"Granted. I'm just presenting alternatives," Sandy said. "And the second alternative is to withdraw from Vietnam right now. Declare victory and leave."

"We can't do that," Newton said. "It would be a disastrous defeat and political suicide for the President."

"I know that," Sandy said. "I'm just setting the limits. The third possibility is to turn the war over to the South Vietnamese."

"ARVN can't handle it," Newton said. "You know that."

"Agreed. Then the last alternative is the only viable choice. We have to adopt a different approach. We have to organize and train our forces to bring ARVN up to speed so they can handle the army from the North."

"How do we do that?" Newton asked.

"The Americanization of the war should cease," Sandy said. "Everybody who has served over there agrees with that. ARVN has to take over the fight, and we have to get out before we kill a lot more American boys. More that that, we need to stop killing South Vietnamese citizens. They are dying at a higher rate than the VC, NVA, and our own guys put together. We're supposed to be saving them, , not killing them."

"That's motherhood and apple pie, Walker. We'd love it if ARVN could carry the fight to the NVA, but they can't. We've tried everything, and they just won't or can't do it. And believe it or not, I don't like killing Vietnamese citizens any more than you do, but this is war."

"I can help you on both counts," Sandy said. "Let's start from where we agree: ARVN doesn't have the men, leadership, materiel, and training to do the job, and we have to find a way to protect the peasants. Okay? I can show you how to do both."

"Don't tell me you're going back to your dumb idea of putting a Special Forces team in every village? I've already told you that won't work."

"Too late for that," Sandy said. "If you'd started it eight years ago, it would be working now, and we'd be winning the hearts and minds of the villagers. No, that opportunity is long gone. Now, we have to do it a different way."

"And what way is that?"

"Double positioning," Sandy said. "Pull the American units back from the borders and jungles and station them with similar ARVN units in the villages. Every ARVN soldier would have an American buddy in his foxhole. Every ARVN officer would have an American officer with him night and day. I mean that our men should stay with the ARVN soldiers all the time, without ever pulling back to an American base camp. ARVN would see how a soldier should live, how officers should lead, and how soldiers should treat civilians. In one stroke, the villages would be twice as secure as they are now. The VC would be cut off from their supply of men and food. Sure, you'd need to provide reaction forces to come to the aid of villages and cities that are attacked, but the Vietnamese paratroopers, helicopters, and tactical air support can do that. The important thing is for us to make the villages secure. Then, as ARVN gets stronger and the villages are secure, we can withdraw American units and let the Vietnamese fight their own fights. It's the only practical way out of the damned mess we're in now."

"That's crazy," Newton said. "It would never work."

"It's already worked," Sandy said. "The 196th Brigade has done just that in the Delta south and west of Saigon. It worked like a charm. The area is secure, and the peasants are happy."

Newton dismissed Sandy and his report. He saw no reason to recommend to his superiors in the Office of the Vice Chief that America should change its current strategy. In his mind, the best course of action was for Americans forces to engage the main force NVA in a conventional war near the Cambodian border, while ARVN was to try to deal with the local villagers. The Pentagon decided to go in the opposite direction from Sandy's recommendation. Thus, just before President Johnson was up for reelection, General Westmoreland once again asked the President to increase men and materiel for MACV, and send more aid to the Vietnamese. As the war protesters in front of the White House chanted "Hey, hey, LBJ, how many kids did you kill today?" Vietnam seemed more and more like a bottomless pit. Faced with stark reality, Johnson made a difficult decision: He decided not to run for reelection.

CHAPTER TWENTY-FOUR

The Pentagon having rejected his ideas about the conduct of the war in Vietnam, Sandy turned his attention to the other challenges he had been given: First, he was to examine the problem of developing "smart" artillery shells. The idea was to use computer chips that could guide a shell in flight and thus zero in on targets illuminated by radar. The goal was to be able to guide the warheads with pinpoint accuracy onto a specific point. Second, he was asked to evaluate the question of putting conventional warheads on tactical missiles that were designed to carry nuclear warheads in Europe. In that way, those missiles could be used in a conventional way if the conflict failed to become nuclear. These problems were complicated and time consuming, and Sandy had trouble in concentrating on them. Because Walter was by now well into his year in Southeast Asia, Sandy's thoughts kept drifting back to Vietnam. And Walter's letters didn't bring good news. The 4th Infantry Division where he was assigned became heavily engaged at Dak To in the Central Highlands. This was near the infamous Ia Drang Valley, the site of the first major battle between an American Airmoblie Division and the regulars of the North Vietnamese Army. It was a crucial area. In 1965, that area was where America's first use of an Airmobile Division was attempted, and the North Vietnamese Army in the hills surrounding the valley had reacted violently. A furious fight had ensued there along Route 19 directly into Cambodia. It had become clear that whoever controlled that part of the Central Highlands would control Vietnam. From the very beginning of that fight, the North Vietnamese had also made it clear that they would fight fiercely for that control. In renewed fighting there, Walter had been injured by mortar fragments. Although his letters described his wounds as superficial, he had to be hospitalized. When he was released after three weeks, however, he was not returned to the 4th Division. Instead, he was reassigned. The Americal Division, newly formed and recently arrived, needed combat veterans to strengthen it as it too prepared to enter combat for the first time. Walter and some buddies were sent to the 11th Brigade of the Americal, with further assignment to its Charlie Company. Shortly after Walter joined his new unit, moreover, the 11th Brigade commenced sweep and destroy operations in the Son My District of central Vietnam near the coast, an area that had been a center of guerrilla activity for some time, and Walter was with them. Sandy was even more concerned, because as Walter again moved into contact with a determined enemy, back at Hilton Head, Cathy was giving birth to Walter's son, Paul. Thankfully, mother and child were fine, but Walter's absence and the obviously dangerous situation he was in made this a difficult time for the entire family.

In the spring of that year, Sandy was upset to hear the beginnings of rumors of possible atrocities in the Son My District where Walter had been fighting. Prominent among the hamlets mentioned was one called My Lai. Sources in the Pentagon spoke of helicopter pilots seeing American soldiers firing on unarmed civilians in and around that hamlet. Apparently, some two to three hundred civilians might have been killed, and women had been raped. The word was that the Army Inspector General was undertaking a fullscale investigation, and soldiers who had been in the vicinity of My Lai were being gathered at Fort Benning, Georgia, for questioning and possible indictment.

In August, Walter came home to Hilton Head for a brief leave and to see his new baby. He had eight months left to serve in the Army, and he was indeed being assigned to Fort Benning. When Sandy pressed him about this more closely him on the phone, Walter reluctantly acknowledged he too was under investigation. Sandy immediately requested and received permission to take two weeks leave, and he went to Fort Benning to see the boy.

"What happened?" Andy asked.

"After I was assigned to the Americal," Walter said, "Four of us who had been in the 4th Division went together to Charlie Company. Our company commander was a Captain Medina and our platoon leader was a Lieutenant Calley. Medina was a nut, and Calley was worse than worthless. I don't know how they ever got commissions."

"That's easy," Sandy said. "It was the result of a political decision by President Johnson."

"What do you mean?"

"He analyzed the political landscape and concluded that if he were to declare an emergency in Vietnam, the American people would reject him and he couldn't be reelected. So he tried to hide from the American people the fact that we were in a major war. Because of that decision, nobody could be required to stay in Vietnam for the duration of the conflict. Everybody had to come home in a year."

"But that's nothing but crazy politics," Walter said. "No way to fight a war. Why didn't the Army object?"

"The Chief of Staff, Harold K. Johnson, almost did," Sandy said. "The day President Johnson announced he was sending the 1st Airmobile Division to Vietnam, the Chief realized it would be madness to send them over and then bring them back in a year. So he decided to resign in public protest. He got in his sedan and told his driver to take him to the White House. On the way, he took the four stars off his shirt in preparation for his resignation. Then he had second thoughts. If the President was crazy enough to try to fight a war under those kinds of restrictions, there was no telling what else he might come up with. So General Johnson decided he could better protect the Army by staying at the President's side and attempting to influence him. He put his stars back on and told the driver to take him back to the Pentagon."

"So he didn't protest?" Walter asked.

"No. And as a result, everybody sent over to Vietnam now stays only a year, and then they rotate home, and a new group of officers and men go over. That's why career professionals and junior officers in Vietnam are scarce commodities. They're either killed or they rotate back to the States. And because of the drastic expansion of combat units over there, up to seven Divisions now, the Army has a far greater need for combat arms officers. At the same time, they have far fewer men from which to choose. Thus, many less qualified recruits like Calley and Medina have been shoved through Officer Candidate School and given infantry commissions. Then they're rushed to Vietnam as combat leaders without further training."

"I don't know anything about that," Walter said. "I can only tell you that Calley had difficulty chewing gum and walking at the same time. As a leader, he was damn near incompetent, and Medina was no better. Our company moved aimlessly, without light or noise discipline, and it suffered casualties almost daily, from mines, booby traps, and snipers, without ever seeing an enemy soldier. Nobody in the chain of command seemed to have any idea of how to fight the VC."

"Again, that's because of the rotation system," Sandy said.

"At the infantry platoon level, the sergeant is usually the one who teaches replacements how to survive, but in Vietnam the NCOS also went home after a year in the field. And they left behind only the smallest of institutional memory of how to fight a guerrilla war in the jungle. The best lessons went home with successful, departing soldiers, and everyone had to learn all over again, the hard way. And too many men died needlessly before they had a chance to absorb and master the new system."

"Well, my buddies and I decided we weren't going to be a part of anything like that. We got together and worked out our own system for staying alive, supplied, and ready to fight. I had the M-60 and a good assistant gunner. We got two guys to act as guards against snipers, and as a team we kept each other alive, in spite of what our platoon leader told us to do."

"And thank God you did," Sandy said. "Tell me what happened that day at My Lai."

"It was March 16th," Walter said. "And you know something? That was the same day Paul was born. It's almost eerie when you think of it. Cathy was suffering back here, while I was in a mess in Vietnam. Not good. Anyway, prior to that operation, we'd been having a really bad time. Guys were getting killed or wounded almost every day, and we never seemed to get a fix on the enemy. The night before the attack, we were briefed by Lieutenant Calley. He said the Captain Medina told him that every living being in Song Be Province was VC, NVA, or an active supporter, and My Lai was supposedly the worst hamlet in the entire province. He warned us that the women in My Lai carried weapons under their dresses, and the kids all had grenades to throw whenever we weren't on guard. He stressed revenge. Our guys were already looking for just something like that. The grunts in my platoon were especially angry because just two days before, one of our best guys was captured at dusk. All night long, we heard him screaming off in the jungle. At dawn, we found his naked body on the trail ahead. All his small bones had been broken. His eyes had been gouged out, his ears had been cut off, and he had been castrated. When we saw what they had done, we were all mad as hell and ready to kill someone. So when Calley told us we would be attacking a fortified village that was heavily mined, we were ready for a fight.

"We were to go in shooting. Before dawn that day, we loaded into choppers and flew to a clearing near the village. Just after daybreak, two platoons of us who were with Calley landed and went toward My Lai as a line of skirmishers. Medina was with the third platoon nearby. We were using marching fire. As we moved forward, everybody was firing his weapon directly ahead. Then an odd thing happened. We took no return fire, and we found no mines. Gradually, most of us stopped shooting and simply moved cautiously through the village searching for enemy soldiers. Occasionally, we would find a tunnel and either fire into it or drop a grenade down the opening. Then, I came to a group of villagers huddled in a ditch, and Lieutenant Calley ordered me to fire on them. When I refused, he grabbed my M. 60 and shot them himself. That was the end of it."

"And you never shot an unarmed villager?"

"No, and neither did any of the guys around me."

"But we're hearing rumors that two or three hundred or more villagers died there. And there are reports of rape."

"Well, all I know is I saw Calley shoot into that ditch. I did hear from the guys that Medina did the same thing in another village. But I never saw any rape, nor heard any of the guys talk about that kind of thing. I think I'd have heard about it if it had happened. You know how the guys will talk after a fight, but I heard nothing about anything like rape or murder. On the other hand, ever since March, all sorts of reporters have been nosing around, and you've always told me how they will not hesitate to exaggerate or distort what they hear in order to make up a juicy headline."

That was the end of it. Walter was not indicted, nor were any of his buddies. In the spring of 1969, he finished his term of service, and he entered the University of South Caroline at Columbia to study law. About the same time, the Army indicted Calley, Medina, and eleven others for murder. That was in September. Two months after the Army had already indicted those thirteen man, Seymour Hersh broke the story of My Lai, for which he subsequently received the Pulitzer Prize.

The tragedy of My Lai shocked the American people, and an outcry for justice ensued. Just vigorously, some elements began to justify what had happened. Congress got into the act by calling involved soldiers before various committees to testify, in the process granting immunity and destroying evidence that could have been used in a subsequent court-martial. Depositions disappeared. Memories faltered. Witnesses left the country. In the end, Colonel Eckhardt, the military prosecutor, had only enough evidence to try the two officers. Medina was acquitted because he had not actually been at My Lai. The only person found guilty was Calley, and he was convicted of the murder of twenty-two civilians. He never had to serve his full sentence. President Nixon pardoned him in 1973, the same year Walter graduated from law school.

CHAPTER TWENTY-FIVE

Sandy spent three more frustrating years at the Pentagon, during which time he accomplished very little. His study of smart artillery shells revealed that they were indeed feasible, but under the prevailing production costs and technology they were far too expensive for widespread use in combat. As a result, the Army's decision was to spend more money on research of ways to reduce costs. In a similar manner, his analysis of the potential European battlefield against the Soviet Union showed that the use of conventional warheads on nuclear missiles would likewise be combat effective, and in this case, the cost would not be prohibitive. When he briefed the latter, however, Pentagon staff officers who had a stake in the use of tactical nuclear weapons objected. They did not want to waste a nuclear missile platform to carry a conventional warhead. Their reasoning was that if we fired a missile with a conventional warhead and the conflict turned into a nuclear one, our ability to fight a tactical nuclear war would have been degraded by our having expended that missile. After some debate, the Soviet threat won the day, and like his study of smart shells, Sandy's report on nuclear warheads was shelved. He accomplished nothing except to prove that the Pentagon was not an appropriate place for a field officer.

He despaired at the stifling inactivity of the Pentagon. Apparently the Army wasn't too happy with him either, for in 1970, to his great relief, he was ordered to report to Fort Jackson, South Carolina, where Walter had trained before going to Vietnam. Jackson was a basic training post, and Sandy's mission was an interesting one. He was sent there to explore the feasibility of conducting basic combat training for women.

After Pentagon service, Fort Jackson was attractive indeed. He would be only two hours from Hilton Head, where Cathy was still living. She had stayed there while Walter was in Vietnam. She had also decided to remain on the island while Walter attended law school in Columbia. Such an arrangement would be better for the kids, for Walter and Cathy now had two children, Paul born in March of 1968 and Beth, born October 3rd the next year. Because Sandy had most of his weekends free, he was able to visit Hilton Head often, and he discovered that it was fun to be a grandfather. He never had to change a diaper, and he could spoil the kids as much as he wanted, leaving them with Cathy for the consequences. He even spoke now and then with Nancy, but he never felt a spark there. That phase of his life was effectively over. He wanted no more failures with women.

Because Walter stayed at the university in Columbia during the week, Sandy was able to share an occasional lunch with him. Walter remained reluctant to discuss the My Lai massacre, and Sandy didn't attempt to break through what was apparently a traumatic barrier for him. The closest Walter came to discussing that tragedy was during a brief discussion of his academic study of the laws of land warfare.

"Do your professors think conventional law applies in time of war?" Sandy asked him. "Or is the full application of law suspended for the duration?"

"Somehow, the subject always comes up," Walter said. "And when they find out I was at My Lai, they won't let it drop."

"It's too soon to forget." Sandy said.

"One part of me wants to," Walter said, "but the other side tells me we have to learn from it."

"Why would we learn from My Lai and not Wounded Knee?"

"Wounded Knee was a long time ago." Walter said.

"But a lot of Indian women and children got killed there, just as many as at My Lai. We didn't learn back then. What makes you think we'll do any better this time?"

"We've got better records now. We aren't too certain of exactly what took place at Wounded Knee, but we sure as hell know what happened at My Lai. I know I'll never forget it, and from what I'm seeing now, my guess is the Army will spend a lot of time and effort in making sure My Lai never happens again."

"I hope you're right, but I have doubts."

"Don't be too cynical," Walter said. "Army schools are already starting to put a lot of emphasis on "Just War" theory, the laws of war, and the handling of noncombatants in a combat theater. I'll bet My Lai will be a case study for every course. From start to finish, we can learn a thousand lessons from what happened."

"Spoken like a good lawyer," Sandy said.

"I rest my case," Walter said, and he wouldn't talk about My Lai again.

If relations between Sandy and Walter were as good as could have expected, so were those with Cathy and the kids. With them, he was simply granddad, with all that entailed. That was certainly not the case either with his father and Sara. They remained problems. Andy spent most of his time in his cottage at Destin drinking his bourbon. Aside from watching television, his main activity seemed to be writing nasty letters to any editor who would print them. He harangued reporters who would listen to him. and he let his health deteriorate. After Sandy visited Walter at Fort Benning, he went by the beach place in Destin to see Andy. He found the old man unremitting in his criticism of nuclear testing in the Pacific and our involvement in Southeast Asia. He rambled on about some old Indian curse that he said the Walker family was carrying. In general, he didn't make much sense, and Sandy was relieved to leave him with his sour mash.

Sara wasn't much better, for she turned aside most of Sandy's attempts to restore civil relations, even though she was at Clemson University, only about three hours from Fort Jackson. She was in her freshman year there, her first time away from home, but she wasn't lonely enough to have Sandy around. She evidently wanted nothing to remind her of things military, and she sure didn't want her peace-loving classmates to know her father had served in Vietnam.

Sandy realized Sara had led a rough life. She wasn't as strong as Walter, and she had always seemed more upset about their many moves and Sandy's frequent absences. When Nancy moved to Hilton

Head, however, Sara seemed to settle down and blossom. For the first time, she began to talk about college, and Nancy took her to investigate schools at Columbia, Florence and Rock Hill. She rejected each one. The University of South Carolina at Columbia was a city school that had little charm. Rock Hill and Florence were more rural, but they seemed drab and colorless. When Nancy took her to Clemson, however, the physical beauty of the place immediately won her over. The university was in the foothills of Carolina, out of the coastal heat and absent the lowland humidity and bugs. The campus was laid out on rolling hills with established trees, plenty of open spaces, and excellent housing. Sara gave Clemson thumbs up, declaring it to be exactly what she was looking for, and she enrolled as a member of the class of 1973.

She decided to study computer science. It was a good choice in a fine Department, and it had great potential for her future. The course requirements promised to keep her busy, and at first that was true. But gradually her college years began to coincide with the violent climax of the anti-Vietnam war movement in the United States, a movement that was particularly strong on college campuses. More and more, all over the country, students were protesting and demonstrating. To a lesser degree, that was were happening at Clemson University. At such a conservative school, however, the war opposition was not great. Size was evidently not important for Sara, however, for she was immediately drawn to the small but vocal element on campus that embraced the peace movement. She enthusiastically joined them and be. came a flower child. She wore love beads and sandals, and when Sandy took the initiative to go to Clemson in an attempt to reconcile, she greeted him with the peace sign. It was as if she wanted to show him she had broken completely away from him and his military background. Sandy tried to understand her motives and not criticize.

"War is terrible," she said. "I hate it."

"Yes, I agree," Sandy said. "That's why we as a nation have to put so much emphasis on preventing wars."

"If war is so terrible, why are you a soldier?"

"Soldiers exist to prevent war," Sandy said. "You see, if war comes, soldiers are the first to die, something we soldiers try to avoid at all costs. But if war comes, soldiers have to be ready to fight. If they aren't, they die."

"That doesn't make sense," she said. "You want to be a soldier so you won't have to fight? Baloney."

"Maybe so, but remember how it was when we were younger," Sandy said. "We discovered that the neighborhood bullies only attacked the kids who couldn't or wouldn't fight back. If a guy was strong and ready to fight, he never had to. That's the way it is with nations. We call it deterrence."

"Well, it sure didn't work in Vietnam," she said.

"Point well made, but it could have," Sandy said. "Four American Presidents made some bad mistakes, ones that we're paying for right now. The military learned some lessons too."

"And what lessons might those be?"

"Leadership really does count," Sandy said. "It's the single most important factor. The Vietnam War is a failure of leadership at the national level, just as My Lai was essentially a failure of leadership at the unit level. Like a big poker game, national leaders have to know when to fight, when to negotiate, and when to throw in the cards. And down at the unit level, company commanders have to know the rules of war and how to enforce them. A President is like the largest unit commander. As the top dog, he has to stop the country from heading in the wrong direction, just as the unit commander has to restrain his men in the heat of war. Early in their terms Truman, Eisenhower, Kennedy, or Johnson could have stopped our involvement in Vietnam. The fact that they didn't was a gigantic failure in leadership."

"I still say that's all baloney," she said. "When you send men to war, you turn them into animals, and they will kill. My Lai was murder. I hate it."

"You started this discussion by saying war was terrible," he said. "I agreed with you, but leadership can prevent things like My Lai."

"Nonsense," she said. "My Lai will happen again. That's why I'm a part of the Peace Movement. We have to stop this war." They agreed to disagree.

CHAPTER TWENTY-SIX

Thankful that Sara had never asked about her missing Saint Christopher medal, Sandy deplored his continuing frustration over the women in his life. He had decided that he couldn't maintain a relationship with a woman because he just didn't understand them. The irony of that was his mission at Fort Jackson. That objective was to produce a report about women in the service, specifically the combat arms. The question under review was whether female recruits could take basic training alongside the men at a place like Fort Jackson. Even more important, should they? In the United States, a rising tide of feminism was insisting that women must be included in every aspect of the military, just as men were. And as that tide rose, opposition to that idea naturally appeared. Every action produces an equal and opposite reaction. The most resistance came from conservative military officers. As they increased their opposition to the idea of women in combat, like-minded civilian groups, both veterans and others not accustomed to the inevitability of change, rendered them ample support. None of them were ready to move toward new ideas in any part of society, much less in the military. For them, the idea of sending women into combat was too much of a change. It would be Sandy's task to ferret out the truth and recommend a course of action.

The first thing he did was to try to see and experience everything the male recruits were doing in basic training at Fort Jackson. To accomplish that goal, he naturally attended physical training and parade drills, but that was not all. More than anything else, he was interested in combat training. To experience that, he put on combat gear and went on road marches with recruits. He camped overnight in the field with draftees. He went through their rifle range courses.

He took gas mask instruction and underwent subsequent surprise attacks of tear gas in the field. He went through recruit drills on how to handle a grenade. After two months, he felt he knew what basic training was all about, and he was ready for the next step.

Armed with readily available statistics about the health of teenagers in the United States, he went to as many high schools in the South Carolina area as he could. He attended their gym classes and watched their sporting events, both male and female. His goal was to understand the limitations each class of athletes had to deal with. He picked the brains of as many physical education instructors and coaches as would put up with him. For homework, he studied reports on physical training and analyzed athletic statistics. He had to know what women could and couldn't do.

His first conclusion was easy, clear almost from the start: The average women lacked the upper body strength of the average man. While it was true that a small percentage of American women could be trained and motivated to exceed the average American male, most women could not. What was somewhat surprising, however, was the fact that a large number of American boys also lacked sufficient upper body strength to perform many of the most basic military tasks. If it was true that most women lacked the strength to change the larger tires on many military vehicles, and he had no doubt about that, he was also convinced that an unusually large percentage of teenaged boys also lacked that strength. He remembered seeing grunts struggle in Vietnam with the heavy loads they had to carry in the jungle. After donning their jungle fatigues, boots, and helmet, they picked up their packs filled with extra rations, socks, and water. Then they added their M-16 with plenty of extra ammunition. His experience told him that a grunt so equipped in Vietnam went into the jungle carrying between seventy-five and a hundred extra pounds. Some of then looked like those small Vietnamese paratroopers loaded down with American gear when they had jumped into combat with him west of My Tho. When they hit the ground so loaded, they could barely walk. That was when he decided to include male draftees in his report.

A second conclusion gradually emerged: A large percentage of today's American women weren't psychologically prepared to be warriors. He watched females break out in tears when their drill sergeants corrected their appearance in ranks. Their feelings were hurt, and they responded as females traditionally have. That was okay in basic training, but it would be fatal in the midst of a North Vietnamese human wave attack against a fire support base the female soldiers might be called upon to defend. And while there were some women who were tough as nails and could handle such a situation, most were not.

He then went back to look more closely at statistics on behavior of young men under stress, and he came to additional interesting conclusions. A certain part of the young male population also responded poorly to the kinds of stress a soldier might be expected to face in combat. The percentage of young men who failed stress tests was much smaller than that of the women, but it was there. His recommendation would therefore have to include the fact that both men and women had serious psychological limitations that might make some of them poor candidates for combat roles.

Pertinent to Sandy's study were the results others had realized by including women in combat missions. He found plenty of literature on the subject. He started with legends about the Amazon warriors of the ancient world, and he found that back then the matriarchs were the strength of their societies. Such females both governed their nations and fought in their armies. He then moved on to the warrior women of history: Zenobia led her soldiers in the Middle East, Greek princesses fought the Turks, and Roman female gladiators fought in the arena. Thus, Joan of Arc wasn't the first female soldier in combat before the modern Russians and Israelis let women into their ranks. In American history, moreover, Sandy found that females had fought in every war their men had, from the Revolution to the present. Thus history clearly revealed that women certainly could and would fight if called upon to do so. It was equally clear, however, that most women who had joined the ranks with their men had subordinated their own femininity, like Calamity Jane, in order to fight. It was also abundantly certain that women who were captured in combat would face harsher penalties at the hands of their captors than did their male counterparts. Even those who were not captured made life more difficult for their own units, just because of the intense sex drive of the young men with whom they lived and served, not to speak of their own needs.

After difficult months of interviews, study, and mental anguish, Sandy decided that the answer had to lie in setting out firm requirements for every job that the Army had to offer. What he recommended, therefore, was that the Army develop explicit mental and physical standards for each and every task a soldier could be called upon to perform. Anybody who wanted a job would have to pass the specific standards for that job. Far more importantly, he stressed that everybody would be allowed to compete for any job he or she wanted. To be considered, all he or she had to do was meet the standards. That way, men as well as women who lacked upper body strength for a specific task would be rejected, and the women could not claim discrimination. Men and women who lacked the mental toughness to fight with the bayonet would be equally rejected, and no one could claim bias. Even after much study and sincere attempts to present a sound analysis, however, he realized there were potential flaws in his recommendations. First, there were those in authority who wanted to include more women in the service. These individuals might be tempted to dilute proposed standards so that more women could meet them, and thus liberal concepts of recruiting quotas could be met. Moreover, in the politically correct rush to create requirements women could meet, pundits might destroy a unit's ability to defeat a determined foe. Second, the problem of sexual attraction in the trenches was a conundrum that could not be resolved by anything other than leadership on the part of unit commanders. It was a serious liability he could not ignore.

After a year, he sat down and wrote a draft report. Upon reading it, the commanding general at Fort Jackson thought enough of Sandy's recommendations that he called for a study group to consider them. Fort Jackson's higher headquarters was the Training and Doctrine Command, TRADOC it was called, at Norfolk, Virginia. TRADOC sent an observer to sit in on the study group's meetings.

That observer was Brigadier General Robert Newton. The conflict between Sandy and Newton that had existed for many years became evident early on.

"You never did make much sense, Walker," Brick Newton said at the first meeting. "How in the hell could you write up a standard for every Army task? There're too many of them."

"Recruiters already have to do that," Sandy said. "A good recruit sergeant has to tell every applicant what he or she will be doing in the job the recruiter wants to fill. All we have to do is codify those jobs with special attention to physical and mental requirements."

"We already have a physical training test," Newton said. "That ought to be enough."

"But it's not," Sandy said. "Guys can pass that generalized test and still not be able to perform specific tasks. That's why we have specific tests for those who want to be paratroopers or rangers. We should expand those kinds of tests to include every task in the Army."

"Well the paratroopers sure don't have any mental tests," Newton said. "Look at you."

"But the Language School has a language aptitude test that you have to pass before you get language training. And clerk typists have to demonstrate manual dexterity."

"But you're talking about psychological testing," Newton said. "Are we going to be a bunch of nuts testing more nuts?"

"I wouldn't open that line of questioning if I were you," Sandy said. "There are those who might say we already are doing just that. No, what I'm recommending is that we look at a requirement for a certain amount of aggression in combat soldiers. It seems obvious to me."

"Well, it's not to me," Newton said. "And I'm dead set against putting men and women in close quarters out in the field away from their husbands and wives for long periods of time. If you do that, you're just asking for trouble."

"It's nothing a good leader can't handle," Sandy said. "The Israelis and Russians have done it."

Newton would not budge, and so Fort Jackson decided there was no use in forwarding Sandy's recommendations. Another of his reports went down the drain. Sandy was becoming as bad at staff papers as he was with women. And he knew that his reputation was getting around higher headquarters. Doubting he would ever be selected for promotion to colonel, he began searching for another career. The answer was thrust upon him by another family tragedy.

In the summer of 1973, when Walter finished his study of the law, he passed the examination for the Bar on his first try. It was a time for celebration, and the family began to gather at Hilton Head to do it right. Andy came up from Florida. Penny and retired General Bob Harrison flew down from New York to be with the party. On the afternoon of September 5th, Walter met his mother and Harrison at the Columbia airport, and they set out for Hilton Head. The South Carolina Department of Public Safety was unable to determine exactly what happened in the intricate maze of high-speed exits and entrances of that complex highway system around the Carolina capitol. The happy, excited little group may have been talking too much, and Walter may have taken his eyes off the road for just a moment. The Vietnamese immigrant driving the other car may have been inexperienced, confused, or unable to control his car. Whatever the cause, Walter's vehicle was hit broadside by that driven by the Vietnamese, who crashed into them at a high rate of speed, almost like a guided missile. The impact killed all four of them instantly.

CHAPTER TWENTY- SEVEN

Funeral services for Penny and Walter were held at the National Cemetery in Beaufort, South Carolina, a beautiful, small, low-country city on the mainland a few miles north of Hilton Head. Two hours away at Fort Jackson, Sandy had been working on several training projects with the South Carolina National Guard, and because of that relationship, he was able to prevail upon its Adjutant General to provide an Honor Guard for the ceremony. Sandy also knew and admired a military chaplain at Fort Jackson, a Catholic officer who had served with Sandy in Vietnam with the Tropic Lightning Division, and he persuaded that cleric to do the honors for Walter. The historic cemetery and its century-old chapel were within city limits of Beaufort, near the stately antebellum plantation houses on Pleasant Point. With plenty of low-country brickwork and black iron fencing, the cemetery had a dignified and classic look that provided a peaceful and solemn setting for the painful ceremony. Penny had been so vivacious and full of life, and she was gone. Walter had been through a terrible ordeal in Vietnam. He was just beginning to emerge from those shadows into the sunshine of a new life. They were both cut down prematurely. Walter was in the prime of life, and Penny was searching for happiness. Their tragic end saddened those that had known and loved them.

Andy came up from Florida to be at the ceremony. Sandy hadn't seen his father for five years, and he was nervous about what the old guy would do or say. Sandy's initial impression did little to lessen that apprehension. He was shocked at the old man's appearance. Andy was overweight, with a bloated ring of flesh around his waist and puffed out cheeks. His sallow complexion showed he had neglected even the basic rudiments of caring for himself. To Sandy's surprise, however, Andy held himself a apart from the family and made an effort to behave by neither drinking too much nor boring everyone with his strange observations about nuclear war, military discrimination, and Indian legends. Sandy couldn't tell if his old man was grieving or just getting senile. At any rate, to Sandy's great relief, Andy didn't cause any problems or embarrass the family, and the rest of the family seemed to accept to old man.

The ceremony was beautifully done. The military chaplain gave a simple homily laced with a bit of Irish humor and strong on the trials of this life being what Joseph Conrad had called sunshine and shadow. He told those in attendance that when they too were called to a final accounting, Walter and Penny would be waiting for them in that glorious garden at the end of a tunnel just a little ways down that long, lonely road. Many listeners were seen wiping tears as he finished. A short time later at the adjacent graves, he tossed some dirt on the coffins. Nancy laid flowers on Walter's grave, while Kathleen did the same for Penny. A bugler sounded taps as a squad of riflemen fired the traditional three volleys. The sharp crack of the rifle fire combined with the haunting bugle notes to spread across the morning observers and otherwise silent cemetery, and Sandy hugged Sara to slacken his sense of loss.

As soon as he returned to Fort Jackson, Sandy put in his request to retire. For him, the Army had lost its appeal, and Cathy would need all the help she could muster in raising Paul and Beth. With his small savings, severance pay, and the money Penny had surprisingly left him, he bought a small villa at Palmetto Dunes, the plantation just north of Sea Pines on Hilton Head Island. The development was called Queens Grant, and his two- bedroom place was bordered on one side by a golf fairway and on the other by a manmade lagoon system. He was thus guaranteed good fishing and an endless scene of passing golfers. The first provided serenity and the second a certain degree of much needed hilarity. He was satisfied. After he earned a license to sell real estate, and Kathleen gave him a job, he set out to be the best he could be in the land business.

Cathy had bought a small house in Port Royal Plantation. It was a one-story ranch with three bedrooms and just enough room for her and the two kids. Port Royal plantation was not far north of Palmetto Dunes. Although it was less grand than Sea Pines, it nevertheless had a security gate, two golf courses, and perhaps the widest, most serene beach on the island. Best of all, it was safe, private, and less expensive than the more well known plantations of Hilton Head. And it was a good place to raise kids. Paul was five, and Beth four. Cathy would have her hands full just putting food on the table, and Sandy wanted to help. He determined to do whatever he could to provide extra funds, transportation, and emergency babysitting. Cathy seemed grateful, and even Nancy reluctantly accepted his presence. And when Sara graduated from Clemson University and came back to the island to live and work, she too seemed almost friendly. Their combined acceptance served to assuage his many, sudden losses. Avril and Joy had disappeared so quickly, and Walter and Penny had gone so suddenly, that he had been stunned and shaken by the vacuum created by their collective absences. Being with the remaining family again helped to bring a small degree of closure. Peace and tranquility did not last.

A year after the funeral, Sandy received a phone call from his father. After years of limiting their contact to perfunctory Christmas greetings, the call was a shock. Even more shocking was the content.

"I wanted you to be the first to know, Sandy," the old man said, "I'm getting married."

"What, who, how on earth?" Sandy stammered.

"Her name is Helen," Andy said. "I met her in the South Pacific during the big war, but lost track of her. With Penny gone, I looked her up, and she's agreed to marry me." "Met her in the Pacific?"

"Yes. She was a civilian Red Cross volunteer. That was before the Women's Army Corps was started. She ran a first aid station in the Fiji Islands."

"While you and Penny..."

"Let's not bring that up..."

"Yes, of course," Sandy said. "You're right. Please accept my, I mean our, heartfelt congratulations and best wishes. When will we meet her? When's the wedding?"

"When we can find time, a justice of the peace will tie the knot up in Alexandria, Virginia. She's selling her house there, and I'm selling the family place down here in Destin. We're moving to South Dakota." "South Dakota! Dad, this is too much. What on earth's in South Dakota?"

"The Standing Rock Indian Reservation," Andy said. "We're going to do some work with the Sioux Indians. You're welcome to visit anytime you want. I'll send you our address and phone number when we find a place to live."

That was the end of the conversation. That evening when Sandy announced the news to the rest of the family, they were as shocked as he had been. All agreed, however, that Andy had been acting strangely for years and that this latest move was just more evidence he was getting senile or worse. The good news in his announcement was that someone would now be living with him in his old age and might take care of him. In addition, Sandy reported a note of renewed strength in Andy's voice. The man actually sounded younger.

Perhaps taking pity on Sandy, Sara became more open with him and more able to discuss things without rancor. They had supper, just the two of them almost once a week, and eventually she was able to talk more about her personal life. He learned that one night at Clemson, in the pot-induced stupor of a midnight campus candle protest meeting, she had met the love of her life. He was a hippie with flowers in his dirty, wild, long hair. He was smart as a whip, and just as worthless. He showered attention on her because coming as she did from a military family, she was living proof of the power of his belief in the anti-war movement. After spending two laid-back years together, however, he graduated with some sort of degree in the behavioral sciences, and he announced that he was headed for California in search of year-round sun and the good life.

Sara was strongly tempted to follow her hippie boyfriend, for she truly loved him, but he offered her no encouragement. He didn't seem to care about her, a family, or anything else. Typical of his unsettled generation, his objective was to float through life with no commitment, no job, and most of all, no responsibilities. His goals were endless summers and great pot. His absence brought Sara to a painful but defining reality. Because of that, in 1973 at her own graduation, she faced the truth and decided not to become a California girl. She came home instead, moving in with Nancy and taking a job with Kathleen. Her assignment was to set up the real estate office with the most up-to- date computer data available. With her programming degree, she knew what she was doing, and she set out to upgrade the operations and records of the agency so that it would boast the best technology on the island. She did a great job, and she seemed content. Over the next few years, she dated various eligible young men on the island, but never seriously, and in her late twenties, it looked as if she would never find a replacement for her lost love.

Surprisingly, she seemed to accept this frustrating verdict, and it helped that she was able to express her maternal instincts by assisting Cathy raise Paul and Beth. Knowing her story and seeing how she dealt lovingly with Cathy's kids made Sandy realize how much she deserved another love, one more responsible than her war protester. He wished her good fortune, even as he determined to forget that lost part of his own life. He had settled down to become a top-flight real estate agent, freed from the painful shackles of the past.

CHAPTER TWENTY- EIGHT

Life as a real estate agent was as tolerable as it could be for Sandy Walker. In the spring of 1977, however, he received a phone call from Jon Bourne that shattered his newly found sense of serenity. Jon was excited, and at first Sandy had difficulty in understanding him.

"We've found her," Bourne said. "She's in California."

"Slow down, Jon. Who's in California?" Sandy asked, not daring to hope.

"A young woman who says she's Joy de Castries," Bourne said. "She came out of Vietnam as a boat person and made it to the Philippines. She says she's your daughter, and our people out there believe her story. After they reported her arrival to us, we dug up the papers you signed back in Saigon. Everything seemed to fit. She's the right age, and she remembered just enough to convince us, so we asked them to ship her from Clark Field to California. Because my name's on the case, they notified me. I really think she's Joy."

"Just this once," Sandy said, "I thank God for the State Department. When can I see her? Is she okay?"

She's tired, underweight, and very apprehensive about being in America. It's a strange, new place for her. Other than that. they tell me she's fine, although she evidently has some pretty bad memories. At any rate, I'm prepared to bring her to you and give you custody if that's what you want."

"Of course it's what I want," Sandy said. "How soon can you bring her here?"

"Now that I have your approval," Bourne said, "We can be at the Savannah airport the day after tomorrow. I'll have some papers for you to sign, but that's about it."

Sandy couldn't believe his good fortune. It was Easter, the time of rebirth, and Joy had been given a new life. Then he began to have second thoughts. She would be about fifteen years old. How would he take care of a teenager, especially one who had never seen America? He had no experience in taking care of a teenager, and he wasn't any good with women. The magnitude of the challenge sobered him. When he began to realize how much help he'd need, he turned to Sara.

"A half sister!" Sara asked. "Who is she? Where did she come from? When can I meet her?"

"First things first," Sandy said. "After the divorce, when I went to Vietnam the first time, I met her mother. Her name was Avril de Castries. We fell in love, but she didn't want to leave Vietnam. When my tour was finished, I left without knowing she was pregnant. During the four years before I went back to Vietnam, she never wrote me or told me about Joy."

"But why on earth would she do that?"

"It's a long story, and someday I'll tell you what I really think, " but the only important thing is that when I went back to Vietnam and found Avril again in Saigon at Christmas of 1966, she introduced me to a beautiful little girl. She said her name was Joy and she was my daughter. For many reasons too difficult to explain, I believed her. We spent that weekend together, and then I had to go back to my men. When I left, I gave Joy the Saint Christopher medal you had given me. Thank God I did, for it must have saved her."

"Saved her from what?" Sara asked.

"Two hours after I left her place in Saigon, the South Vietnamese authorities raided the compound. They killed her security guards and took Avril and Joy prisoner.

"My God! What for?" Sara asked.

"They said Avril was a North Vietnamese spy and had stolen secrets from people like me and from the American Embassy where she worked."

"Oh come on, dad, a spy? You're putting me on. How could that happen? It's too much.

"It's all true, Sara. I swear."

"How terrible for you!"

"Believe me, it was a shock."

"What happened to Avril?"

"At a military summary court-martial the day after they captured her, they convicted her of treason. The day after that, they executed her."

"Oh dad, that's horrible," Sara said, and she hugged him as hard as Joy had on the day they had said goodbye. After a moment, she recovered.

"And you had to keep it from us all this time."

"I couldn't think of a way to tell you."

"What happened to Joy?"

"Evidently the Viets put her in some sort of indoctrination camp," Sandy said. "But they wouldn't ever tell me where she was or how she was doing. When I had to leave Vietnam, I signed papers saying that she was my daughter and that I would take full responsibility for her. I wanted her brought to me. After Saigon fell in 1975, I never thought I'd see her again, but she evidently got out of Vietnam on a smuggler's boat and made it to the Americans in the Philippines. After the State Department checked her out, they moved her to California, and my contact called me. She'll be here tomorrow. That's why I need your help. She's a teenager, and she knows almost nothing about America. And I know nothing about teenagers, especially female teenagers. Help me."

"If anybody ever needed help, dad, you do," Sara said. "That poor gal is probably scared to death, and if I know you, you'd make her worse. I'm her only hope, and of course I'll help. What time does she arrive?"

Sara arranged to go with him to the airport. When he picked her up at Nancy's place well over two hours before the flight was due, Sara was grim faced.

"What's the matter," he asked her.

"Mother's not happy about all this," Sara said.

"You told her?"

"Of course I told her," Sara said. "Did you plan on keeping Joy a secret?"

"No, I just hadn't thought about it. Of course you had to tell her. Did she take it real bad?"

"She's not a happy camper," Sara said. "She said some bad things about you guys in Vietnam having oriental mistresses and illegitimate children. She's hurt."

"But she'd already divorced me," Sandy said. "You just don't get it about women, do you, dad?"

Rebuffed again, he lapsed into silence and forgot the lecture he had planned for Sara on how to handle Joy. At the airport, they waited quietly by the arrival gate. Then he saw Bourne coming up the ramp holding hands with a beautiful young girl, a very thin, young version of Avril. A lump appeared in his throat. and he had to hold back tears. When Bourne saw Sandy, he said something to Joy. The girl hesitated and then came slowly toward him. Sandy didn't want to frighten or overwhelm her, but he couldn't stop himself, and he held out both arms to offer a hug. With a cry, she hurled herself into his arms. Tears ran down her face as she squeezed him very hard, while he kept repeating that everything was okay. When she took a breath and backed off to look at him, he saw Sara's Saint Christopher medal, and he had to hug her again. Finally, he took her arm and introduced her to Sara. After a moment, the two of them went off to the lady's room, and Sandy was left alone with Bourne.

"Thanks, buddy," Sandy said. "I owe you big. Now tell me. What did they do to her?"

"Evidently the Vietnamese took her to an indoctrination camp at Ban Loc on the river south of Saigon. They kept her there for almost nine years, until Saigon was about to fall. It was evidently pretty bad, like a prison, work gang, and military school combined. At the end, the prison was just was like the rest of the country. Everything was in chaos. When the VC came to the camp, they told everybody they were free, and she went with some other former prisoners back to Saigon. There, she discovered that Avril's house was almost completely destroyed, and she couldn't find anybody she could trust. She stayed on the streets with other refugees, sort of like a gang of homeless people. Gradually the new regime began to crack down, however, and the kids knew they would be discovered sooner or later. So they pooled everything they could find, steal, or beg and hired a boat captain to take them to the Philippines."

"Why the Philippines?" Sandy asked.

"Well, you may recall that just before the collapse of South Vietnam, we took as many refugees as we could to Clark Field on Luzon and to Guam. Mostly we ferried them out by helicopter, although the Coast Guard and the Navy also helped. At any rate, all those who didn't make it before the end immediately started planning to get there by themselves."

"How many got out?"

"Over a hundred thousand in that first wave, but now we are seeing a continuing mass exodus from Southeast Asia. It's pretty bad. Those that find an honest boat captain to carry them out into the South China Sea stand a darned good chance of being caught by pirates. When that happens, they are robbed, killed, or even worse. So many are making it through to the Philippines, however, that Congress has just passed and President Ford has signed the Indochina Migration and Refugee Act. That act allows refugees to enter the United States under a special status. Those who have sponsors like you can become citizens quickly. Based on current forecasts, the State Department is gearing up to take in a million of them."

"So many? What will happen to them?"

"We start processing them in the Philippines and on Guam. Then they're sent to military bases in California, Arkansas, and Florida where we try to find homes and jobs for them. It's a humanitarian need and a gigantic task. It would take me hours to bring you up to date on it, and I'd be happy to brief you later, but I don't have much time right now, Sandy. You need to sign these paper."

"First, do you know anything more about Avril's death?"

"I can add nothing to what you already know," Bourne said. "Let's not look up a horse's ass. Just sign these things so Joy's legally here and I can make my return flight." Frustrated by Bourne's reluctance to discuss Avril, Sandy turned his attention to Bourme's papers. Just as he finished, Sara and Joy returned. Arms interlocked, they appeared to be deeply engrossed in conversation. From what he could tell, they were already the best of friends. At any rate, Joy seemed

-186-

much more relaxed than when she had emerged from the plane. She almost started to cry again, however, as she said goodbye to Bourne. Then Sandy retrieved her pitifully small bundle of luggage and tossed it into the trunk of the Olds. When the girls got in the back seat, Sandy started to object, but Sara told him to shut up and drive. As they headed for the island, Joy began to talk. Like a dam burst, the words rushed out.

"I don't remember much, daddy, but after you left that Sunday, some wild men jumped over the walls around our house. They were screaming and shooting. They killed several of our guards, including Cousin Ba and Uncle Ly. When they finished shooting, they took mother away and put me in a truck. We drove south for an hour or so to a compound with barbed wire, and they put me in a wooden barracks building with other children. The next day, they told me my mother had been executed for treason and I had to stay there. I wanted to die too, but I couldn't figure out how to kill myself. I was miserable. We had guards and more barbed wire. There were fifty of us in every barracks. Each of us had a bunk, and we shared the showers and toilets. We had a mass kitchen where we helped cook and clean up after the meals. Every day, we had to march and sing patriotic songs. And every morning, we had indoctrination sessions where we had to repeat slogans and chant patriotic poems. In the afternoons, we worked in the garden and rice paddy. If the guards didn't like what we did, they beat us and tortured us. For the next ten years, when any of the children got old enough, they were transferred either to the army or the women's volunteer corps. Even then they were still in prison, because the parole system guaranteed that if you made trouble, they would bring you back to our camp and put you in solitary confinement where the food was even worse."

"Did the guards abuse you?" Sandy asked.

"What kind of a question is that?" Sara asked.

"No," Joy said. "It's all right. Many were abused, but for some reason, they left me alone."

"How did you get out?"

"It was in 1975," Joy said, "and the government in Saigon was losing control of everything. One day, some VC soldiers appeared around our camp, and the ARVN soldiers guarding us surrendered. The VC came into the barracks and told us we were free. Then they left, taking the ARVN soldiers away as prisoners with them. At first, we didn't know what to do, but then we decided we had to take a chance and get away. So those we trusted gathered together and worked out a plan. We hitchhiked to Saigon. I went to our house near the Continental, but it was smashed to the ground in rubble, and nobody was around. Most of us ended up in the Chinese section of Cholon, and we sort of organized a gang. We hustled money and even stole things we could sell. We lived together in abandoned buildings and talked about what we should do. Then Saigon fell to the Communists, and the new regime started to crack down on crime and the homeless people like us. We had to try to escape before we were rounded up and put back in prison. We heard stories about people who were leaving illegally by boat, and we decided to try that. We would have done almost anything rather than stay there. We were miserable and frightened, so when we had the bare minimum amount of the money they said we needed, we contacted a smuggler. He agreed take us, and we gave him everything.. to At first we were afraid he would just take the money and disappear or betray us, but we were lucky. He kept his word and met us on anyway, the river south of Saigon. There were too many of us for his boat, and we didn't have enough to eat, but we went just to get away. After five days on the water, we were all starving and seasick, when a motorized junk appeared. We hoped they would save us, but they turned out to be pirates. They came after us and quickly captured our little boat. Then they began shooting, raping, and killing, and then two of them grabbed me and I thought I was going to die. Then suddenly, a big coast guard ship showed up. They must have been following the pirates. They were Americans, and the massacre stopped as quickly as it had started. Thank God the Americans took us on board, fed us, and carried us to the Philippines. Once we were there, the refugee camp at Clark Field was almost luxurious after the ARVN indoctrination camp in the Delta and the empty buildings in Saigon where we had hid. I was just happy to be safe and have enough to eat. They asked me questions, and I told them what I remembered about you.

I showed them the medal you had given me. Then they took my fingerprints and told me everything would be okay. I didn't know whether to believe them or not, but after Mr. Bourne contacted me, I knew I would be all right. He was wonderful. He got me through, and now, everything is going to be fine."

She stopped talking. And when Sandy looked in the rear view mirror, she was asleep in Sara's arms. Tears were flowing down Sara's face.

CHAPTER TWENTY-NINE

Over the course of the next five years, Sandy's expanded family dramatically changed his life for the better. These were times of great happiness. Joy lived with him in the Queen's Grant villa, and with the resiliency of youth, she rapidly assimilated American culture. Understandingly, she had the most difficulty with her schoolwork. After all, she had had no formal schooling for ten years, and so she had much to make up. Add to that an overwhelming culture shock and a significant language challenge, and you would have expected her to have problems. After a few months, however, she began to show signs of steady improvement. Hard work, native intelligence, and an innate desire to excel drove her. Most of all, she seemed happy to be reborn as an American teenaged girl. Glorying in her newfound freedom, she discarded the Vietnamese au dai for blue jeans and a sloppy shirt. She cheered the Sea Pines basketball team and learned all the current dance crazes. In short, she became an outwardly normal girl. Yet Sandy knew she wasn't. She had unpleasant memories, and Sandy worried about her repression of them. Whenever he mentioned the subject to Sara, however, his daughter reassured him that Joy was happy just to be alive and rapidly becoming well adjusted.

The change in Sara was even more miraculous. Whether it was because Sandy was no longer in the Army she hated or because she had assumed responsibility for Joy, she was fundamentally a very different person. She took a direct interest in Joy's education, both in high school and in American life. Gone was her pessimism about the United States and the "fascist" government that she had protested against during the years of the Vietnam War. In its place was a cheerful young lady who was ready to assume responsibility for herself, her work, and others. She took more care in her personal appearance, and men began asking her out more often. Joy too shared in the happiness of that change, and Sandy marveled at it.

Both Sara and Joy helped Cathy raise Paul and Beth. Although Paul was emerging into his teen years as a fine young man, Beth was the one who matured first. Maybe girls tend to cover up their struggle toward maturity, but to Sandy, Beth seemed to make the transition more quickly. Even though she was the younger of the two, moreover, Beth had Sara and Joy to help her through the difficult adjustment into young adulthood. While Paul was still an awkward boy struggling to become a man, Beth was therefore rapidly becoming a beautiful young lady who awed her friends and intimidated the boys. Both she and Paul were a pleasure to watch, and Sandy was a happy grandfather indeed.

Over those same five years, Sandy's understandably cool relationship with Nancy began to warm. Once Sara explained to Sandy how difficult it was for Nancy to accept the fact of Avril's past role in his life and the mere existence of Joy, he took care to mollify Nancy and attempt to be positive whenever they met. After all, they were both involved in Kathleen's real estate firm, and it was in everybody's interest they work well together. At any rate, when Nancy saw what a lovely young lady Joy was turning out to be and how much help she gave to Cathy and Beth, Nancy mellowed considerably. Sandy was grateful for that. He needed no more conflict as he worked at his transformed life and in his new career. He thought he was doing a good job of converting himself from the dangers of combat to the challenges of civilian life. He told himself he was grateful for the difference and resigned to a peaceful life in retirement, and he settled down to be a good family man and island citizen. He was able to enjoy life without stress until the spring of eighty-two, when Jon Bourne called once again.

"I'll be in Savannah tomorrow," he said. "We have to talk."

"What about?" Sandy asked. "It's not about Joy, is it? She doesn't have to leave does she? She's doing really well."

"No, it's not entirely about Joy," Bourne said. "Don't worry about it. Just meet me at the airport, alone. Let me emphasize that again: come alone."

How could he not worry? Sandy didn't like Bourne's saying they had to talk. And alone. About what? And why such insistence on secrecy? Sandy thought he had heard an urgent tone in the other's voice, and he didn't like the sound of it. His stomach knotted, and the old stress started all over again. Bourne was a strange one, and his call had bought back memories, bad memories that made for a restless night. Because of his lack of sleep, Sandy was up early and waiting when Bourne showed up at the Savannah Airport departure gate. To Sandy's great relief, moreover, Bourne seemed cheerful, friendly, and eager to talk. They moved to a small conference room in the terminal, where Jon lost no time in starting at Sandy.

"I have some bad news and some good," Bourne said.

"And it is very important that I have your cooperation about both. As you military guys say, do you Roger that?"

"Roger, Wilco," Sandy said. "Remember, I owe you."

"Then I'll tell you the bad news first," Bourne said. "I have been less than truthful to you on a very important matter, and 1 want to apologize for that. I can only tell you that national security needs concerning sensitive operations in Vietnam dictated that I had to conceal certain things from you. I hope you can accept that."

"Apologies accepted," Sandy said, fearing the worse. "No matter what happens from now on, I owe you for bringing my daughter to me."

"Thanks. Now before I tell you the good news," Bourne said, "I must ask that you not repeat what I say to anyone. Again, it's a matter of national importance."

"You're being mighty mysterious, buddy. What's up?"

"I'm about to tell you," Bourne said, "but first I need your word not to reveal what I'm about to say. Okay?"

"Okay," Sandy said. "You have my word."

"First of all, I have to confess to you that I'm with the Agency, and I have been for some years. And that included the time when we were in Vietnam together and I had a cover job at the American Embassy."

"You mean the Agency in McLean?"

"That's the one," Bourne said. "But if you tell anybody, I'll have to kill you."

"Very funny. That can't be the good news."

"No, the good news is that Avril's alive."

CHAPTER-THIRTY

Stunned and not quite comprehending what Bourne had just said, Sandy didn't react at first. He stared at the man as if he wanted to be sure of what he had heard and exactly what it meant. Finally, he found his voice.

"Say that again, will you?"

"Avril's alive, and she needs your help."

"But you told me repeatedly that she'd been killed."

"I had to. We had to protect her."

"You're lying."

"I had to, back then. I'm telling the truth now."

"How can I tell?" Sandy asked. "You're not making much sense, and I don't understand a thing you're saying. Why don't you start all over again? Take it from the top?"

"Okay, but this is the part you can't repeat. Avril was my agent in Vietnam. She worked for us. For almost ten years, I was her control officer."

"She was an agent?" Sandy asked. "I thought she was an agent of the Communists."

"We wanted them to think that."

"The Communists?"

"Yes. We needed her as a double agent."

"How did all this happen?"

"When the North Vietnamese first contacted her," Bourne said, "back in the mid-fifties, she came to me and asked what she should do. I decided she should play along with them and see what kind of information she could turn up for us. She agreed, and that was when she became our agent."

"And when did you say that was?"

Sandy's War

"The mid-fifties. Well before you came on the scene. By the time you met, she had been working for us and doing a great job for almost five years, and we had to protect her. She knew the system inside and out, and because of her contacts, she was invaluable."

"But Joy said that the South Vietnamese stormed her house, captured her, and killed the men guarding her. Why would they do that if she was working for us? It doesn't make any sense."

"The ARVN intelligence officers didn't know she was working for us, and I couldn't tell them. They had too many leaks. Half of them were NVA sympathizers, and the rest talked too much. She would have been killed by the Communists."

"But you said they tapped her phone?"

"That's right. ARVN began hearing strange rumors, and when people started pointing at her, they thought they'd caught a big one. We had no way to stop them without revealing to the other side that she was a double agent. That would have destroyed our network, compromised the other agents she was working with, and killed a lot of good people, including her."

"But how could you let the South Vietnamese try her?"

"We had to let the trial play out. When they convicted her and sentenced her to death, that's when we stepped in. We bribed a few people and had her smuggled out to a halfway house up at Da Lat. In the chaos that was South Vietnam, she was able to stay there until Saigon fell, but we couldn't tell anybody. Too much was involved."

"Then how'd you explain when she showed up alive?"

"We got to her last brother, the one who didn't die during the Tet Offensive. We persuaded him that she had been under interrogation the whole time. The cover story was that she'd been tortured but hadn't ratted on his guys. He believed us, and she came out a heroine."

"You're a prick, a big red one," Sandy said. "It takes a sick, devious mind to do what you do. At least you could have told me."

"No, I couldn't," Bourne said. "You know that. You'd have raised bloody hell with the wrong people. And when you did that, the word would have leaked out, and a lot of our people would have died. Many of our most productive operations would have been compromised, ceased, or cancelled. Worse yet, we'd have never gotten Joy to you. As it was, we were able to protect her while she was in that camp all those years, and we were looking to help her when she and her group made a break for it." "I'm not sure whether I should hit you or kiss you."

"Neither, please," Bourne said. "The best is yet to come, old man. She's here in the States, and she wants to see you."

"When? How?"

"The new government in Ho Chi Minh City, the place you called Saigon, wants desperately to improve relations with the United States, and they've quietly sent over an exploratory team to see what can be done. It's a cultural exchange, and Avril had all that experience with our cultural attaché in the American Embassy. So she was a natural for this mission, and because she was a national hero to the Communists, they included her. We feel that she can defect without compromising what's left of her contacts in Vietnam. We're ready to set it up if you'll go along with us and not spill the whole story. How about it?"

"You have my word," Sandy said, holding out his hand. "Just let me be a part of it. Do it as fast as possible, and give her refugee status."

"That's been done," Bourne said. "Everything's already been set up. At a cultural conference in Washington next week, we'll grab her, and you can help. Then we'll bring her down here. I'll have all the necessary papers. We'll release her to your custody, and it'll be up to you to protect her after that."

"Do you have to kidnap her, or will she defect?

"She's going to defect, but we'll make it look like we kidnapped her."

"How are you going to do all this?"

And so they began to discuss the details and work out how the defection-kidnapping would be attempted. Sandy listened and answered Jon's questions, contributing what her could. All the while his mind was working a mile a minute, as he considered the possibility that at the age of fifty-six, he was about to jump-start his life again.

CHAPTER THIRTY-ONE

All during the following week, Sandy had to remain silent about a trip he was suddenly planning to Washington D.C. By the time he left for Washington National Airport, his anxiety had grown, yet he couldn't talk to anyone. Bourne had repeatedly warned him not to say a word about his real purpose for going to the nation's capital. Jon stressed that if even the slightest hint of Avril's defection were to leak out, the Vietnamese would react by closely guarding her until they could put her back on a plane to Vietnam. There, she would be subject to torture and intimidation, the real thing this time. Thus, Sandy had made up a lame excuse about needing to check his retirement papers at the Pentagon, and he slipped away quietly. Now, at National Airport, he nervously watched fellow passengers and people who had met the plane at the gate, trying to make sure that no one was watching or following him. As planned, he stopped at a small airport bar for a beer and a burger, all the while surveying those around him. When he was finally satisfied that no one had noticed him, he went to meet Bourne just outside the baggage retrieval area. Acting the part of an amateur spy, he felt foolish, but he took no chances. As arranged, Bourne was waiting in an unmarked, black limousine at the curb. Sandy ducked inside and the vehicle quickly sped away.

"I'm not made for this kind of work." Sandy said. "I don't know who the enemies are. I don't think anybody followed me, but I can't be sure."

"Not to worry," Bourne said. "We'll take care of them. You did great. Now that you're safely here, we can fill you in on the final plan to rescue Avril."

"When do we do it? Where?" Sandy asked.

"Saturday at the Jefferson Memorial next to the Tidal Basin and immediately adjacent to the Potomac River. It's the perfect time and place. The cherry blossoms are in full bloom, and that area is a favorite place for tourists like the Vietnamese delegation."

"When did you say?" Sandy asked.

"This Saturday. The cherry blossoms are especially colorful this year, a vivid pink, and large crowds will be wandering around the memorial. While they're taking pictures, enjoying what the weather forecast says will be a fine spring day and picnicking on the lawns, we'll use them as cover."

"Why would the Viets go there?" "Because of Uncle Ho," Bourne said. "The Vietnamese delegation had to include a visit to the memorial because of Ho Chi Minh's great admiration for Thomas Jefferson and our Declaration of Independence. You may not know it, but during Ho's thirty years of exile and struggle, first against the French and then against the Japanese, he had plenty of time to study how a nation like the United States might become and remain free. In doing so, he learned of Jefferson's many achievements, including the drafting of the Declaration. Ho's respect for Jefferson became so great that after World War Two when he took over North Vietnam, he opened his first speech as the leader of that newly freed nation with American OSS officers standing beside him as he quoted freely from the Declaration of Independence. So now, North Vietnam's current leaders want to see for themselves what Uncle Ho was talking about. The memorial commemorates Jefferson's many achievements, and so they put it on their itinerary. When I learned that they would actually come to the site, I decided to set up Avril's escape there. While the others are taking in the memorial, we'll take Avril."

"But the place will be crowded," Sandy protested.

"And that will make it easier for us. You'll see."

The Saturday in question was the 11th of April, right in the middle of that two-week period when the Japanese cherry blossoms were indeed in glorious full bloom. When that day arrived, the memorial and Tidal Basin were crowded with thousands of visitors taking in that vivid beauty. And the weather forecast proved to be correct. Many picnic blankets were spread on the grass, lovers wandered with cameras in hands, and couples paddled their rented pontoon boats around the quiet tidal basin next to the memorial. The large numbers of visitors fit well into Bourne's abduction plan. Because of them, and well before the arrival of Avril's group, the Agency was able inconspicuously to place twenty-five agents in the area. An escape limousine with darkened windows and a uniformed driver was parked under police guard at the curb nearest the Fourteenth Street bridge on the western side of the complex. As Sandy waited within that car, he reflected on the irony of the moment. His family migrated to western Ohio in the early nineteenth century after Jefferson's Louisiana Purchase created new opportunities on the American frontier. Theirs and many other lives were forever changed by Jefferson's foresight. Today, the great President's memorial would offer a new life to a fugitive from Vietnam.

Bourne's plan of operation was simple. Avril didn't know how or when she would be freed. She only knew that when she saw Sandy, she was to go quietly to him. The simplicity of the plan appealed to Sandy, because in love or war, KISS, keep it simple stupid, had long been a favorite axiom for him. At Bourne's signal, Sandy's job was to get out of the car and walk toward Avril until she saw him. When she came to him, he was to take her by the arm and walk, not run, with her to the waiting car. Bourne's men were poised to close quickly in behind the couple and prevent anyone from seeing where they went and following them. Bourne expected no trouble. Even so, his men were armed. Sandy was not.

Fortune smiled on them, for when Saturday arrived, the day was bright, with a moderate breeze that gently dispersed the sparkling sunshine. The glorious cherry blossoms were a good omen, Sandy thought, as he waited in the car and marveled at the crowd in and around the memorial. So many visitors were out enjoying the day that Sandy began to worry about being able to locate Avril in the midst of the crowd. He need not have concerned himself, for shortly after noon, an escorted bus appeared. Carrying the Vietnam delegation, it was clearly visible as it came down Fourteenth Street and turned into the Bureau of Printing and Engraving, where a special parking area had been set up for it. Waiting guides then ushered the Vietnamese out of the bus and began to herd them through the other tourists toward the memorial. As they went, the guides tried to explain about Jefferson and his many achievements. They were approaching the site from the east, and that put the majority of the dense crowd between Sandy and Avril. The congestion was both good and bad. It prevented the Vietnamese from seeing his limousine, but it also made it difficult for Sandy to keep track of them. He craned his neck to see Avril, but at first he couldn't find her, and he worried that the rescue attempt might have to be aborted. Then he thought he caught a glimpse of her, more graceful and beautiful than he remembered. Almost shaking with eagerness and anxiety, he waited for Bourne to radio the signal. Then the driver spoke.

"Okay, Colonel," he said, "Now it's up to you."

Trying to hold his anxiety in check, Sandy deliberately got out of the car and walked slowly toward her, pretending to admire the Japanese cherry trees, and trying not to attract attention. Then he saw her more clearly. Like the first time they had met, she was wearing a white au dai with a high collar. She seemed tired, but she had the same black hair, high cheekbones, and bronzed complexion he had remembered all these years. The remainder of the Vietnamese delegation was clustered around her, and Sandy was afraid she wouldn't see him and he couldn't reach her. The entire group was busily engrossed in interpretation of the inscription etched into the white-marble, circular band around the upper rotunda. It read "I have sworn upon the altar of God eternal hostility against every form of tyranny over the mind of man," and the guides were struggling to explain that concept. Sandy moved closer, hoping she would notice him while the rest were focused on the memorial and the words of their guides. For the longest time, he was unable to catch her attention, yet he hesitated to approach closer for fear of attracting the attention of her guards. Because she was wearing dark sunglasses, moreover, he couldn't see her eyes and know exactly where she was looking. He knew she was searching the crowd, however, because she wasn't following the words of the tour guide who was explaining the inscription on the memorial. For what seemed an hour, she stood there casually, glancing around. Then she turned her head his way, and suddenly her body language changed. She stiffened and her whole aspect tensed. The difference was so clearly evident that Sandy was afraid it would alert one of the men with her. They were clearly bodyguards, and they looked as if they could cause trouble. Avril paused for an instant, as if measuring her chances. Then she moved toward Sandy, carefully threading her way through the people around her. She seemed to be in a daze, for she moved stiffly, as if hypnotized. As he reached out to her, the crowd around them suddenly surged and cut off the other Vietnamese. Sandy took hold of her arm to guide her toward the waiting car. Heart about to burst, he moved slowly and deliberately. At any moment, he expected to hear shouts and the sounds of sudden alarm and pursuit. Nothing happened, however, until he had almost reached the car. Then he heard the sounds of some sort of commotion coming from the direction of the delegation behind them. Quickly, he shoved her into the back seat and dove in behind her, and the vehicle roared away from the curb, heading for the bridge to Virginia. He took her in his arms.

"You're safe now," he said.

She collapsed against him, sobbing without attempting to stop. She had broken from the land of her birth. The transition had been hazardous, even painful, yet she had done it. In some sort of mystical way, her child had led her to this new place. It was Easter, and like Joy before her, she had been reborn. She had been holding back her emotions for so long. Now she was free, and she couldn't hold back the tears.

CHAPTER THIRTY-TWO

He continued to hold her as the pent-up emotions of years gushed out and she sobbed almost hysterically. By the time they reached the National Airport ten minutes later, however, her tears had subsided and she had quieted, although she looked crushed and small, barely able to breathe. When the driver had maneuvered the limousine into a special parking area, Bourne's agents were waiting to usher the two of them quickly into a small conference room just inside the departure building. By then, she was almost calm. That was important, because a video camera had been set up and was waiting for her. Bourne's agents were to question her and record her statement.

"Today, April the eleventh, 1982, I, Avril de Castries, a citizen of Vietnam, am defecting to the United States and asking for asylum. I do this of my own free will because I fear for my safety in my country. I have a daughter living in the United States. I want to join her and become an American citizen."

The tape was to be held in reserve in case the Vietnamese attempted to go to court, the United Nations, or the Congress to press for her return. While the agents made sure their tape was clean and its sound good, Avril and Sandy signed papers that cleared the way for her to remain in the United States with him. Within the last year, Congress had set up procedures that would speed and ease her path to American citizenship. The papers having been signed, Bourne took Sandy aside. "They may come after her, Sandy." He said.

"I'll get a concealed carry permit," Sandy said.

"We can help," Bourne said. "We'll always be around, but you need to stay on the alert. Don't let your guard down. If you see even a hint of the bad guys, just call."

Then Bourne and the agents escorted Sandy and Avril out to an executive jet waiting on the tarmac. It was all very safe, secure, and businesslike, but Sandy couldn't relax until they were in the air and headed for Savannah.

"Where are we going?" she asked. "Is Joy there?"

"Hilton Head," he said. "You remember I told you about that island on the South Carolina coast. Yes, she's there. Well, actually, she's at school, at a college not too far away."

"She's in college?"

"She sure is," he said. "She's worked hard and done well. She passed the entrance exams, and she's at a place called Clemson University, in the mountains about five hours away. That's where my daughter Sara went. I'll explain later, but for now Bourne has sent some guys there to pick her up and bring her home. They're probably in the car and on the way right now. She should be home not much after we arrive."

"Is she okay? What's she like? You realize I haven't seen her since she was four years old?"

"She's a beautiful young woman," Sandy said. "You may be in for a shock, tho, 'cause she's an American teenager, with all that means. She's in her freshman year, living in the dorm where Sara lived. The two of them are the best of friends, and they've been great for each other."

"Does she know I'm here?"

"No, none of the family does," Sandy said. "We couldn't tell anybody about you until you were safe. If anything had leaked, those goons with you would have reacted immediately, and that would have killed your rescue chances, maybe even you. But I suspect that by now Bourne will have called his men and told them to give her the news."

"It's been such a long time," Avril said. "They kept me a prisoner in that house for more than eight years, until Saigon fell. And then I had to work for the new Communist government and help them take control in the south."

"Where did you live?"

"Because they thought I was a hero of the State, they let me rebuild the house in Saigon. It was a slow and difficult process, and through it I lost another seven years. And now I've lost the house again. I'm so tired, and I feel so old."

"Why don't you rest?" Sandy asked. "We'll talk later."

"I can't stop thinking about it," she said. "When you came to see us that last time, watching informants immediately passed the word that you were there. And even as you were getting to know Joy, they were planning to kill you. I wanted to tell you, but Jon said I couldn't. I'd expose my friends and they'd die. I was going to tell you anyway, but he said he'd have an ARVN unit protect you. I wasn't sure about him. I never was. So even in spite of what he said, I whispered to you and tried to warn you when we said goodbye, without anybody knowing."

"Well, you did. It worked," Sandy said. "I knew something was up, and when they came at us, we were ready for them. They hit us out near Hoc Mon. It was a scary moment, but Jon's three armored cars showed up just in time. My driver got hit, but he's okay now."

"But I didn't know what had happened. Even when they put me on trial the next day, I didn't know if you were alive or dead. When they convicted me of spying and sentenced me to die the following day, I was ready to go, because I thought you were already dead and I had killed you. The morning after the trial, when they came to get me, I thought they were going to put me in front of a firing squad. Instead, they took me to a sedan. Jon was waiting in the car. He told me you were alive. He had bribed a few people, and I was going to the hills of Da Lat under house arrest. I was to stay there and never to talk to anyone about what I had been doing for him. He told me that he had Joy under protective surveillance and he could keep her safe as long as I didn't talk. But if my story got out, he couldn't stop them from killing her. Being up there and keeping quiet about everything was agony. At first, when the North Vietnamese took over, I thought I would be able to find her, but she had disappeared. Nothing changed. Then my brother came to get me. Jon had found him and arranged for my release, but I couldn't tell even him the real story. He still believed I was an NVA agent. That was why he helped me get a job with the new government. And still I couldn't tell anyone. It was all hidden inside of me. Jon told me Joy had fled as a boat person. Then he sent a message that she was safe in America. He was also smart enough to know that the North Vietnamese would want to start an effort to restore relations with the United States. He told me they would need people like me for that effort, and he urged me to prepare for that. So I worked myself into a job with their task force. It paid off when they decided to send a delegation to Washington. I was frantic with worry until I got the word that they wanted me with them. I was to help with translation and the people I had known at the American Embassy in Saigon. After we arrived in San Francisco, our first efforts were to contact some of the North Vietnamese agents who had fled among the others and were living in California. That gave Jon time to contact me and tell me you would be able to help me defect. Still I had to keep quiet, until now. Now I can talk about it, and be with you, and see Joy after all these years. It feels so good. I'm so happy." Exhausted, she fell asleep. As he looked into her face, he could see the lines of fatigue and worry. Those would eventually go. She had a struggle ahead. She had never been out of Vietnam. Now she had left her country behind and had come to him with nothing except herself. It was enough. With the bad years and many tears behind her, she would prosper as Joy had. Life would be full again.

CHAPTER THIRTY- THREE

At the Savannah airport, Bourne's agents escorted them to the car Sandy had left there. They stood guard as Sandy loaded Avril and his luggage into the car. Then they let him use their radio-phone to call Sara.

"Meet me at the villa in an hour," he said.

"Why? What's wrong?" she asked.

"Nothing. Everything's right," he said. "But please come. It's important."

Then he shook hands and thanked the agents. They offered to follow him over to the island, but he declined, and they stood by watchfully as he got into the Olds and pulled away. Suddenly, he felt very much alone. He was unarmed, yet he was responsible for her. He looked in the rearview mirror to see if anyone was following him. Nobody. The poor woman. Bourne had packed a bag for her and put it in the plane, and that was her only luggage. Sandy was now the only person she knew in this strange land. What a shock it all must have been for her. She had left her whole life behind her, and she owned only what she had on her back. It must have taken a great deal of courage. His heart went out to her. She had a lot of catching up to do. They both did.

The hour's drive from the airport was uneventful. Avril spent most of the time staring in wonder at the passing scene of the South Carolina low country, so different from the flooded Vietnamese rice paddies and bustling Saigon. He wanted to comfort her, reassure her, bring her back to reality.

"Sara has done a great job of helping Joy make the transition to life in America," he said.

"How Joy has suffered," she said.

"Yes, but that's over now," he said. "She made it, and so can you. You'll see."

"So many have died," she said.

"Too many," he said. "Walter's gone, you know. That's why I left the Army. I wanted to help Cathy raise Paul and Beth."

"How did he die?" she asked.

"A car accident," he said. "But Sara and Joy stepped in to help Cathy with Beth. And that helped them too, made them more mature. They are all very close now, a stronger family. You'll be a part of that, and it will be even stronger."

When they were almost to the island, she asked only one more question. It was the obvious one.

"And your wife, Nancy," she asked, "how is she taking all this? Are you seeing her?"

"You mean my ex-wife. Well, Sara explained to me that it would be only normal for Nancy to be jealous of Joy and angry about you, so I have been careful to make sure she had no reason to harbor resentment. Over the years, Joy won her over, and she has let me off the hook. But no, I'm not seeing her. Or anyone else for that matter. I couldn't erase your memory. Nobody interested me. I'm glad, now that you're here. I want you to stay with me."

She reached over and put her hand on the back of his neck, gently rubbing. Then she put her other hand on his leg and lightly caressed him.

"It's been a long time," she said. He was smiling as he drove into Palmetto Dunes and up to the Queen's Grant villa. He half hoped that Sara wouldn't be there and that he and Avril could be alone for awhile, but Sara's little Volkswagen beetle was out in front. When she heard the Olds pull up, she came to the door.

"Sara," Sandy said. "I have another surprise for you. This is Joy's mother, Avril. She's defected from Vietnam, and we're going to be married."

"She's not dead. ." Sara began. Then she stopped and stared, the many questions implicit.

"No, the CIA faked her death to save her life. She couldn't tell anyone. Not me, not even Joy. She's been in prison for fifteen years, but all that's over now, and she's free."

"My God. Does Joy know?"

"The Agency sent some men up to school to get her," Sandy said. "She's on her way home as we speak, and they must have told her by now."

Sara slowly came down the steps and went to Avril as if in a daze. At first she simply held out a hand, but then she reached out her arms to offer an embrace. Avril began to cry again as she fell into Sara's arms. Sara took her into the house. And when Joy arrived an hour later, Bourne's agents had indeed told her everything. She came flying into the villa for another tearful reunion. The two of them lapsed into a mixture of Vietnamese, French, and English. Even Sara somehow seemed able to join in, but Sandy was excluded. The women had shut him out again. All he could do was to send out for pizza.

Avril and Sandy were married at the little church on Highway 278 across from Port Royal Plantation. Somehow, the media got word of Avril's background and did a story about the happy couple. Thus, the chapel was filled with family, friends, clients, and curiosity seekers. So many of these last came that some attendees even had to stand in the rear and around the sides under the high, stained-glass windows. At first, Sandy worried that the unwanted publicity might come to the attention of a terrorist Vietnamese agent bent on revenge, but Jon Bourne volunteered to attend along with a few friends from the Agency, and Sandy was able to relax. The local minister was a slim, handsome man with a down-to-earth preaching style, and he did the honors for the ceremony. The Walkers were well represented. Paul brought his girlfriend, Jo, and Cathy came with Beth, Joy, and Sara. This wasn't unusual, for more and more, the women had taken to hanging out together. Sandy's sister, Kathleen, came with her husband, even though lately she had been complaining of fatigue and high blood pressure. And in the end, even Nancy relented and agreed to attend, mostly because Joy insisted she be there. After the ceremony, the newlyweds didn't leave the island for a honeymoon.

Avril assured Sandy that after spending so many years in wartorn, now Communist, Vietnam, Hilton Head was a wondrous getaway vacation for her, and she had had enough travel. To allow the newlyweds a small measure of intimacy, Joy elected to move out of Sandy's Queen's Grant villa. She and Sara rented a small villa in Palmetto Dunes. And so the Walker family settled down to their new lives on Hilton Head, which remained beautiful even as it added paved streets, traffic lights, new developments, and ever more tourists.

Because the women were such a closely-knit group, however, Sandy had time to take more and more interest in Paul. Over the years, Sandy's relationship with the boy began to ease the pain of losing Walter. He found that Paul was an all-American guy. Smart and serious in high school at Sea Pines Academy, he also played varsity quarterback in the T-formation. Like most of the Walker men, he was big, calm under fire, and quick with his hands. Sandy took some credit for Paul's ability to throw a football, because they played catch in the back yard almost daily, but that may have been presumptuous, because Paul was a natural athlete. Although he was strong and coordinated, however, he wasn't speedy or quick, so he never ran for the Sea Pines track team. Instead, he was a field man, putting the shot, hurling the discus, and throwing the javelin. He stayed in great shape all year round, and he kept Sandy fit by insisting that they exercise and run together whenever they could. Paul liked people, and he had many friends. Intellectually curious, the military fascinated him, and whenever he asked, Sandy told him stories about weapons, radios, combat, and the like, always emphasizing that soldiers were nothing more than kids from hometowns all over America. Just like him, they were real guys with hopes and fears. Sandy got as much from their relationship as Paul did, and he hoped it would never end. That hope was not realized, for the end came sooner than he had ever thought possible.

The day after his eighteenth birthday, Paul drove to Fort Jackson and volunteered for the Army.

CHAPTER THIRTY-FOUR

Paul's sudden act, carried out with no advance warning, startled his family and friends. Sandy in particular was taken by surprise. At the first opportunity, he questioned the boy.

"It's time for me to see more than Carolina," Paul said. "Do you realize that except for Savannah, I've never been anywhere outside of South Carolina? There's a big world out there. You know that, 'cause when you were in the Army, you were all over the world. I'd just like to see more of it."

"But your education? How about college?"

"Maybe later," Paul said. "Right now, I'm going to be a soldier, like all the Walkers. Time and again, I've heard you say that serving your country was one of the finest things a man can do."

"But how about West Point?"

"If I went to West Point, I couldn't marry Jo," Paul said. "We want to get married now."

"You're that serious about her?" Sandy asked.

"I sure am, and she feels that way too."

"But you'll be off on basic training, and then the Army will send you overseas. What will Jo do?"

"I struck a deal with the recruiter," Paul said. "I get my choice of assignment. So after basic training, she'll be able to join me at Fort Bragg. We'll make it work."

Sandy saw that the boy's juices were flowing and there was no way to stop him. What did the poet say? It's time "for your boots and horse lad, to all the world away. Young blood must have its course, lad, and every dog his day." He realized how the boy wanted to have his day and do something on his own. Every generation does. And Jo was a fine young lady; Paul just couldn't do any better. Seen in that light, his volunteering for the Army made sense. At any rate, Sandy discovered that what Paul had said was true: because Paul had enlisted, he indeed had choices. He had selected Special Forces, so after he finished his basic training at Fort Jackson, he was sent to Fort Bragg, only five hours from Hilton Head. And when he successfully completed airborne and Special Forces training there, he came home to marry Jo in the same church where Sandy had married Avril. Then he announced that he had been put on a fast track for the rank of sergeant. That meant promotion the following year and subsequent assignment to the Tenth Special Forces at Bad Toltz, in West Germany. Jo would be allowed to accompany him. Sandy remembered the Special Forces in Vietnam, and he wondered about Paul's duties in West Germany. When the opportunity came, he asked Paul what the overseas Special Forces assignment would entail.

"Most of it's classified," Sandy said. "But I can tell you that I'm trained on the SADEM, and my area specialty is the Middle East. My language specialty is Arabic."

"The SADEM?" Sandy asked. "Isn't that the small atomic bomb that a guy can carry? Special Atomic Demolition Munitions, acronym SADEM. We learned about them back at Fort Sill. And you intend to use them in the Middle East?"

"That's the one," Paul said. "But my area specialty has nothing to do with the SADEM. The Middle East mission is simply an additional assignment, 'tho it too is classified."

"Well, a lot of this stuff has been unclassified," Sandy said. "I have seen open military journals that describe the SADEM as small, easy to use, and very powerful."

"That's right," Paul said. "We break one SADEM into two loads, put the two on backpacks, and jump out of planes with them strapped to us."

"And as I remember, it has two yields," Sandy said. "Two guys could set one up and then move a switch to select a small or a large yield."

"Yeah, but 'small' is probably a poor word. The smaller yield is about five times more powerful than the bomb we dropped on

Hiroshima, and the larger is ten times more powerful than that. It's all relative."

"But isn't it true that they're plutonium fission weapons? That means they're 'dirty' weapons that have lots of radioactive fallout, doesn't it?"

"That, and the fact that we dig them into the ground. So that when they go off, they throw up a large radioactive cloud of dust and debris."

"But that would mean the ground in that area and everything downwind of the blast would be contaminated for a long time."

"Right. And if we used them in response to a Soviet attack, the Russians would have to avoid the contaminated areas. That's the idea: to cut off advancing Soviet armor and force their tanks into killing zones where we can position weapons to destroy them."

"But if we used one, the ground would be poisoned. So even if we won the war, the ground would be radioactive for years. And if we used them in West Germany, that would destroy the Germans' own land. I don't see how that makes much sense."

"Did war ever make much sense?"

"Good point," Sandy said. "But I'd think our allies would have a problem with our ever using this weapon, because it would be their land that would be poisoned."

"Believe me they do," Paul said. "But in spite of that, we train their own soldiers on how to use it. And the Soviets also have such weapons, almost an exact copy of ours."

"Now, that really worries me," Sandy said. "If two men are all that's needed to set one up and detonate it, a SADEM in the wrong hands, like those of a terrorist, would cause big trouble. What if one were set off in New York City, maybe to knock down a large building like the Empire State?"

"Well, for one thing, there are safeguards," Paul said. "Each SADEM has a special code, and both operators have to have separate keys. A terrorist would have to steal a weapon, its specific codes, and the individual keys. To prevent that, everything is stored separately, under very heavy guard."

"But stored in Europe?"

"That's classified and not for publication," Paul said. "It's a political thing, and very sensitive to host countries. But actually, we've got about three hundred of them over there in special depots."

"You know something else that's strikes me as particularly bad?" Sandy said, "The Soviets may not have as many safeguards over theirs weapons as we do ours."

"I'm sure they don't," Paul said. "But Soviet laxity is something I have no control over. And you once told me not to worry about things over which I have no control."

"Didn't you say your specialty was the Middle East?" Sandy asked. "We're not going to use those atomic things in that part of the world, are we?"

"Naw. Each Special Forces team has several missions," Paul said. "My team's job there would be nation building. It wouldn't include the SADEM. Special Forces Atomic weapons aren't targeted on the Middle East."

"Thank God for that," Sandy Said. "But there's another thing you might have to worry about. You probably don't remember back when I was telling you about our family and the Plains Indians way back in the last century. Well, it may be nothing to concern you, but you may recall my telling you that in an absurd leap on reasoning, my father linked the Indian Wars with the testing of atomic weapons in the Marshall Islands. He claimed tree were treating the native islanders out there badly, the way we treated the Sioux."

"What does that have to do with me?" Paul asked.

"As I said, probably nothing. But Andy told me that after his great-grandfather fought for twenty-five years against the Sioux, a Medicine Man named Sitting Bull put a curse on the Walkers, including those yet unborn, like you. The old guy was apparently getting senile, and he supposedly forecast that the Walker men who became soldiers would die violently because of their crimes against people of color. Once Andy had seen the destruction caused at Hiroshima and Nagasaki, he began to worry about that old story. Now, you're a soldier carrying that SADEM. As I said, the story is probably nonsense, especially since you're not going to use it against dark-skinned people in the Middle East."

"That's way out, dad. Indians and curses aren't part of my Special Forces training. Have you been drinking?"

That ended the discussion, and Sandy never had a chance to bring it up again. Jo gave birth to her first child, Steven, on December 15, 1988. In the summer of the following year, Paul took his young family to West Germany. That was the same year Kathleen had a stroke and became too sick to continue in the real estate business. She wanted to sell the firm, and Nancy wanted to buy it. Unfortunately, she didn't have enough money, so Kathleen and Dan asked Sandy if he wanted to take control. He didn't know what to do.

"I'd like to buy it," he told Avril, "but if I do, Nancy might get mad, because she wants it. And I don't want to start another family fight all over again."

"Ask her to be your partner," Avril said.

"Partners? That's crazy."

"Why? It's just business. And it would keep the family together. You've always said that the strength of the family is the important thing. And the firm is doing well. It seems good both as an investment and for family relations."

"And you wouldn't object?"

"Not if you don't stay late at the office."

CHAPTER THIRTY-FIVE

Avril's idea worked. Sandy used his retirement funds to buy Kathleen's interest in the firm, and he made Nancy a junior partner. It was a good move. Oceanfront lots on Hilton Head were now selling for over a million dollars each, and more tourists than even were deciding that Hilton Head was their first choice for a retirement home. Every one of them needed a real estate agent, and the Walker family business boomed. As the firm's managing broker, Sandy was deeply immersed in the day-to-day operations of the business when, a year later, he took a phone call from his father.

"Helen is dead," Andy said. "I need you. Please come."

The news was a shock, a real bolt out of the blue. Except for perfunctory exchanges at Christmas and on birthdays, Sandy hadn't heard from his father for years, yet now the old guy needed him. Nancy insisted that she would have no problem in running the business, and Avril told him to go. She would follow if he needed her. And so it was that a week later, on September 5th, he was able to wind up his personal commitments, break free, and fly to Pierre, South Dakota. When he exited the departure gate, he saw a sturdy, dark-skinned man holding up a homemade sign that displayed the name "Sandy Walker" in large letters. The man turned out to be the Sioux, Joe Bearclaw, that Andy had told him about. Joe was a strong-looking man with a compact body. He had the smooth skin and straight, black hair of a full blooded Indian. He wore, as he apparently always did, blue jeans, denim shirt, and a black bowler hat with a feather. Sandy decided he couldn't even guess at Joe's age. The man seemed to be timeless, a throwback to an earlier age. After they threw Sandy's luggage in the back of Joe's ancient Ford pickup, Joe set off north, roughly paralleling the Missouri River, toward the town of Mobridge. As they began the ride, Sandy probed for information, but Joe wasn't a talker, and he answered only reluctantly.

"My father," he asked. "How's he doing?"

"The colonel's a good man," Joe said. "Need's help."

"How did Helen die?"

"Breast cancer."

"Was it bad?"

"At the end."

"How's dad doing?"

"Not good. He misses her."

"Does he have a doctor?"

"Nope."

"Well, does he eat, or exercise?"

"Not much. Tired."

"Who takes care of him?" Sandy asked.

"My woman, Reva. She cares."

"Is there enough money to pay bills?"

"Don't know about money."

And then Joe lapsed into silence and responded to further questions with monosyllabic grunts. Left in silence to his own thoughts for the next hundred miles, Sandy tried to absorb the wide-open landscape, so different from Vietnam or the low country of South Carolina. How inspired Lewis and Clack must have been coming up the great Missouri two hundred years before. Inspired and maybe even crazy and discouraged at the immensity of the challenge that lay before them as they tried to find a water route to the Pacific. The immense obstacles would have stopped lesser men, but they pushed on, into an unknown land full of savages. At any moment, Sandy expected to see a Sioux war party coming over the next ridge, led by the ghosts of Crazy Horse and Sitting Bull. It wasn't until over two hours later, after they turned into a ranch on the eastern side of Mobridge, that Joe broke his silence.

"This is home," he said. "The colonel's waiting for you on the porch."

Sandy hadn't seen his father since the memorial service in the cemetery at Beaufort seventeen years before. As Andy slowly rose to greet him, Sandy saw that his father's hair was now completely white, his movements were hesitant, and his hand shook ever so slightly. When Sandy had last seen him, Andy had stood erect, but now he was slightly bent over, as if his back ached painfully. He held out his hand.

"It's been a long time," Andy said quietly.

"Too long, dad," Sandy said, ignoring the hand and putting his arms around the old man to hug him.

"Careful," Andy said. "I bruise easily. Have a seat. This here's Reva. She's going to bring me a Coke. You want one?"

Sandy nodded to the short, stocky woman who had come out of the ranch house. She was round-faced with clear, brown skin and black hair pulled back in a bun. She stood straight and looked as if she were almost as strong as Joe, and Sandy could easily visualize her in a teepee mending buffalo hides by the fire. As she went into the house, he took a seat in the wooden rocker that was apparently meant for him. At least, he thought, Andy was apparently well cared for.

"We were sorry to hear about Helen," Sandy said. "Did she suffer a lot?"

"She was in a lot of bad pain until Joe got her some marijuana," Andy said. "Then she was okay until the very end."

"Marijuana? Is it legal here?"

"Nope, but it sure helped." Andy paused as if he was lost in his memories. After a moment, he shook himself and continued, "I'm grateful to Joe for risking himself to help her, but then, he's been a rock of strength over the last fifteen years. And of course, Reva, she was too. I want you to take care of them when I'm gone."

"Stop that," Sandy said. "What kind of talk is that? You're not going anywhere."

"Well something's been happening to me," Andy said. "I've felt pretty bad over the last year. Maybe that was because it was so painful to have to watch her suffer and not be able to help. I can't seem to get over it, and I get very tired now, all the time. That's why I called you. I need your help."

"I'll do anything I can," Sandy said. "I can't get you any pot, but aside from that, what do you want me to do?"

"Well, Helen and I were working on some things, and I'd like you to take them over and keep them going. I'll give you power of attorney and make you the executor of my will if you'll agree to carry on."

"I'll do whatever's needed," Sandy said. "What kind of projects are you talking about?"

"I'm ready for a nap right now," Andy said, finishing his drink. "While I'm resting, why don't you go through the papers on the table inside? Then we'll talk some more."

Over the next few weeks, this became a pattern. Andy would rest or rock in his favorite rocker on the front porch. Sandy would go through the pile of papers and the never-ending stream of mail, all the while listening as Andy muttered to himself or labored to breathe as he napped. As he reviewed Andy's papers, he tried to organize them, and a pattern began to emerge. Sandy started by segregating the correspondence into similar stacks. First were the outstanding bills. For these, he found that a lawyer had prepared a durable power of attorney giving Sandy authority to act for his father. As for money, a bank account showed a checking account with a sizeable balance. Once he had verified with the bank that the balance was indeed correct and that he could sign its checks, he worked the stack of bills down. Only occasionally did he have to ask Andy if a particular bill was valid. They all apparently were.

Sandy then moved on to the remaining correspondence. He divided the letters into piles that seemed to deal with similar subjects. First was what appeared to be a religious group based way out in the Pacific, in the Fiji Islands. Then there seemed to be letters from individual students at various colleges. Next were those from a variety of military sources. And finally, he found many requests for charitable donations. His task was then to find out about each stack, so he began to question Andy whenever the old man seemed strong enough to respond.

"What is this correspondence from Fiji?" he asked.

"That's where Helen and I first met," Andy said. Then he paused as if trying to remember. "That was a long time ago, in the big war, 1942 I think. After we got married, after Penny died, we returned to the same island for our honeymoon. We loved it so much that we tried to go back each year."

"But this is some sort of religious group."

"That's a Foundation we set up. We wanted to build a chapel on the main island. It was to be a memorial to some natives who died fighting against my battalion when we were moving dirt to construct a military airfield. It was a religious thing. An argument over the deaths of those natives caused Helen to leave me for over thirty years. We wanted to heal that wound."

"You actually built a chapel?"

"Yes, and it really helped."

"But a chapel must have cost a lot of money."

"Not as much as you'd think," Andy said. "We built it back in the seventies, right after we were married. Land was cheap, and many volunteers were anxious to help build it. And really, anything it cost was money well spent. Recently, we've only been sending funds for repairs, landscaping, and maintenance. It's beautiful. I hope you'll go see it someday. The people down there are good folks. Try to give them what they ask for." And then Andy was too tired to continue. He shook his head, rose slowly from his chair, and headed for his room. Sandy started to get up to help the old man, but he knew his father wanted to be on his own as long as possible. Stubborn, he had to do it his own way. It ran in the family. So he remained in his chair and watched anxiously as Andy made his way unassisted. When he was assured that his father was safely sleeping, he turned to the next stack of papers.

These seemed to be from students, many of them away at college. From the various contents, he surmised that Andy and Helen had been sending them money. They wanted to tell him how sorry they were about Helen's passing and much they appreciated her counsel about their education. They thanked Andy for his assistance and told him how well they were doing in their studies. From their names and many references to other Native Americans, Sandy guessed that most of them were Indians, and mostly Sioux from the Standing Rock Reservation. Later, Andy confirmed this and explained.

"We wanted to help these people. For over a hundred years, the White Men have given them such a hard time. And all this time, the government hasn't dealt fairly with them." He paused and seemed to be trying to recall something. Then he nodded and began again. "I've told you about your great-great-grandfather Joseph, and how he fought these people for many years. They hated him back them. One of their medicine men put a curse on him. I guess I told you the story. Well, I wanted to change that hatred, so a while back, I began given their young people scholarship money. Helen was a teacher, you know. She helped. You're seeing the results, very positive results."

"But there seem to be so many of them," Sandy said.

"Almost a hundred by now, over these last fifteen years. It's been very successful, filled a great need. We have been very proud of them."

"But dad, these scholarships and that chapel in the Fijis must have cost a lot of money. Was Helen very rich?"

"No. She was a schoolteacher. Most of the money came from what my parents left me. When Dad died sixty-five years ago, he gave me twenty-five thousand dollars. That was a lot of money back then. I put it in a mutual fund, all of it, and I never touched it. Same thing with what Mom left me when she died just before the war. And Penny hadn't changed her will. She was very rich, you know, and she left her fortune to you kids and me. And our houses, Helen's and mine, sold very well. I never spent much, and the stock market has been very good to me, especially these last ten years under Reagan. You'll have plenty of money to continue what we've done. I hope you do."

The military letters came from a variety of sources. The military attaché from the Fiji Islands wrote expressing his sorrow at Helen's death and his gratitude for her work on the chapel and her service in his islands during World War Two. The Superintendent of West Point sent his condolences and thanked Andy for recommending several fine young men for the Academy. The Adjutant General of the South Dakota National Guard offered his sympathy, as did the Army Deputy Chief of Staff for Personnel at the Pentagon. When

Sandy considered that Desert Shield was taking place in the Persian Gulf and most of these people were fully occupied with preparations for that conflict, the letters seemed all the more remarkable. He asked Andy to explain.

"Helen experienced discrimination in the service," Andy said. "And I remembered Joseph's and Junior's relationship with the Buffalo Soldiers, who served so well and were treated so badly in World War One. And back when Helen was in the WACs during World War Two, women weren't given a fair shake. They were like the Buffalo Soldiers, always getting the short end of the stick. It has gone on for a long time, too long. We wanted to help."

"What did you do?"

"We gave money to memorialize the Buffalo Soldiers, and we supported efforts to let women attend West Point. Things like that."

"Well what about these requests for charitable donations?"

"We always did what we could," Andy said. "I wanted to advance research against breast cancer. Helen suffered so much. It's a cruel and heartless disease. Blacks, Indians, women: we wanted to help them get what's fair. We tried to help, but I'm not up to it now. Not without her. So now it's your job. Use your own judgment."

Sandy was amazed to find that Andy's bank and security accounts totaled over two million dollars. The various piles of letters testified to the many good works he and Helen had been involved in. It wasn't the picture that Sandy had expected. Maybe the old guy wasn't as nutty as the rest of the family had thought all these years.

CHAPTER THIRTY-SIX

During the next three months, Andy's attorney prepared the papers needed to transfer ownership of the ranch, the Fiji Foundation, and his various investment accounts to joint control with Sandy. During the same period, Sandy gradually took over the daily operations of the ranch, paid the bills, and answered the substantial correspondence. Always consulting with Andy, he responded to various requests for contributions and began to make decisions required by the trustees of the Fiji trust and Andy's many other responsibilities. When Sandy finally felt comfortable with Andy's affairs, and the old man seemed more relaxed and content, Sandy decided to make an attempt to have the old man talk about his early days. He did this not only because he wanted to know about the family, but also because he realized that his father was far more comfortable talking about the past than the present. Like many older people, Andy could remember what had happened fifty years ago, but forget what had taken place just yesterday. When he was gone, those early memories would die with him, and they were priceless. So Sandy wanted him to talk. But he also realized that Andy relaxed most when he was reminiscing about the earlier Walkers, and Sandy especially wanted to hear more about the old story of an Indian spell that Andy had mentioned several times over the years.

"Tell me about Joseph and Sitting Bull," Sandy said. "I don't know if I can remember," Andy said. "It was so long ago. So many things have happened."

"But is there a Sioux curse?" Sandy asked.

"I'm not really sure," Andy said. "Maybe I'm just getting old. My mind plays tricks now, but I know that odd things have happened to the family."

"Like what?" Sandy asked.

"Like repeated coincidences in dates," Andy said, and then he paused for several minutes as if trying to recall, before he continued. "When Joseph met Sitting Bull in September, back in 1890, the two of them had been fighting in various campaigns since they first met at a battle on the Yellowstone River in 1774. And the day they last met, September 5th, 1890, was the same date that government agents had murdered Chief Crazy Horse in an Army prison at Fort Robinson, thirteen years before. They were supposed to be guarding him, and they killed him. It was a coincidence that on the anniversary of that murder, General Miles sent Joseph out west to Sitting Bulls' remote cabin in the hills of the Standing Rock Indian Reservation. Miles wanted Joseph to persuade Sitting Bull to stop the Ghost Dance craze then sweeping through the seven Sioux nations. And the old Indian could have done it. He had the power, because he had led them against General Custer, but stubbornly he rejected Joseph's pleas. Instead, he used that opportunity to forecast that any Walkers who became soldiers would die violent deaths. I never paid much attention to that story until I learned that in 1906, Joseph had chosen that same date, September 5th to commit suicide. And when in 1925, Junior expired from the effects of a stroke on that same day, it seemed odd."

"Pure coincidence," Sandy said.

"That's what I thought," Andy said, "until Walter died on that exact date in that car crash in Columbia. And remember that a person of color, a Vietnamese immigrant, was driving the car that killed him."

"You're stretching it, dad."

"Maybe so," Andy said. "But what day did you arrive at the airport here for Joe Bearclaw to pick you up?"

"September 5th," Sandy admitted, a little puzzled.

"And what day was Paul born?"

"March 16th...."

"The date of the massacre at My Lai."

"Oh, come on, dad...."

"And what day was Steven born?"

"December 15th.

"That was the day Sitting Bull was murdered after he gave his approval for the Sioux to embrace the Ghost Dance. After he had sewn the seeds of rebellion, government agents killed him, just like they did Chief Crazy Horse."

"And you actually believe an Indian curse is doing all this?" Sandy asked. "Why would that be?"

"According to Junior, it was retribution for the terrible things we did against the Indians, all the women and children we killed. And if we continued to harm people of color, the curse would also continue."

"But from what I have read, after he left the Army, Joseph tried to help the Sioux. Why would he be cursed?"

"He was the primary symbol of repression," Andy said. "Sitting Bull was reacting to Whites invading his lands for so many years. The White Men meant the end of independence for the Plains Indians. Joseph had fought them for such a long time that he was an easy target."

"But Junior? You think he merited a curse?"

"He was at Wounded Knee with Pershing, and he fought the Filipinos in the Insurrection in those islands after the Spanish-American War. He was involved in the courts-martial that led to the hanging of twenty-nine black soldiers after the riots in Houston in 1917."

"And you? What did you do?"

"Fiji natives died at the airfield I was building."

"And that must mean I'm cursed too. What did I do?"

"You fought the North Koreans and the Vietnamese," Andy said. "Always people of color."

"And I suppose you blame Walter?"

"It's not for me to blame anybody, but remember that Walter was present at the tragedy of My Lai. And if any of this is true, Paul and Steven face the same danger."

"Dad, I've got to tell you," Sandy said, "that all these ideas are nothing but biased manipulation of historical fact. If it were true that the Walkers were cursed, you'd have been dead a long time ago."

"You'll need to ask Tashunka about that," Andy said. "Actually, you're probably right not to accept anything as far fetched as a curse. Just remember what I've said. You're the patriarch now. It's in your hands."

After that discussion, Andy lost interest and wouldn't discuss Sitting Bull or the legend any further. On the other hand, Sandy couldn't put the idea out of his mind. He decided he'd go see the Sioux shaman, Tashunka, the one both Andy and Joe Bearclaw had mentioned. Thus, the next week he asked Joe to set up a meeting. The week after that they drove west across the Missouri River, then past Sitting Bull's grave, and finally up into the hills west of Mobridge. At the end of a dirt road, they stopped in front of a rundown ranch house. They walked past an old fence badly in need of paint and a dilapidated car put up on granite blocks. On the porch, an ancient version of Joe Bearclaw waited. Tashunka had long, white hair, a lined face, and gnarled hands, but he rose with dignity to greet them. After Joe had made the introductions, Joe took his place on the steps in front of them, Sandy took a rocker beside Tashunka, and an Indian woman passed Cokes around.

"Excuse my ignorance," Sandy said. "What is a shaman?"

"A priest," Tashunka said. "Someone you can turn to."

"And you have a congregation?"

"No, I just help those who need me."

"How?"

"Any way I can. I rely on the collective wisdom of our people, and I pray often to the Great Spirit for answers." "Did you pray to the Great Spirit about my father?"

"Yes, and what Andy told you is true. A curse is on the Walker family."

"If that is so, why is Andy still alive?"

"Because he has done so many good things for so many people, he is an exception. Others of his family are not as fortunate. You yourself and the rest remain under a dark cloud."

"And could that ever change?"

"Probably. Follow your father's lead, take his path."

"I'm not sure what that means. How would I find out?"

"Ask the Great Spirit.'

"But how does a person consult the Great Spirit?"

"In many ways. Some have found answers in visions brought about by rituals like the Sun Dance. Prayer, meditation, or abstinence can sharpen a person's senses. Some use drugs. No one knows all the paths."

"And you take guidance from visions?"

"All our people do. From visions, dreams, and even stories. Andy's father used to tell him stories about life and learning. Wisdom can be found in them too."

"What kind of wisdom?"

"How to live your life. What the good things are. What to look for as you pass through this world. What are the values. Much more than I can tell you."

"Then how should a person live?"

"Listen well to others, to the animals, to the wind. Walk with the soft breeze and savor the red and purple sunsets of a mottled sky. Seek the peace that comes only through silence. Love, and express that love. Rise and rest with the sun. Walk life's path, but leave no tracks that would mar the land. Take responsibility. Have eyes that see and the wisdom to understand. Those are some ways."

"But how does a person do these things?"

"Clean the waters. Replenish the earth. Restore humanity. Speak the truth quietly. Respect your brothers. Realize we are all related, every rock and leaf. Seek the strength not to judge or criticize your neighbors. Walk a good road until on that final day when the great stillness comes, you go to the Great Spirit without shame. For he is our Father and the Earth is our Mother."

"And Andy did these things?"

"Yes, and they saved him. He did what was right. He dedicated a part of himself to a greater good. He led a remarkable life. He was a warrior, and he fought many battles, but he chose to be an engineer, one who built things. And he could love with a love that lasted over many years. My vision showed him standing in a single ray of sunlight while surrounded by great clouds of evil and darkness. In the midst of chaos, he remained untouched."

As Tashunka talked, his voice took on a singsong, hypnotic quality. Sandy felt as if he was in a dream, and he was not sure how long they spent on that porch that day. When he left, he only knew that he had experienced something unusual. And when he next spoke with his father, Sandy was less critical.

"Tashunka is a remarkable man," he said.

"He and his people have endured much sadness," Andy said. "That is tragic, because they are good human beings. Reva and Joe have been a great blessing to me. I hope you will take care of them and their people after I am gone."

He seemed reconciled, almost eager, to follow Helen, as if he believed she was waiting for him to join her at the end of a long, lonely road or perhaps just around the next bend in the light beyond the tunnel. Andy grew weaker each day, as if he was ready to move on. Sandy tried to tell him how much everyone loved him, and that may have helped, but Andy evidently missed Helen very much and wanted to be with her. His wishes were granted on December 15, 1990, exactly one hundred years after Sitting Bull had been killed at Standing Rock. Sandy wondered if by an act of will, Andy had somehow chosen that date himself.

Many people came to Mobridge for Andy's funeral service. Most of them were Indians: tribal chiefs, religious leaders, and many common members of the tribe. They came quietly, mostly to shake Sandy's hand and offer words of praise and support. Joe and Reva took care of all of them. Many members of the local communities, Mobridge and Pierre, prominent and otherwise, also attended. They were of all types: common people, businessmen, and civic leaders. The local Congressman and both Senators paid their respects. In spite of the expanded war in the Persian Gulf, many military came from Washington, and the Dakota National Guard was well represented. Sandy was impressed, but it was a difficult time for him. The constant press of strangers, even though they meant well, upset him at a time when he wanted to be alone. He needed support, and so he sent for Avril.

CHAPTER THIRTY-SEVEN

Together, they decided he needed to remain on the ranch, at least for the foreseeable future, and so Avril stayed on to take over the household management and supervise Reva and the chores. Realizing he could not remain at the ranch and still do justice to his Hilton Head business, Sandy decided to sell his interest in that real estate business to Nancy. That was easily done, for he gave her very favorable terms. When Sara and Joy moved into his Queen's Grant villa, Sandy was freed from entanglements back east. He was then able to focus on Andy's estate.

From the very beginning, Avril and Reva Bearclaw hit it off, and the house began to shake off the somber effects of Helen's and Andy's deaths. When Joe saw that Sandy was sincere, moreover, in trying to carry on Andy's work with the Sioux, he too began to warm up. Soon, the entire ranch was humming along efficiently and harmoniously, and Sandy was able to achieve a small degree of peace. One problem that he couldn't shake off, however, was the Desert Storm conflict in the Persian Gulf. Sandy kept thinking about Andy's warning that Paul might be in danger there. Sandy knew that Paul and his Special Forces team would almost certainly be sent from Germany to the Middle East because the boy could speak Arabic, and the team was trained for work in that part of the world. And so Sandy feared for the worst. Andy and Tashunka had warned about danger to Paul, and Sandy fretted about it constantly. When he confessed his concerns to Avril, she shared his apprehension, not because she believed in some kind of Indian curse, but because she knew that during the coming months, Paul would be exposed to the inherent dangers of combat. Together they watched anxiously as the war intensified, and they waited each day for news. To their great delight, however, the war ended more quickly than anyone had thought possible. Soon Paul was able to call home and tell them he was safe. Their prayers were answered in the summer of 1992, moreover, when the Army transferred Paul back to Fort Stewart, near Savannah. He would be less than two hours from Cathy and the rest of the family on Hilton Head. When Paul, Jo, and Steven were safely home, Sandy and Avril flew to Hilton Head for a reunion. The occasion was more meaningful because Paul's safe return meant that Andy's ideas about an old Indian curse were nonsense.

When they had an opportunity to spend some time together, Paul told Sandy about the operations his team had carried out in Iraq during the brief but violent conflict just concluded.

"We flew down from Germany to a base south of Riyadh," Paul said. "It was a place called Al Kharj, in central Saudi Arabia. There, we gathered data on Iraqi Scud missile sites and communications centers located well behind the front lines around Kuwait. When the command selected a target, the usual operation followed an established pattern. Following a joint briefing, our Air Force fighter-bombers strafed and bombed Iraqi military targets like antiaircraft sites on and around the objective. After enemy resistance was sufficiently softened, we went in by helicopter. Once on the ground, we destroyed any Scud missiles, warheads, or control centers we found. The emphasis was on speed, so the waiting choppers could extract us before any nearby Iraqi security forces could react."

"Dangerous work," Sandy said.

"Yeah, but we knew what we were doing." Paul said. "When you get into Special Forces, you accept the risk. Training carries you through, and in the end I was proud that we had carried out some fifteen operations with only minor losses. It's better to be part of a good outfit. That reduces risk."

Their discussion and visit ended too soon, for Andy and Avril found that their responsibilities forced their return to South Dakota. Back at the ranch, they discovered that the problems that had brought them back simply required a little attention and a few decisions. Soon, they had time to discuss Paul's experiences.

"Paul's survival under such dangerous conditions," Avril said, "is proof that your stupid Indian curse means absolutely nothing. It's utter nonsense.'

"I'm not so sure, maybe Andy had helped."

"How?"

"Maybe all the good things Andy did removed the curse."

"I don't think a curse is like a mortgage," she said. "You can't just kind of pay it down. And remember, Paul was fighting Iraqis, people of color again. If you believe Andy's story, Paul was continuing to violate the curse, yet he survived."

"But there were no violations like My Lai in Desert Storm. We learned painful lessons in Vietnam. As a result, although the Gulf War was a major fight involving thousands of soldiers and many nations, we had no stories of atrocities or massacres."

"How about cruise missiles in downtown Baghdad?"

"They were targeted on military sites."

"Like schools and hospitals?"

"You know better than that," Sandy said. "Sure, people got hurt by errant missiles, but those munitions weren't aimed at civilians. They weren't premeditated murder like what Calley and others did at My Lai. We had none of that."

"You can't be sure," she said, "because the Army didn't let any reporters actually accompany combat units. They were kept out of the combat zone so the army could feed the public a sanitized script put out by Stormin Normin."

"I think you're selling us short," Sandy said. "The great majority of soldiers are honorable people doing a nasty job under very difficult circumstances. My Lai was an aberration. We learned from it. Desert Storm proved that."

"Whether you learned anything or not has nothing to do with Andy's stupid Indian curse," she said. "That remains a figment of Walker imagination."

They couldn't agree, except for the fact that they were happy that the family was safely together again in South Carolina, far from potential harm. Their serenity was shattered, however, the following summer when Paul and a Ranger unit he had joined at Fort Stewart were put on alert for a possible mission to Somalia. Paul and the other members of his Ranger battalion didn't hesitate. This was the type of mission they had been trained for, and they set about preparing for it professionally. Then Paul called Sandy to tell him about the assignment.

"It's a peacekeeping mission," Paul said.

"So was Vietnam at the start," Sandy said. "But the bad guys changed that pretty quickly. Peacekeeping goes out the window when the bullets start."

"Well, we know there are bad guys over there too," Paul said. "We may have to go after one of them, a Somali chieftain named Aideed."

"Be damned careful if you do," Sandy said. "Somali bullets kill just like Viet Cong's."

"We're an outstanding unit. We can handle him."

"Promise me you'll take care," Sandy said. "Let someone else win the medals. You come home safe."

"You got it, gramps," Paul said, and he was gone.

Mail from Africa came regularly. At first, Paul's letters described several successful missions. He was justifiably proud of his unit and confident of his own ability. Sandy read such accounts with great reservations. He remembered how enthusiastic Walter had been before going to Vietnam, and he crossed his fingers and waited. In the second week of October, the worst happened. Sandy and Joe watched anxiously from the porch as a black sedan drove up the long driveway and a stranger emerged. Obviously not a local, he wore a black suit and dress shoes. As the man came toward them, however, Sandy observed how fit he looked, as if he was an athlete. He moved easily, and his jaw was set firmly. He didn't have an ounce of fat on him. This guy's trouble, Sandy thought, and he was correct.

"Name's Matt Prce," the man said, holding up some sort of identification badge. "Jon Bourne's a friend of mine. Before he left the firm, Jon told me about you and asked me to keep tabs on you and stay in touch."

"Pleased to meet you," Sandy said. "This here's Joe Bearclaw. Mrs. Walker's inside. What can we do for you?"

"I need to tell you a painful story," Price said. "Maybe Mrs. Walker should hear it."

Avril and Reva came out. Introductions were made, and the group settled down nervously to hear what Matt had to say.

"The Agency sent me here," he said, "because of the long relationship it had with Mrs. Walker in Vietnam and more recently because of the work Colonel Walker had been doing out here. We respected Mrs. Walker's service, and we admired the good work your father did in these last years before his death. We're glad you're carrying on. Now, I know you're not the next of kin. Others are talking to Cathy now, but I wanted to tell you myself. Paul's dead."

"I knew it," Sandy said, putting his arm around Avril. "As soon as I saw your car, I knew you had bad news."

"Let me tell you what I know," Price said. "The mission of his Rangers battalion in Mogadishu was to capture the Somali clan chieftain Mohammad Aideed."

"Paul told me about him," Sandy said.

"Well, as background, you should remember that the capture of Aideed was not the original United Nations goal in Somalia. In 1992, the UN went there with food, medicine, and United States Marines to restore order and save thousands of natives from starvation. By early 1993, the marines had accomplished their mission, and they went home in May. Then the UN commander on the scene, American Admiral Jonathan Howe, was faced with a difficult task: how to build law and order in Somalia without the muscle needed to enforce anything. He tried for a national Somali consensus, but he quickly discovered that clan chief Aideed was not the least bit interested in sharing power. He wanted it all. In June, Aideed's men ambushed and killed twenty-four Pakistani soldiers of the UN forces. When the bodies were recovered, moreover, several had been skinned alive. It was an atrocity reminiscent of those of the Indian Wars in the early days of the American West, some not far from where we sit right now."

"Walter told me about the same things in Vietnam," Sandy said. "In his unit, the horrible treatment by the VC carried out on one of

Walter's buddies who had been captured was part of the fuel that ignited the massacre at My Lai."

"Well, in this case, the CIA clearly identified Aideed as the source of the atrocity, and thus Admiral Howe cut him out of all negotiations aimed at governing the country. In July, moreover, the admiral retaliated against Aideed's violations by directing a TOW missile attack on a clan meeting being held in a downtown Mogadishu hotel. Sixty of Aideed's clan leaders were killed. Unfortunately, that included most of the moderates who were arguing for accommodation with UN forces. After they died, Aideed declared war on the United Nations. Howe in turn wanted Aideed's caught. In early August, after the clan set off remote controlled land mines that killed four American soldiers and wounded seven more, President Clinton authorized the use of Army Rangers and the Delta Force to capture Aideed."

"That's when Paul was alerted," Sandy said.

"Right. Paul and the Rangers were quickly airlifted to Somalia and set up a base camp at the Mogadishu Airport. Acting immediately, they launched a series of raids aimed at Aideed's clan. They inflicted severe casualties, succeeded in capturing Aideed's banker, and forced Aideed himself into deep hiding. These operations continued for a month. At the beginning of October, the UN Command assigned them a target in downtown Mogadishu near the Bakhara Market. They were to strike the Olympic Hotel there where agents had located two of Aideed's major clan leaders. Plans called for an assault by helicopter units. The Delta Forces were to land on the hotel while Paul's Ranger units were to secure the surrounding streets and prevent any counterattack. Armored vehicles were then to move from the airport to the hotel, a distance of just three miles, and extract the Delta Force, the Rangers, and their prisoners. The task force commander, a General Garrison, estimated he would need just two hours for the whole mission. But when Defense Secretary Aspin personally denied Garrison's request for additional armor and an orbiting aerial gunship, the stage was set for tragedy."

"Why would Aspin do that?" Sandy asked.

"He seemed to think the additional units would look too much like we were starting a full scale war."

"My God, man, if you start a fight, you're supposed to win, not think how it would look."

"No question about that," Price said. "Aspin seemed to think we were on a peacekeeping mission, and he didn't want to expand the conflict."

"Peacekeeping! What a bunch of bull," Sandy said. "Soldiers are supposed to create havoc and inflict casualties, not keep the peace."

"I suppose his idea was to avoid our guys taking any casualties," Price said.

"If you think you can fight without taking any casualties, you'll send our guys in harm's too casually, thinking there won't be consequences. That's just plain wrong."

"Agreed, but there we were, and the attack was launched early on the morning of Sunday, October 3rd. In an ironic coincidence of dates, October 3rd was the ninth anniversary of the founding of Paul's 3rd Rangers, the ones who would be making the assault. By midday, the Delta Force had descended on the Olympic Hotel and easily captured the two targeted clansmen. The Americans had gone in during daylight, because General Garrison had thought the mission would be over quickly, in spite of the fact that the Americans had special equipment and training for night combat. The Rangers prepared for a very brief fight, but they ran into trouble immediately. In their descent from the choppers, several Rangers were injured and two units landed in the wrong area. There they were quickly surrounded by thousands of tribesmen who pinned them down with AK-47s and rocket grenades fired from what seemed like every window in that densely crowded neighborhood. Plans had to be changed so that the relief convoy could split its force and dispatch several vehicles to rescue the trapped and injured Rangers. And to make matters worse, as that was happening, Somali shoulder-fired missiles shot down two American helicopters nearby."

"Screwed from the start," Sandy said. "Where was Paul?"

"He was with the injured Rangers, okay, but surrounded. But that's not all. At this point, everything that could go wrong, did. Radio frequencies didn't allow the command elements orbiting overhead to talk to the men on the ground, nor to the relief convoys heading their way. The trapped men couldn't talk to the rescue convoys. Constant ambushes and swarms of tribesmen tore up those convoys, and instant blockades sprang up along the relief routes. Conflicting orders on the radios that did work spread confusion among the Americans and their UN allies. The Malaysian tankers, fearing mines, refused to force their way through the blockades, and the Rangers were on their own." "How many of them were there?" Sandy asked.

"By this time they had managed to join up with the other unit that had been lost," Price said. "They had about one hundred and twenty guys, but over thirty were wounded, some very badly. They were being attacked by thousands of armed tribesmen, who often hid behind women and children in the streets. The rules of engagement instructed the Rangers to shoot only those Somalis who actually aimed a weapon in their direction. But as massive crowds of men, women, and children charged the few Rangers who were able to return fire, the Americans had to abandon the rules and lay down protective fires. More men died."

"Where was the command and control?" Sandy asked. "Why weren't reinforcements rushed in?"

"Radios either didn't work, or they were on the wrong frequencies. Contradictory orders kept everyone in a state of confusion. Paul and his buddies hunkered down to hold their position. By now, they had two dead and almost forty wounded. Several times, tribesmen launched mass charges at them. Women and children formed shields for the gunmen to hide behind, and the Rangers were forced to fire into the crowds. They began to run out of ammunition and water. Orders continued to come by radio in confusing sequences. Time was against them."

"How long did this go on?" Sandy asked.

"Far too long. It took more than ten hours for the UN command to organize its Turkish trucks, Pakistanis soldiers, Malaysian armor, and the American Tenth Mountain Division into a partially effective relief force. During that agonizing delay, Paul was hit in the chest by a rocket-propelled grenade. Ranger medics on the spot did their best to save him, but by the time the relief column arrived the next morning, Paul was gone. All I can tell you that he fought well and died a hero. In addition to his Purple Heart, he has been posthumously recommended for the Distinguished Service Cross, our nation's highest award next to the Medal of Honor."

"A tragedy," Sandy said.

"Agreed," Price said. "And a multiple one at that, so many errors occurred that the UN command looked like Keystone Cops. Paul's Rangers weren't given the armored vehicles, airborne support, and men needed to do the job. The Delta Force and the Rangers on the scene were not placed under a single commander on the ground, and confusion resulted. Back at the airfield, senior commanders, trying frantically to control the battle from that remote location, simply created more confusion. The attack was poorly conceived in that it took place in broad daylight and gave away the advantage the Delta Force and the Rangers had because of their extensive night training and night vision devices. Finally, disparate United Nations elements could not be quickly and effectively controlled and organized into a relief force at a time when speed was a major factor."

"Somebody should pay for that," Sandy said.

"We concur," Price said. "There can be no excuse for such a mishandled operation. The Administration knows that. Already we have seen talk that Secretary Aspin must resign, and General Garrison will be called to account. And President Clinton is reexamining the whole concept of our operations in Somalia. I realize that these things are coming too late for Paul, but I thought you'd want to know."

"Sandy, do you realize that Paul died on Beth's birthday?" Avril asked. "What a terrible thing."

"That isn't the only coincidence in dates," Price said. "Earlier, another tragedy had occurred in Somalia. It was so notorious that it became known as the Canadian My Lai. Based on reports of mass killing of twenty natives by its soldiers, the Canadians government had conducted an inquiry. At that inquiry, Canadian soldiers were found to be at fault, in a scenario eerily similar to that of My Lai. The Canadian judge who held the investigation was the first to call the atrocity a second My Lai. One reason for that name was the fact that the date of that atrocity in Somalia was March 16th, the anniversary of My Lai. It was a strange coincidence."

"Strange indeed," Sandy said. "And you know something else? Way back in 1876, General Custer foolishly led two hundred and fifty men of the Seventh Cavalry as they charged into an Indian village on the Little Big Horn. Estimates vary, but there might have been as many as three thousand Sioux, Cheyenne, and Arapaho warriors waiting in that village. And here we are a hundred years later, and General Garrison sends three hundred Rangers into that Bakhara Market, where thousands of Somali warriors were waiting for them. Just about the same ratio as the Little Bid Horn. What a waste of American's best, young men with their lives before them. We never learn."

CHAPTER THIRTY-EIGHT

Sandy and Avril flew down to Hilton Head for the funeral. The beautiful little chapel on Highway 278 was filled with mourners for the occasion. The media had published lurid accounts of the American debacle in Mogadishu, and several of those in attendance voiced outrage over the circumstances of Paul's death. In response, Sandy tried to emphasize the positive by asking those protestors to remember that Paul had died honorably, doing what he had volunteered for: his duty in defense of his country. Privately, he had to admit that it was a stretch to call the pursuit of a Somali chieftain in Mogadishu a defense of the United States. In spite of Sandy's attempt to be positive, the sense of unnecessary loss was very sharp among those who came to the service, and even Sandy had to admit his contempt for those in leadership positions whose multiple failures had caused such a painful tragedy. They had forgotten that loyalty must flow down as well as up, and that leaders had to take care of their men first and foremost. The loss of so many fine young soldiers saddened him. The memorial service helped to ease that sadness, however, for the minister had a comforting way with words.

"Our fate is written in a script far too large for us to fully comprehend," he said. "Put your trust, therefore, in the Author, Who sees into the hearts of us all. He will render the final verdict. Vengeance is His, not ours. Soften your hearts with sympathy for those who sorrow, suffer and err. A heart filled with hate has no room for love."

Comforted by the service, Sandy turned to the needs of Jo and Steven. He found that Paul had had insurance, and the Army was committed to providing substantial benefits to Paul's survivors. Jo could buy a place to live, and Steven would be raised among friends and family. Reassured that Jo and Steven were mentally, physically,

Sandy's War

and financially stable, he and Avril headed back for South Dakota. On the airplane, he turned to the subject of the old Indian legend. "Do you realize how many Walkers have died violently?" he asked her.

"Paul and Walter are the ones I know about," she said.

"There were others," he said.

"I don't doubt it," she said. "Soldiers lead violent lives. It's part of war."

"It wasn't just combat," he said. "Don't forget Joseph's suicide and Junior's stroke. And always, there were questions about the dates. Joseph and Junior both died on September 5th. And remember the car accident that killed Penny and Walter was on that same date."

"Where are you going with all this?" she asked.

"Do those deaths concern you?" he asked.

"You mean more than the sense of loss? Not really. All except Walter and Paul had led long, good lives. And remember that if there was a curse on the Walkers, Andy wouldn't have lived as long as he did and died so quietly. And you yourself seem to be doing just fine."

"That old Indian priest, or I guess they call him a shaman, told me that through good works, Andy had paid for more than his fair share of the family sins."

"What about you?" she asked.

"I guess I'm an open book," he said. "My final chapter hasn't yet been written. That doesn't worry me, but Andy also warned me that Steven would be in danger, and that does concern me, a great deal."

"You believe all this?"

"Not really," he said. "But those funny dates worry me. Not only are we talking about family deaths on September 5th, but also there's December 15th, the date of Sitting Bull's murder, Steven's birth, and Andy's death. And March 16th was the date of My Lai, Paul's birth, and the Canadian massacre in Somalia. Then add Paul's death on Beth's birthday. It's so odd that it's beginning to defy probability."

"No, it's the selective use of coincidence," she said.

"There are too many of them for me," he said. "I think I'll ask Joe to take me to see Tashunka again."

By the time Joe could arrange the meeting, however, it was almost Thanksgiving, and the Dakota weather had turned very cold. The highways were half frozen, and many of the back roads were slick with ice patches. Joe had to drive the old truck with great care. As they traveled west of the Missouri, the roads turned to dirt, and its frozen ruts jolted them. Joe had done it before, however, and at least the heater worked. After two hours, they reached Mahto. Soon they were on the western side of town, and Sandy saw Tashunka's place. A dusting of snow covered the weeds, and that actually made the place look more inviting, although Sandy could still see the rust on the old Ford resting on blocks in the front yard. Like a Christmas postcard, however, the windows of the house were covered for the winter, and a column of smoke rose from the single chimney.

Joe honked the horn, and the two of them hurried through the frost toward the porch, trying not to slip on the ice. When they banged on the door, a voice from within called out that it was open, and they entered. Tashunka was sitting in his rocking chair by the fire. He was wrapped in a blanket. His woman stood by the kitchen door.

"Come. Sit," Tashunka said. "Have some coffee."

Sandy took the second rocker, and Joe went into the kitchen to find the coffeepot. Then Sandy settled in to try to warm himself, waiting for the old Indian to speak. Tashunka just sat there by the fire, pulling quietly on his pipe and occasionally grunting. His long hair was even whiter than Sandy remembered, and the lines in his bronzed face were etched more deeply. At times, Sandy thought the old man had fallen asleep. It seemed an hour before Tashunka finally spoke.

"How can I help?" he asked.

"My father told me that Sitting Bull had forecast violent deaths for my family," Sandy said. "When you explained that Andy had done many good deeds, I hoped the legend would die with him. It didn't. A month ago in the streets of Mogadishu, in Somalia, the worst came true: African gunmen killed my grandson. Except for me, my great-grandson is the only one left. I don't want him to suffer. What can I do?"

"You yourself are still at risk," the old man said. "Aren't you concerned for your fate?"

"I'll be okay," Sandy said. "I've had a good life. I'd like to save Steven."

For what seemed another hour, Tashunka was silent, maybe even asleep. Sandy remained quiet, fearing to break the spell that had taken over the dark, smoky room. His coffee was long cold when Tashunka spoke again. Now, the ancient Indian began to ask questions.

"You killed North Koreans and Chinese?"

"And Vietnamese," Sandy said.

"Do you hate them?"

"Maybe I did back then," Sandy said. "Most likely because they were killing a lot of my friends. Now, I guess I just feel sorry for them."

"Sorry?"

"A lot of them died, mostly noncombatants. Those that are left don't have very much. They paid dearly to fight us."

"You've changed," Tashunka said.

"Maybe 'mellowed' is the better word," Sandy said.

"Do you hate the Somali people who killed Paul?"

"I don't have any feelings about them," Sandy said. "If I hate anybody because of what happened there, it's the leadership that sent our guys far from home and let them down when they really needed help."

"And you aren't concerned for your own safety?"

"Sure, but this is really about Steven."

"Tell me about him."

"He was born on the anniversary of Sitting Bull's death," Sandy said. "He's five now, and when he grows up, he'll have only dim memories of his father. We'll try to keep them alive, however, because Paul was a fine man, and Steven needs to know that. All the family is helping his mother take care of him. I'd like to think he's not going to be a part of any Indian legend."

Tashunka lapsed again into silence. After a few minutes, he opened his eyes and gazed directly at Sandy. Now his eyes had changed, and their intensity was startling, almost angry. As if he was looking into Sandy's soul, he seemed to be probing and measuring. After an eternity, he spoke again.

"I will ask the Great Spirit for guidance. When I have an answer, Joe will bring you here again."

The meeting was over, and Joe drove in silence back to the ranch to await Tashunka's summons. In the interim, winter arrived with a bitter, wind-driven fury. Show began falling regularly, and great snowdrifts piled up. Sandy and Avril were house bound. Sandy kept busy with the paperwork needed to assure that Andy's many projects continued. Avril had taken over part of the finances, and between investments, banking, and taxes, her hands were full. Joe and Reva stayed in the guesthouse and made sure the ranch functioned. When a great storm took out the local power, Joe started the generator and kept electricity available. The fireplace burned constantly. They kept in touch with Hilton Head. In short, they survived.

At Christmas, Joe came to Sandy to say that Tashunka was ready to see them again. They drove in four-wheel drive through blistering cold and massive snowdrifts across the Missouri and west of Rattlesnake Butte. At Mahto, they hit deep snow that almost caused them to turn back, but Joe was a skilled driver, and they finally reached Tashunka's small, frame house. The front yard with its dilapidated wooden fence was almost buried in snowdrifts, and just the roof of the old Ford was visible in front. Because of the snow and fog, Sandy could hardly make out the chicken coop and barn behind the house, and he was thankful to see smoke rising from the chimney. The fire would be welcome. As before, Tashunka waited inside. He tried to rise in greeting, but had to settle back into his rocking chair. His woman offered coffee, while Tashunka lit his pipe. Sandy took a seat beside the old man and near the fire. Joe went into the kitchen. After Sandy had thawed and Tashunka had his pipe going, he spoke.

"I have prayed many times for guidance," he said. "Wakonda, the Great Spirit, has revealed that the Walker curse still has strong medicine. I believe that Steven is the target."

"How do you stop a curse?"
"You appeal to the Great Spirit."
"How?"
"Usually by a ritual ceremony," Tashunka said.
"What kind of ceremony?" Sandy asked.
"It is a ritual of cleansing," Tashunka said. "There are many such ceremonies, but the most powerful among them would be the Sun Dance. That was the ceremony that the great Medicine Man Sitting Bull performed just before the Sioux triumph at the place of the grassy grass near the Little Big Horn. To cleanse your family from his spell, a person would have to perform the same dance. It could not be some fake illusion a tourist might see. It would need to be the real thing. And it would have to be in May, as close as possible to the time of year that Sitting Bull danced before the yellow-haired Custer and his men died."

"What's this Sun Dance like?" Sandy asked.

"The dancer would be offering himself as a sacrifice," Tashunka said. "Because Wakonda has truly cursed the warriors of your family, Steven is in great danger. He is too young to cleanse himself. You would need to take his place and undergo the ritual for him, but that would be a great danger for you. The Sun Dance is for young men. It is a ceremony based on torture and pain as a path to freedom. Pain brings about an altered state of mind and is a bridge to self-knowledge. For a long time, our people have used such torture as a ritual of initiation, a path to truth. Even today, men and women of several African tribes mutilate their bodies, and the Australian Aborigines still practice genital mutilation. Indian devotees of Siva pierce their flesh. Our Sun Dance is like all of those, although each of our ceremonies differs based on its purpose. The version that Sitting Bull performed was primarily a search for his own vision. It emphasized severe pain and fasting to reveal truth and bring about spiritual cleansing. You must understand that only the strongest can survive such a ritual. That is the one we would have to use. A weak man would fail, achieve no vision, perhaps even die. Think about all this very carefully. If after you consider all these things, you still wish to continue, you must undertake intense preparation so that next May you will be strong. The Sun Dance will test your body and search your heart as never before. When you believe you are ready, we will meet again. If you then tell me you wish to attempt the dance, I will make the arrangements."

Sandy had five months, and he began physical preparations immediately. He bought an aerobics video and a portable step that could be adjusted for height and difficulty. After he fell a few times and when he became adapted to the music and its pace, he did aerobic exercise each day he couldn't be outside. For the better days, he bought snowshoes and cross-country skis. Relying on the training the Army had given him in the Army Arctic Indoctrination Center at Tok Junction, Alaska, he worked out a track around the ranch. Alternating between the snowshoes and skis until he gained proficiency, he gradually increased the length of his sessions. He started with just a twenty-minute workout, but by the time the snow melted in the spring, he could stay at it for hours. He coupled his daily physical routine with a diet that emphasized fruits, water, and reduced fat. Finally, he went to the small public library at Mobridge. It wasn't an extensive library, but it had a large section devoted to the American Indians, especially the Sioux, and he was able to read about the various versions of the Sun Dance. He traveled to the two nearby Reservations, Standing Rock and the Cheyenne River Sioux. There, he talked with representatives of the Department of the Interior and of the tribes themselves. He heard conflicting stories and some silly myths, but he found nothing to reassure him. As practiced by the Sioux, the ceremony was apparently painful and dangerous. That knowledge gave him incentive not to relax his preparations. He knew he would need to be in top shape just to survive what Tashunka might have in mind for him.

By the time May arrived, Sandy had lost fifteen pounds and was feeling as fit as he could remember. He was ready when Joe came to him and said Tashunka was waiting. Back at Mahto, they found that Tashunka too must have undergone intense preparation for the ceremony, because he now seemed more fit and alert, as if he had a purpose to sustain him. His eyes were sharp and clear. He moved more briskly and held himself more erectly. The deep lines were still there in his face, but he seemed to have shed twenty years.

Inside Tashunka's house, nine young Indian men were waiting. Tashunka introduced each one by his Indian name, but because of the unusual pronunciation, Sandy could not reproduce them. He wondered if they had intentionally concealed their names to make it more difficult to trace them if something went wrong. Dressed in blue jeans, T-shirts, and work boots, they looked very much alike. Except for their smooth, dark skin and straight, black hair, they resembled any other group of country boys in America. They shook hands firmly as if testing him, all the while examining him with somber, dark eyes.

"If you are ready," Tashunka said, "these men will dance with you. They are grateful for what you and your father have done for them and others of our people who want a better life.

But I must warn you that the ritual you are to undertake is a sacred one and it cannot be diluted. Do you understand?" Sandy nodded.

"Very well, here is what we will do," Tashunka said. "Your Sun Dance will be a ceremony meant for warriors. Before you, Sitting Bull was the oldest man ever to perform it. Thus there is danger in your even attempting the ritual. It will cover three days. During that time all of you will fast, consuming only water for fully seventy-two hours. Second, you will sleep under the stars or in teepees of your own making. You will go barefoot and wear only loincloths, wrapping yourselves in blankets by your own fires at night. You will rise with the sun each day, work throughout the daylight hours, and retire at nightfall. On the first day, you will construct the ceremonial arena, using only handmade tools and ropes. On the second day, under the heat of the sun, you will dance to the beat of drums for twelve hours. On the final day, you will undergo ritual piercing."

By the time Tashunka had finished, Sandy was having second thoughts. Sure, he had read about the Sun Dance, but the written words had lacked impact. Tashunka's solemn demeanor and serious presentation added another, more alarming dimension to the written accounts. This was going to be serious business, and for the first time, Sandy began to realize that he might not be able to go through with the ceremony. The hazing of Plebe year at West Point had been rough, and jump training for parachute and Special Forces qualification had been even more arduous. They were nothing compared to what Tashunka described as his Sun Dance. Finally, the presentation was done.

"Do you understand?" Tashunka asked.

Under the intense scrutiny of the shaman and the young men watching, Sandy hesitated and then nodded.

"And yet you wish to proceed?" Tashunka asked. This was beginning to feel like the worst moment of his life, and it was then that Sandy almost backed out. Unable to speak, he looked around at the serious Indian faces watching intently. Finally, he nodded once again.

"Since you agree, I must confer with the warriors," Tashunka said. "Please join Joe Bearclaw outside. In a few moments, we will decide, and we will call for you."

When Sandy told Joe what had happened inside the house, Joe replied that they were probably voting on whether they would proceed with the ceremony. The decision would depend on how each of the ten had sized Sandy up. Events proved Joe correct. In about fifteen minutes, Tashunka called Sandy into the house and informed him that the ritual would take place as planned. Joe was to bring Sandy back in two weeks. The first day of the Sun Dance was to be May 26th, as close as possible to the time of the year that the Sioux had gathered at Wolf Mountain before the momentous Sioux victory over the Seventh Cavalry at the Little Big Horn.

CHAPTER THIRTY-NINE

Two weeks later, on May 25th, Sandy ate a good breakfast. In was to be his final meal before Joe drove him back to Tashunka's house and the ordeal waiting for him at Standing Rock. During the trip to the old man's farmhouse, Joe was silent as usual, and Sandy was lost in his own thoughts about the upcoming ritual. At Tashunka's place, the old shaman and one of the young men were waiting beside an old Ford truck. Sandy had one last chance to back out, but he got into Tashunka's truck and left Joe behind. When that happened, his last link to civilized life was gone. The three of them then drove on a dirt road away from Mahto to Bullhead, then farther west on back roads and trails that seemed to double back on themselves. After a half an hour, Sandy was completely lost. If his host was trying to confuse him, the plan worked, for he could never have retraced his steps. Sandy guessed they might be near the cabin where Sitting Bull had been killed, but he had no way to tell. After more than an hour, they came to a small teepee camp in a valley where they apparently were to spend the night.

Before dawn the following day, barefoot and dressed in loincloths, Sandy and the Indian boys assembled below an eastern hill on the top of which Tashunka waited for the sun. When the rising sun silhouetted him against the newly orange sky, Tashunka gave the signal, and they rushed to begin construction of the stage for the ceremony. A telephone pole and some tools lay on the ground waiting for them. For the next twelve hours, they labored, with only water to sustain them, to erect that pole. Without machinery to assist, they dug a hole and used ropes attached to nearby trees to insert one end of the pole in the ground and raise it to the vertical. By mid-day, they had it firmly in its hole. Then they had to climb it and apply clean bands of alternating red, yellow, white, and black paint. As they worked, Tashunka emphasized that those bands represented the four directions of the winds and the four races of the world. To secure the sacred pole, they attached long guy ropes. On those ropes, they hung Indian blankets and buffalo hides to provide some small amount of shade. Then they cleaned off the brush within the great circle and leveled the dance floor. Well after sunset, Tashunka led them in prayers of consecration. In spite of the hunger that gripped him, Sandy was ready for the blankets thrown on the ground for him. Exhaustion drove him to a fitful sleep.

The second day came too quickly. Having spent the night on the hard earth, Sandy was cold and stiff when he rose before dawn. He had already gone over forty hours with only water to nourish him. As Tashunka again announced the arrival of the sun, four of the Indian boys began to pound on great drums. They started slowly and softly as the five other young men and Sandy began their dance around the great pole. They had painted their bodies black, red, and yellow, and they wore amulets on beads around their necks. To bands on their arms and ankles, they had attached eagle feathers that rose and fell rhythmically as they danced by rising on their toes and bending their knees in time to the drums. At first, it was easy. The morning was cool, the drums beat slowly, and they rested every fifteen minutes. As the sun rose, however, the heat began to press down on them. By noon, still with only water for nourishment, it was hot, and Sandy felt lightheaded. Flies bit at him, and perspiration drained his body. As the afternoon passed and the drums beat louder and faster, he experienced several dizzy spells. He was not sure of the time or place, and his mind wandered. Once he fainted, only to revive as Tashunka splashed water over him and forced him to drink. He did not know how long he had been unconscious, but it seemed hours later that the welcome darkness finally fell over them, and Tashunka offered a closing prayer for their safety on the third day.

Even more exhausted than before, Sandy wrapped himself in a blanket and closed his eyes. Fatigue caused him to drop off into a strange, violent world of darkness, flashing lights, whistles, and bugle calls. His men had deserted him. The Viet Cong and the Chinese were on the fences, and he couldn't find his rifle. As the yellow hordes swarmed over him, he tried to flee, but he couldn't run, and they seized him. An enemy soldier hit him in the stomach with a rifle butt, and he fell unconscious to the ground. The sharp hunger pangs became a dull, empty ache in his belly as he dozed fitfully through the night.

When he rose before dawn of the third day, Sandy's whole body ached. He gulped water to fill his stomach and stumbled toward the sacred pole. Tashunka announced the sun, and six of them danced together in a great circle around Tashunka in the center of their little universe while the others beat the great drums. Then Tashunka selected one young man. In the midst of the ceremonial stage, the two of them faced each other, as the rest made a circle around them. Tashunka seized the boy by the flesh between his shoulder and breast and raised a handful of skin. With a knife, Tashunka pierced the flesh and tied a thong through it. Then, he repeated the piercing on the boy's other breast. Finally, he tied the thongs and fastened them to a line from the top of the center pole. The rope secure, he released the boy, who fell backwards. The impaled and exhausted warrior was only kept upright by the thongs secured in his bleeding flesh. As the remainder of the group circled around him chanting and the great drums beat ever more loudly, he threw himself back again and again, attempting to tear his flesh and break free. Groaning and screaming, he lurched back and forth. Then with one final, great thrust, he freed himself, ripping his flesh, and fell bleeding to the ground.

The others waited, watched, and rested while Tashunka tended to the wounded warrior. Then the shaman selected another young man, and the ceremony began again. Each supplicant took a different amount of time to break free, and several required extensive medical treatment after piercing. Thus it was mid-afternoon before Tashunka turned to Sandy. He had seen the torture of the others so he knew what would happen, but he was in no condition to resist. Already dizzy and hallucinating, he was in a dream world. That world was shattered when Tashunka pierced his flesh and pain tore through him. He screamed as Tashunka released him and then shoved him backwards. The sharp agony in his chest intensified as the thongs pulled against his impaled chest. He staggered drunkenly as he attempted to hurl his body backwards and free himself from the monster gripping him, but he did not have the strength to wrench free. The heat was overwhelming. Dust rose and choked him. Flies swarmed over him. He could neither see nor breathe, and he lost track of time. Suddenly, he saw the others circling around him, each holding a bow and arrow. As they raised their weapons to fire, he knew the truth. He had been betrayed. He was to pay for the sorrows the White Man had brought upon the Sioux, and they meant to take final revenge by fulfilling Sitting Bull's angry curse. In was Sandy's turn to die at the hands of the Indians. He screamed as their arrows flew toward him. As sharp pains shot through his body and blood cascaded down his chest, he fell once more to the ground unconscious.

When he awoke, the shadows were long, and dusk was falling. Tashunka had bandaged him, and the great Indian drums were silent. The peaceful quiet told him that his betrayal had been imagined. In his hallucination, he had dreamed his execution. Now, Tashunka helped him up, and the ten of them knelt so they faced the final rays of the setting sun as it lit the clouds above them in a glorious pink hue. Tashunka prayed aloud, sometimes in English and sometimes in a native dialect, asking Wakonda to protect them. He urged each of them to search their hearts for a vision to guide them. Dizzy with pain, heat, and hunger, Sandy closed his eyes and fell over to the ground. In a moment, he was asleep again. When he awoke, it was to the sound of a violent surf pounding. He was on the beach at Hilton Head, and a storm was crashing over him. Suddenly through the mist he saw Steven in a crowd of dark figures. It was bitter cold, and rain was falling. Without the sun, darkness was over them, but wherever Steven walked, a prism of sunlight followed him like a laser. Steven stood tall in the midst of chaos. Sandy reached for Steven, but could not break through the dark crowd around him. The vision disappeared, and he fell into an exhausted, dreamless sleep.

When Sandy again awoke and had eaten, he felt better, and Tashunka gently questioned him.

"Did you dream?" he asked.

"I think so, yes," Sandy said.

Sandy's War

"Can you remember it?" Tashunka asked.

"It's all fuzzy, kind of vague," Sandy said.

"Tell me what you can," Tashunka said.

"I remember a storm," Sandy said. "I think it was on the beach at Port Royal, on Hilton Head. I may have been under some sort of shelter. And I was looking out at the people on the beach. They were scrambling around, as if the storm was a surprise, and they were trying to gather up their stuff and run to my shelter. The clouds were very black, and there was a driving rain. Then suddenly I saw Steven. He was standing still. A beam of light was shining down on him, and no rain penetrated that bright beam. He seemed happy."

"Steven is free," Tashunka said, smiling. "The Great Spirit has spoken. You are cleansed. The legend is finished. The long Walker journey is over."

EPILOGUE

Once upon a time not so long ago, we were warriors, boys who became men as we marched toward the sounds of the guns. In the exuberant enthusiasm of our youth, we were tireless, and we considered ourselves invincible. With arrogant ignorance, some of us even thought that we were immortal. All of that changed in the first furious firefight that set off a terrible, bloody battle against our fierce, fanatical, determined foes. Mostly they were small, yellow men: Koreans from the hills just south of the Yalu River, Chinese swarming down from the vast steppes of Outer Mongolia, Vietnamese fresh from their victory over the French Foreign Legion at Dien Bien Phu. They came at us during the night, in waves of hundreds and eventually thousands, driven relentlessly into our lines by the whistles, drums, bugles, lights, and shouts of their leaders. And as they threw themselves on our protective barbed wire, they set off our mines, and we used artillery, mortars, machineguns, grenades, rifles, and bayonets to kill them by the hundreds, eventually by the thousands. As the conflict deepened, we found that they were different from us: they killed any captured wounded, while we sent their casualties to the MASH unit or the MEDEVAC choppers for the best of care. But no matter how many we killed, it made no difference, for there was apparently an inexhaustible supply of them. For every one of them who fell, more still swarmed into our killing fields. And then we too began to die, far too many of us. In ten years of active combat in Korea and Vietnam, in places like the Chosin Reservoir and Ia Drang Valley, we lost over a hundred thousand of our best young men. Yet the enemy suffered far more. The North Vietnamese alone tell us they lost over a million men, and reports indicate that more than five million Asian civilians died: noncombatants, old men, women, and children. Many of those were innocents caught on those cruel, indiscriminate killing fields. Some were without doubt Viet Cong who merited their fate, but a few died because of the stupidity, anger, fear, and incompetence of a small number of craven, cowardly Americans who thereby dishonored our country. Their crimes became an obsession of the press, which then neglected to tell the story of the courage and sacrifice of the rest of us.

Most of our soldiers who perished were young, with their lives before them, not old enough to vote for the politicians who had sent them to their fate in Asia. They died in many horrible ways, and those of us who survived had to fight on from bunkers made slimy by their blood and body parts. In the long hours that became years we watched the cruel, heartless bullets tear apart their strong, young bodies. And as that happened, the boundless enthusiasm of our youth changed to a dull acceptance of our fate and the reality of the death that was everywhere around us. Gradually the sharp, clear vision of that better time before combat changed to shock. The eager gleam in our eyes was replaced by a blank, unfocused stare. Yet still we fought on. Partly we may have endured because we felt we were serving grander concepts: a commitment to what we thought was our duty, for a personal sense of honor, or out of loyalty to our country. You cannot imagine our dismay when we saw that the press had rejected our service by insisting that our country appreciated neither our sacrifice nor our loyalty. Nor can you possibly comprehend our frustration at not being allowed to carry the fight to our enemies. Seething in anger, we obeyed the rules that prevented us from attacking those who were killing our friends.

Yet we still continued to fight, perhaps not so much for our country, but for our families: wives, sweethearts, parents, and children, in the naïve belief that maybe our sacrifice was creating a better world for them. Most of the time, in reality, we fought for the only people who really mattered: the men who shared our foxholes. Those around us who endured our thirst, fear, hunger, exhaustion, heat, and cold inspired a fierce loyalty. And so, immersed in the stench of the dead bodies, friendly and enemy, rotting on the wires in front of our guns, we fought on rather than let our buddies down. For them, even as we were splattered by their blood and shared our trenches with their shattered limbs, we killed far more of the enemy than they killed of us, seventeen times as many. It made no difference. The other side was willing to take casualties, while we abhorred the very idea. Each year we spent in Vietnam took a terrible toll on us and on the nation. Those of us who survived that horror seemed well past middle age by the time we came home. And when it was finally over, we returned, not to a triumphant, ticker-tape parade down Fifth Avenue, but to the Vietnam Memorial, a terribly evocative place that most of us still cannot bring ourselves to visit. Even today, when a few of us do summon up the courage to view those massive, stark, somber, black-granite slabs, we invariably break down in tears as we trace our fingers over the etched names of our departed fellow soldiers who gave their lives, only to be abandoned. And when you ask, we cannot bear to talk about it.

For some of the grunts who fought in Korea and Vietnam, the consummate image of combat is that of a great, angry, gray, bull elephant that suddenly materializes at night out of the mist and fog of war. The irate monster trumpets a deafening war cry before launching a lumbering, thunderous charge directly at our lines. Those who have looked into the bloodred eyes of the elephant are forever changed. We must never forget those who have been trampled and crushed by that crazed beast.

POSTSCRIPT

Hawk Kiefer encourages readers to comment on "Sandy's War" or "Soldiers Never Sleep." To do so, please E-mail him at Hawkkiefer@aol.com or write him at 22880 Virginia Trail, Bristol, VA 24202. He will make every attempt to answer.

www.ingramcontent.com/pod-product-compliance
Ingram Content Group UK Ltd.
Pitfield, Milton Keynes, MK11 3LW, UK
UKHW020906181224
452569UK00012B/851